THE
MIDNIGHT
STAR

A YOUNG ELITES NOVEL

MARIE LU

PENGUIN BOOKS

PENGUIN BOOKS

UK | USA | Canada | Ireland | Australia
India | New Zealand | South Africa

Penguin Books is part of the Penguin Random House group of companies
whose addresses can be found at global.penguinrandomhouse.com.

First published in the USA by G. P. Putnam's Sons,
an imprint of Penguin Random House LLC,
and in Great Britain by Penguin Books 2016

001

Text set in Palatino Linotype
Printed in Great Britain by Clays Ltd, St Ives plc

A CIP catalogue record for this book is available from the British Library

PAPERBACK
ISBN: 978-0-141-36184-0

INTERNATIONAL PAPERBACK
ISBN: 978-0-141-36194-9

To those who, in spite of everything,
still choose goodness

SKYLANDS

BELDAIN
Hadenbury

KENETTRA

The
Sun
Sea

Anjou
Campagnia
Serrata
Estenzia
Golden Valley
Triese di Mare
Udara
Dalia
Falls of
Laetes
Petra

The
Sacchi
Sea

SEALANDS

The Ember Isles

SUNLANDS

I saw her, once.

"She passed through our village, through fields littered with dead soldiers after her forces overwhelmed the nation of Dumor. Her other Elites followed and then rows of white-robed Inquisitors, wielding the white-and-silver banners of the White Wolf. Where they went, the sky dimmed and the ground cracked—the clouds gathered behind the army as if a creature alive, black and churning in fury. As if the goddess of Death herself had come.

"She paused to look down at one of our dying soldiers. He trembled on the ground, but his eyes stayed on her. He spat something at her. She only stared back at him. I don't know what he saw in her expression, but his muscles tightened, his legs pushing against the dirt as he tried in vain to get away from her. Then the man started to scream. It is a sound I shall never forget as long as I live. She nodded to her Rainmaker, and he descended from his horse to plunge a sword through the dying soldier. Her face did not change at all. She simply rode on.

"I never saw her again. But even now, as an old man, I remember her as clearly as if she were standing before me. She was ice personified. There was once a time when darkness shrouded the world, and the darkness had a queen."

—*A witness's account of Queen Adelina's siege*

on the nation of Dumor

The Village of Pon-de-Terre

28 Marzien, 1402

Tarannen, Dumor
The Sealands

Moritas was sealed in the Underworld by the other gods. But Amare, the god of Love, took pity on the young, dark-hearted goddess. He brought her gifts from the living world, rays of sunshine bundled in baskets, fresh rain in glass jars. Amare fell in love—as he was frequently wont to do—with Moritas, and his visits resulted in the births of Formidite and Caldora.

—An Exploration of Ancient and Modern Myths, *by Mordove Senia*

Adelina Amouteru

I have had the same nightmare for the past month. Every night, without fail.

I am asleep in my royal chambers at the Estenzian palace when a creaking sound wakes me. I sit up in bed and look around. Rain lashes the windowpanes. Violetta sleeps next to me, having crept into my chambers at the sound of the thunder, and under the blankets, her body is curled close at my side. I hear the creaking again. The door of my room is slightly ajar and slowly opening. Beyond it is something horrifying, a darkness full of claws and fangs, something I never see but always know is there. The silks I'm wearing turn unbearably cold, as if I am neck deep in a winter sea, and I cannot stop myself from trembling. I shake Violetta, but she does not stir.

3

Then I jump out of bed and rush to close the door, but I can't—whatever is on the other side is too strong. I turn to my sister.

"Help me!" I call to her desperately. She still does not move, and I realize that she is not asleep, but dead.

I startle awake, in the same bed and same chambers, with Violetta sleeping beside me. *Just a nightmare,* I tell myself. I lie there for a moment, trembling. Then I hear that creaking sound, and I see the door is starting to open once more. Again, I jump out of bed and rush to close it, shouting for Violetta. Again, I realize that my sister is dead. Again, I will bolt awake in bed and see the door opening.

I will wake a hundred times, lost in the madness of this nightmare, until the sunlight streaming through my windows finally burns the scene away. Even then, hours later, I cannot be sure I am not still in my dream.

I am afraid that, one night, I will never wake. I will be doomed to rush to that door over and over again, running from a nightmare in which I am always, forever, lost.

⁂

A year ago, it would have been my sister, Violetta, riding at my side. Today, it is Sergio and my Inquisition. They are the same white-robed, ruthless army that Kenettra's always known—except, of course, they now serve me. When I glance back at them, all I see is a river of white, their pristine cloaks contrasted against the somber sky. I turn around in my saddle

and return to gazing at the burned houses that go by as we ride.

I look different from when I first took the throne. My hair has grown long again, silver as a sheet of shifting metal, and I no longer wear a mask or an illusion to hide the scarred side of my face. Instead, my hair is pulled back in a braided bun, jewels woven into the locks. My long, dark cape billows behind me and down my horse's quarters. My face is fully exposed.

I want the people of Dumor to see their new queen.

Finally, as we pass through an abandoned temple square, I find who I'm looking for. Magiano had initially left me and the rest of my Kenettran troops right after we entered the city of Tarannen, no doubt wandered off somewhere in search of leftover treasures from homes abandoned by fleeing citizens. It's a habit he picked up soon after I became queen, when I first turned my sights on the states and nations around Kenettra.

As we approach, he rides through the empty square and slows his horse to a trot beside me. Sergio shoots him an annoyed look, although he says nothing. Magiano just winks back. His mess of long braids is tied high on his head today, his menagerie of mismatched robes replaced with a gold breastplate and heavy cloak. His armor is ornate, dotted with gemstones, and if one didn't know better, one would assume at first glance that *he* was the ruler here. The pupils of his eyes are slitted, and his expression is lazy under the midday sun. An assortment of musical instruments is looped across his shoulders. Heavy bags clink at his horse's flanks.

"You are all looking magnificent this morning!" he calls out cheerfully to my Inquisitors. They just bow their heads at his arrival. Everyone knows that openly showing any disrespect for Magiano means instant death at my hands.

I raise an eyebrow. "Treasure hunting?" I say.

He gives me a teasing nod. "It took me all morning to cover one district of this city," he replies, his voice nonchalant, his fingers floating absently across the strings of a lute strapped in front of him. Even this small gesture sounds like a perfect chord. "We'd have to stay here for weeks for me to collect all of the valuables left behind. Just look at this. Never saw anything this finely crafted in Merroutas, have you?"

He edges his horse closer. Now I see, wrapped in cloth in the front of his saddle, bunches of plants. Yellow thistle. Blue daisies. A small, twisted blackroot. I recognize the plants immediately, and suppress a small smile. Without saying a word, I untie my canteen from the side of my saddle and hand it to Magiano so that the others don't see. Only Sergio notices, but he just looks away and guzzles water from his own bottle. Sergio has been complaining of thirst for weeks now.

"You slept poorly last night," Magiano murmurs as he gets to work, crushing the plants and mixing them into my water.

I had been careful this morning to weave an illusion over the dark circles under my eyes. But Magiano can always tell when I've had my nightmares. "I'll sleep better tonight, after this." I motion at the drink he's preparing for me.

6

"I found some blackroot," he says, handing my canteen back to me. "It grows like a weed here in Dumor. You should take another tonight, if you want to keep the . . . well, *them* at bay."

The voices. I hear them constantly now. Their chittering sounds like a cloud of noise right behind my ears, always present, never silent. They whisper at me when I wake in the morning and when I go to bed. Sometimes they speak nonsense. Other times, they tell me violent stories. Right now, they're mocking me.

How sweet, they sneer as Magiano pulls his horse slightly away and goes back to plucking at his lute. *He doesn't like us very much, does he? Always trying to keep us away from you. But you don't want us to leave, do you, Adelina? We are a part of you, birthed in your mind. And why would such a sweet boy love you, anyway? Don't you see? He's trying to change who you are. Just like your sister.*

Do you even remember her?

I grit my teeth and take a drink of my tonic. The herbs are bitter on my tongue, but I welcome the taste. I'm supposed to look the part of an invading queen today. I can't afford to have my illusions spinning out of control in front of my new subjects. Immediately, I feel the herbs working—the voices are muffled, as if they have been pushed farther back—and the rest of the world comes into sharper focus.

Magiano strums another chord. "I've been thinking, mi Adelinetta," he continues in his usual, lighthearted manner, "that I've collected far too many lutes and trinkets and these

7

delightful little sapphire coins." He pauses to turn around in his saddle and digs some gold from one of his heavy new satchels. He holds out a few coins with tiny blue jewels embedded in their centers, each one equivalent to ten gold Kenettran talents.

I laugh at him, and behind us, several Inquisitors stir in surprise at the sound. Only Magiano can coax joy out of me so easily. "What's this? The great prince of thieves is suddenly overwhelmed by *too* much wealth?"

He shrugs. "What am I going to do with fifty lutes and ten thousand sapphire coins? If I wear any more gold, I'll fall off my horse."

Then his voice quiets a little. "I was thinking you could dole it out to your new citizens instead. It doesn't have to be much. A few sapphire coins each, some handfuls of gold from your coffers. They're overflowing as it is, especially after Merroutas fell to you."

My good mood instantly sours, and the voices in my head start up. *He's telling you to buy the loyalty of your new citizens. Love can be purchased, didn't you know that? After all, you bought Magiano's love. It is the only reason why he's still here with you. Isn't it?*

I take another swig from my canteen, and the voices fade a little again. "You want me to show these Dumorians some kindness."

"I think it could reduce the frequency of attacks on you, yes." Magiano stops playing his lute. "There was the

assassin in Merroutas. Then we saw the beginning of that rebel group—the Saccorists, wasn't it?—when your forces set foot in Domacca."

"They never got within a league of me."

"Still, they killed several of your Inquisitors in the middle of the night, burned down your tents, stole your weapons. And you never found them. What about the incident in northern Tamoura, after you secured that territory?"

"Which incident did you have in mind?" I say, my voice growing clipped and cold. "The intruder waiting in my tents? The explosion on board my ship? The dead marked boy left outside our camps?"

"Those too," Magiano replies, waving his hand in the air. "But I was thinking about when you ignored the letters from the Tamouran royals, the Golden Triad. They offered you a truce, mi Adelinetta. Their northern strip of terrain in exchange for releasing their prisoners and the return of the farmlands near their only major river. They offered you a very generous trade deal. And you sent their ambassador back bearing your crest dipped in the blood of their fallen soldiers." He gave me a pointed look. "I seem to remember suggesting something subtler."

I shake my head. We already argued about this, when I initially arrived in Tamoura, and I'm not about to debate it again. "I'm not here to make friends. Our forces successfully conquered their northern territories regardless of their deals. And I will take the rest of Tamoura next."

"Yes—at the cost of a third of your army. What will happen when you try to seize what remains of Tamoura? When the Beldish strike at you again? Queen Maeve is watching you, I'm sure." He takes a deep breath. "Adelina, you're Queen of the Sealands now. You've annexed Domacca and northern Tamoura in the Sunlands. At some point, your goal should be not to conquer more territories but to keep order in the territories you *do* have. And you won't achieve that by ordering your Inquisitors to drag unmarked civilians out into the streets and brand them with a hot iron."

"You think me cruel."

"No." Magiano hesitates for a long moment. "Maybe a little."

"I'm not branding them because I am *cruel*," I say calmly. "I'm doing it as a reminder of what they've done to *us*. To the marked. You're so quick to forget."

"I never forget," Magiano replies. This time, there is a slight sharpness to his tone. His hand hovers near his side, where his childhood wound continues to plague him. "But branding the unmarked with your crest will not make them any more loyal to you."

"It makes them fear me."

"Fear works best with some love," Magiano says. "Show them that you can be terrifying, yet generous." The gold bands in his braids clink. "Let the people love you a little, mi Adelinetta."

My first reaction is bitterness. Always *love* with this insufferable thief. I must appear strong in order to control my

army, and the thought of handing out gold to the people who once burned the marked at the stake disgusts mc.

But Magiano does have a point.

On my other side, Sergio, my Rainmaker, rides on without comment. The color of his skin looks pallid, and he seems like he still hasn't fully recovered from the chill he'd taken several weeks ago. But other than his silence and the way he wraps his cloak around his shoulders even in this mild weather, he tries not to show it.

I turn away from Magiano and say nothing. He looks ahead too, but a smile plays at the corners of his lips. He can tell that I'm considering his suggestion. How does he read my thoughts so well? It irritates me even more. I'm at least grateful to him for not mentioning Violetta, for not confirming out loud that part of why I am sending my Inquisitors to force the unmarked into the streets. He knows it is because I am searching. Searching for *her*.

Why do you still want to find her? The whispers taunt me. *Why? Why?*

It's a question they ask over and over again. And my answer is always the same. *Because I decide when she can leave. Not her.*

But no matter how many times I answer the whispers, they keep asking, because they don't believe me.

We've reached the inner districts of Tarannen now, and although it looks deserted, Sergio's eyes stay focused on the buildings surrounding the main square. Lately, the insurgents known as the Saccorists—taken from the Domaccan

word for anarchy—have attacked our troops on several occasions. It has left Sergio searching constantly for the hidden rebels.

A tall archway leads into the main square, its stones engraved with an elaborate chain of the moons and their various shapes, their waxes and wanes. I pass under it with Sergio and Magiano, then pause before a sea of Dumorian captives. My horse stamps the ground in impatience. I sit straighter and lift my chin, refusing to show my exhaustion.

None of these Dumorians here are marked, of course. The ones in chains are those with no markings at all, the sort of people who used to throw rotten food at me and chant for my death. Now I lift a hand at Sergio and Magiano; they guide their stallions away from me to stand at either end of the square, facing the people.

My Inquisitors spread out too. Our captives shrink back at the sight of us all, their stares fixed hesitantly on me. It is so quiet that if I closed my eye, I could pretend that I am standing alone in this square. Still, I can feel the cloud of terror blanketing them, waves of their reluctance and uncertainty beating against my bones. The whispers in my head dart out like hungry snakes at scurrying mice, eager to feed on the fear.

I nudge my stallion forward several steps. My gaze travels from the people up to the roofs of the square. Even now, I find myself searching instinctively for a sign of Enzo, crouched up there like he used to do. The pull between us, the tether that binds him to me and me to him, tenses, as

if from somewhere over the seas he knows that Dumor has fallen to my army. Good. I hope he senses my triumph.

My attention turns back to the captives. "People of Dumor"—my voice rings out across the square—"I am Queen Adelina Amouteru. I am *your* queen now." My gaze goes from one person to the next. "You are all part of Kenettra and can consider yourselves Kenettran citizens. Be proud, for you belong to a nation that will soon rule all others. Our empire continues to grow, and you can grow along with it. From this day forth, you shall obey all laws of Kenettra. Calling a marked person a *malfetto* is punishable by death. Any abuse, harassment, or mistreatment of a marked person, for any reason, shall bring not only your own execution, but the execution of your entire family. Know this: The marked are marked by the hands of the gods. They are your masters and untouchable. In return for your loyalty, each of you will receive a gift of five Dumorian safftons and fifty gold Kenettran talents."

People murmur in mild surprise, and when I look to my side, I see Magiano glance at me in appreciation.

Sergio jumps down from his horse and moves forward with a small team of his former mercenaries. They go through the crowd, picking out a person here and there, then drag them forward where Sergio forces them all to kneel before me. Fear washes over these chosen ones. As well it should.

I peer down at them. As expected, all those chosen by Sergio and his team are strong, muscled men and women. They tremble, their heads lowered. "You have the chance to

join my army," I tell them. "If you do, you will train with my captains. You will ride with me to the Sunlands and the Skylands. You will be armed, fed, and clothed, and your families will be looked after."

To make my point, Magiano descends from his stallion and approaches them. At each one, he makes a show of digging into his bag and dropping heavy satchels of gold Kenettran talents in front of them. The people only stare. One of them grabs his satchel so frantically that the coins tumble out, glittering in the light.

"If you refuse my offer, you and your family will be imprisoned." My tone deepens. "I shall not tolerate potential rebels in my midst. Pledge your loyalty, and I will make sure that promise is worth your while."

From the corner of my eye, I see Sergio stir uneasily. His eyes turn to the perimeter of the square. I stiffen. I've become very good at knowing when Sergio senses danger. He mutters to several of his men, and they head off into the shadows, disappearing behind a door.

"Do you pledge?" Magiano asks them.

One by one, they answer without hesitation. I motion for them to rise, and a patrol of Inquisitors comes to lead them away. More able-bodied men and women are brought before me. We repeat the same ritual with them. Then, another group. An hour passes.

Someone in one of the groups refuses to pledge. She spits at me, then calls me some name in Dumorian that I don't

understand. I turn my glare on her, but she doesn't back down. Instead, she curls her lips. *A defiant one.*

"You want us to fear you," she growls at me, speaking now in accented Kenettran. "You think that you can come here and destroy our homes, kill our loved ones—then make us grovel at your feet. You think we will sell you our souls for a few coins." She lifts her chin. "But I am not afraid of you."

"Is that so?" I tilt my head at her curiously. "You should be."

She challenges me with a smile. "You can't even bring *yourself* to spill our blood." She nods in the direction of Sergio, who has already started to draw his sword. "You have one of your lackeys do it for you. You're a *coward queen*, hiding behind your army. But you cannot crush our spirits beneath your Roses' heels—you cannot win."

At one time, I might have been intimidated by words like these. But now I just sigh. *You see, Magiano? This is what happens when I show kindness.* So while the woman continues her speech, I swing down from my stallion. Sergio and Magiano watch me in silence.

The woman is still talking, even as I stop before her. "The day will come when we strike you down," she's saying. "Mark my words. We will haunt your nightmares."

I clench my fists and fling an illusion of pain across her body. "I *am* the nightmare."

The woman's eyes bulge. She lets out a choked scream as she falls to the ground and claws at the dirt. Behind her, the entire crowd flinches in unison as eyes and heads turn away

from the sight. The terror flowing from her feeds directly into me, and the voices in my head explode into shouts, filling my ears with their delight. *Perfect. Keep going. Let the pain force her heart to beat so rapidly that it bursts.* So I listen. My fists clench tighter—I think back to the night when I'd taken my first life, when I'd stood over Dante's body. The woman convulses, her eyes flickering about wildly, seeing monsters that are not there. Crimson drops fly from her lips. I take a step back so that her blood doesn't reach the hem of my dress.

At last, the woman freezes, falling unconscious.

I calmly turn back to the rest of our captives, who have become as still as statues. I could slice their terror with my knife. "Anyone else?" My voice echoes in the square. "No?" The silence lingers.

I lean down. The bag of coins that Magiano had originally thrown at the woman's feet now lies untouched next to her body. I pick the bag up delicately with two fingers. Then I walk back to my stallion and swing up into the saddle.

"As you can see, I keep my word," I call to the rest of the crowd. "Do not take advantage of my generosity, and I will not take advantage of your weakness." I toss the woman's satchel of coins to the closest Inquisitor. "Chain her up. And track down her family."

My soldiers drag the woman away, and a new group is brought before me. This time, they each accept their gold quietly and bow their heads to me, and I nod my acceptance in return. The procedure continues without incident. If I've learned anything from my past and my present, it's the

16

power of fear. You can give your subjects all the generosity in the world, and still they will demand more. But those who are afraid don't fight back. I know this well enough.

The sun rises higher, and two more groups pledge their loyalty to my army.

Suddenly, a sharp object glints in the light. My gaze darts up. *A blade, a needlelike weapon, hurled from the roofs.* On instinct, I pull on my energy and whip an illusion of invisibility around myself. But I do not react quickly enough. A dagger flies right past my arm, slicing deep through my flesh. My body lurches back at the impact, and my invisibility flickers out.

Shouts from the captives, then the sound of a hundred swords scraping against sheaths as my Inquisitors draw their weapons. Magiano is at my side before I can even sense his presence. He reaches for me as I sway in my seat, but I wave him away. "No," I manage to gasp out. I can't afford for these Dumorians to see me bleed. It's all they need to rise up.

I wait for more arrows and daggers to rain from the roofs—but they don't. Instead, in the far corner of the square, Sergio and his men reappear. They drag four, five people between them. Saccorists. They're dressed in clothing the color of sand to blend in with the walls.

My anger rises again, and the pain in my bleeding arm only fuels my energy. I don't wait for Sergio to bring them to me. I just lash out. I reach for the sky, weaving, using the fear in the crowd and the strength inside myself. The sky turns a strange, deep blue, then red. The people shrink away, screaming. Then I reach out for the rebels and send an

illusion of suffocation around them. They hunch forward in the grips of Sergio's men, then arch their backs as they sense the air being pulled straight out of their lungs. I grit my teeth and strengthen the illusion.

The air is not air at all, but water. You are drowning in the middle of this square, and there is no surface for you to breach.

Sergio releases them. They fall to their knees, struggling to breathe, and thrash on the ground. I expand my illusion, reaching out for the rest of the captives in the square. Then I lash out with all of my power.

A net of pain blankets all of the captives still sitting on the ground. They shriek all at once, clawing at their skin as if hot pokers were burning them, yanking at their hair as if ants were crawling through the strands, biting at their scalps. I watch them suffer, letting my own pain become theirs, until I finally wave the illusion away.

Sobs wrack the crowd. I don't dare reach up to clutch my own bleeding arm—instead, I focus my hard stare on the people. "There," I say. "You have seen it for yourselves. I will tolerate nothing less than your loyalty." My heart pounds in my chest. "Betray me, or any of my own, and I will make sure you beg for your death."

I nod for my troops to come forward and round up the crying rebels. Only then, with the Inquisitors' white robes swirling around me, do I turn my stallion and ride out of the square. My Roses follow. When I'm finally out of sight, I let my shoulders droop and descend from my mount.

Magiano catches me and I lean against his chest. "Back to

the tents," he murmurs as he puts an arm around me. His expression is tense, full of an understanding that goes unspoken. "You need to have that wound sewn up."

I lean against him, drained after the sudden blood loss and whirlwind of illusions. Another assassination attempt. Someday, I may not be so lucky. The next time we enter a conquered city, they may ambush me before any of my Roses can react fast enough. I am not Teren—my illusions cannot protect me from the cut of a blade.

I will need to root out these insurgents before they can become a real threat. I will need to make a harsher example of their deaths. I will need to be more ruthless.

This is my life now.

Raffaele Laurent Bessette

The sound of the surf outside reminds Raffaele of stormy nights at the Estenzian harbor. Here in the Sunland nation of Tamoura, though, there are no canals, no gondolas that have drifted away from their moorings to bob alongside the stone walls. There is only a beach of red and gold sand, and land dotted with low shrubs and sparse trees. High on a hill, a sprawling palace overlooks the ocean, its silhouette black in the night, its famous entrance illuminated by the glow of lanterns.

Tonight, a warm early spring breeze comes in through the windows of one of the palace apartments, and the candles burn low. Enzo Valenciano sits on a gilded chair, his figure hunched over, his arms resting on his knees. Waves of his dark hair fall over his face, and his jaw is clenched tight. His eyes stay shut in pain, his cheeks moist with tears.

Raffaele kneels before him, carefully undoing the white cloth bandages that run all the way up to the prince's elbows. The smell of burned flesh and cloyingly sweet ointment fills the room. Every time Raffaele pulls the bandage from a segment of Enzo's arm, tugging on the wounded skin as it goes, Enzo's jaw tightens. His shirt hangs loose, slick with sweat. Raffaele winds the bandages in a roll. He can sense the agony hovering over the prince, and the feeling scalds his own heart as surely as if he were wounded himself.

Underneath the bandages, Enzo's arms are a mass of burns that never seem to heal. The original scars and wounds that had always covered the prince's hands have now spread upward, aggravated by his spectacular display during the battle against Adelina in the Estenzian harbor. Destroying almost all of Queen Maeve's Beldish navy with fire has taken its toll.

A piece of skin tears away with the bandages. Enzo utters a soft groan.

Raffaele flinches at the sight of the charred flesh. "Do you want to rest for a moment?" he asks.

"No," Enzo replies through clenched teeth.

Raffaele obeys. Slowly, painstakingly, he removes the last of the bandages from Enzo's right arm. Both of the prince's arms are now exposed.

Raffaele lets out a sigh, then reaches for the bowl of cool, clean water sitting beside him. He places the bowl in Enzo's lap. "Here," he says. "Soak."

Enzo eases his arms into the cool water. He slowly exhales. They sit in silence for a while, letting the minutes drag

on. Raffaele watches Enzo closely. Day by day, the prince has grown more withdrawn, his eyes turned frequently and longingly to the sea. There is a new energy in the air that Raffaele cannot quite put his finger on.

"You still feel her pull?" Raffaele asks at last.

Enzo nods. He turns instinctively toward the window again, in the direction of the ocean. Another long moment passes before he answers. "Some days, it is quiet," he says. "Not tonight."

Raffaele waits for him to continue, but Enzo falls back into his deep silence again, his attention still on the ocean outside. Raffaele wonders whom Enzo is thinking about. It is not Adelina, but a girl long gone, from a happier time in his past.

After a while, Raffaele takes the bowl of water away and gently dabs Enzo's arms dry, then applies a layer of ointment to the burned skin. It is an old salve that Raffaele used to request back at the Fortunata Court, when Enzo would visit him at night to have his hands bandaged. Now the court is gone. Queen Maeve has returned to Beldain to lick her wounds and restore her navy. And the Daggers have come here, to Tamoura—what is left of Tamoura, at any rate. Adelina's Inquisitors dot the hills in northern Tamoura, holding strong.

"Any news of Adelina?" Enzo asks as Raffaele reaches for a fresh set of bandages.

"Dumor's capital has fallen to her army," Raffaele replies. "She rules all of the Sealands now."

Enzo looks back to the sea, as if searching again for the eternal pull between him and the White Wolf, and his gaze seems very far away. "It won't be long before her attention returns here, to the rest of Tamoura," he says at last.

"I wouldn't be surprised if her ships show up next at our borders," Raffaele agrees.

"Will the Golden Triad meet us tomorrow?"

"Yes." Raffaele glances up at the prince. "The Tamouran royals say their army is still weakened from Adelina's last siege. They want to try negotiating with her again."

Enzo gingerly moves the fingers of his left hand, then winces. "And what do you think of it?"

"It will be a waste of time." Raffaele shakes his head. "Adelina turned down their last attempt without a moment's hesitation. There's nothing to barter—what can the royals offer her that she cannot simply take by force?"

Silence falls over them again, perhaps the only answer to Raffaele's question. As Raffaele continues to wrap Enzo's arms in fresh bandages, he tries to ignore the waves outside. *The sound of the sea beyond the window. A pair of candles burning bright in the darkness. A knock on the door.*

The memory comes unbidden and unrelenting, breaking through the walls Raffaele has put around his heart since Enzo's death and resurrection. He is no longer tending to the prince's wounds but standing, waiting, frightened in his bedchamber at the Fortunata Court years ago, looking out at a sea of masked people.

It seemed as if the entire city had turned out for Raffaele's

debut. Noblemen and noblewomen, their robes of Tamouran silks and Kenettran lace, fanned out across the room, their faces all partially hidden behind colorful half masks, their laughter mingling with the sounds of clinking glass and shuffling slippers. Other consorts moved amongst them, silent and graceful, serving drinks and dishes of iced grapes.

Raffaele stood in the center of the room, a demure youth dressed and groomed to the height of perfection, his hair a curtain of dark satin, his gold-and-white robes flowing, black powder lining the rims of his jewel-toned eyes, staring out at a sea of curious bidders. He remembers how his hands trembled, how he'd pressed one against the other to steady them. He had been trained in the types of expressions to allow on his face, a thousand different subtleties of the lips and brows and cheeks and eyes, regardless of whether they reflected his actual emotions. So, in this moment, his expression had been one of serene calm, of shy allure and gentle joy, silent as snow, absent of his fear.

Now and then, the energy seemed to shift in the room. Raffaele turned his head mechanically in its direction, unsure of what he was sensing. He thought at first that perhaps his mind was playing tricks on him—until he realized that the energy focused on a young stranger gliding between the crowds. Raffaele's eyes followed him, mesmerized by the power that seemed to travel in his wake.

The bidding started high and spiraled higher. It soared until Raffaele could no longer make out the numbers, the sights and sounds around him beginning to blur. Other

consorts whispered to one another in the audience. He had never heard such amounts tossed back and forth at an auction before, and the strangeness of it all made his heart pound faster, his hands shake harder. At this rate, he could never live up to the winner's payment.

And then, as the bidding began to trickle down to a few—a young manservant hidden in the crowd doubled the highest offer.

Raffaele's calm expression wavered for the first time as murmurs rippled through the room. The madam called again for an offer to top it, but none did. Raffaele stood in the silence, willing himself to remain still as the manservant won the auction.

That evening, Raffaele lit a few candles with unsteady hands and then sat alone on the edge of his bed. The blankets were silken, trimmed with gold thread and lace, and the scent of night lilies lingered in the air. The minutes dragged on. He listened for the sound of footsteps approaching his chambers and repeated to himself lessons that older consorts had given him over the years.

After what seemed like an eternity, he heard the sound he had been waiting for in the hall outside. Moments later, there was a soft knock on the door.

It will be all right, Raffaele whispered, unsure of the truth of these words. He got up and raised his voice. "Come in, please."

A maid pushed the door open. Behind her, a masked young man walked into his chambers with the grace of a

seasoned predator. The door closed behind him, right as he reached up to remove the mask from his face.

Raffaele's eyes widened in surprise. This was the same stranger he'd noticed in the crowd. He realized, embarrassed, that the stranger was quite handsome—dark curls of hair tied back into a low tail, long black lashes framing his eyes, scarlet slashes in his irises. He stood tall, and he did not smile. The energy Raffaele had sensed during the bidding now enveloped the stranger in layers. *Fire. Flames. Ambition.* Raffaele flushed. He knew he should be inviting the stranger to come closer, to sit on the bed. But, in this moment, he couldn't think.

The young man stepped forward. When he stopped before Raffaele, he folded his hands behind his back and nodded once. Raffaele felt the energy shift again, beckoning at him, and he couldn't help but return the stranger's gaze. Raffaele forced himself to give the young man a smile, one he had been trained to give for years.

The stranger spoke first. "You noticed me in the crowd," he said. "I saw your eyes following me around the room. Why is that?"

"I suppose I was drawn to you," Raffaele replied, turning his eyes down and letting the heat rise to his cheeks again. "What is your name, sir?"

"Enzo Valenciano." The stranger's voice was soft and deep, silk hiding steel.

Raffaele's eyes shot back up to him. *Enzo Valenciano.* Was that not the name of the disgraced prince of Kenettra? Only

now, in the dim light of the chamber, did Raffaele realize that the boy's hair glinted with a hint of deep red, so deep it looked black. A marking.

The former crown prince.

"Your Highness?" Raffaele whispered, so startled that he didn't think to bow again.

The young man nodded. "And I'm afraid I have no intention of fulfilling your debut night."

The scene evaporates as a knock sounds on the door. Raffaele and Enzo look over at it in unison and Raffaele lets out a long breath, pushing the memory to the back of his mind as he puts down the bandages. "Yes?" he calls out.

"Raffaele?" a timid voice answers. "It's me."

He folds his hands into his sleeves. "Come in."

The door opens, and Violetta steps hesitantly inside. Her eyes first meet Raffaele's, then dart to where Enzo sits with his elbows leaning against his knees. "I'm sorry to interrupt," she says. "Raffaele, something strange is happening down by the shore. I thought you might want to have a look."

Raffaele listens with a frown. So, Violetta has sensed something ominous as well. She looks pale tonight, her olive skin ashen, her full lips pulled into a tight line, hair secured behind a Tamouran wrap. She had found the Daggers with her power almost a year ago, all on her own. It'd taken her a week to find the words to tell Raffaele what had happened between her and her sister, then another week still before she begged them through her tears to find a way to help Adelina. Since then, she has stayed at Raffaele's side, working with

him as he tested her alignments and taught her how to concentrate her ability to sense others' energy. She was a good student. A *fantastic* student.

She reminds him so much of Adelina. If he let himself, Raffaele could imagine that he was staring at a younger version of the Queen of the Sealands, before she turned her back. Before she was beyond help. The thought always saddened him. *It is my fault, what Adelina has become. My fault that it is too late.*

Raffaele nods at Violetta. "I'll come in a moment. Wait for me outside."

As Violetta retreats to the hallway, he finishes bandaging Enzo's arms, then rubs his own neck in exhaustion. Too many nights in a row he's spent like this, weeks that stretched into months, all trying in vain to repair Enzo's wounds. But every time they began to heal, they would worsen again. "Try to sleep," Raffaele tells him.

Enzo doesn't respond. His face is drawn, pale from the pain. He is both here and not.

How long ago was it that they had first lost him in the arena? Two years? It seems a lifetime ago, eons, since the last time Raffaele had seen his prince truly alive, the fire in him burning bright and scarlet. He does not want to give Enzo more reason to suffer right now, to let him know how much his presence—half in the living realm, half in the Underworld—hurts those who love him. Instead, Raffaele walks to the door and quietly lets himself out.

The night is warm, a prelude to Sunland summers, and the

28

heat from the day still lingers in the corridors. Raffaele and Violetta walk in silence under the lanterns, passing through the light and the shadows. At each door, he can sense the energy of every one of his Daggers staying inside the apartments. Michel, who after Gemma's death has locked himself away for days at a time, losing himself in his paintings. Lucent, whose chamber has a ripple of disturbance in it. Raffaele can sense that she is still awake, perhaps gazing out of her bedchamber window down at the shores. Lucent's bones have continued to hollow, and now she aches constantly, a development that has made her bitter and short-tempered. Maeve had stayed at first, begging Lucent to return to Beldain with her, even tried bribing and commanding her—but Lucent had refused. She would remain with the Daggers and fight alongside them until her dying breath. After a while, Maeve was forced to lead her soldiers home. But the Beldish queen's letters still arrive weekly, asking about Lucent's health, sometimes sending along herbs and medicines. Nothing has helped. Raffaele knows it will *never* help, for Lucent's illness is caused by something deep within her own energy.

The last chamber once belonged to Leo, the bald boy whom Raffaele had recently recruited to the Daggers, who had wielded the power to poison. Now the chamber sits empty. Leo died a month earlier. The doctor told Raffaele that it was because of a lingering lung infection. But Raffaele wonders about another possible reason—because Leo's body had turned on itself, poisoning him from within.

What weakness will soon manifest in him?

"I heard about Adelina's latest conquest," Violetta says when they finally reach the stairway leading out of the palace. Raffaele only nods.

Violetta glances at him furtively. "Do you think . . . ?"

How hard she tries. Raffaele can feel his heart reaching out to her, wishing to comfort her, but all he can do is take her hand and soothe her temporarily with a tug of her heart-strings. He shakes his head.

"But —I hear she is offering generous payments to the citizens of Dumor," Violetta replies. "She's been more generous than she could be. Perhaps if we could only find a way to—"

"She is beyond help," Raffaele says softly. An answer he has given many times. He is not certain that he believes it, not entirely, but he cannot bear to raise Violetta's hopes only to see them crushed. "I'm sorry. We need to concentrate on defending Tamoura against Adelina's next move. We must make a stand somewhere."

Violetta looks back toward the shoreline and nods. "Of course," she says, as if convincing herself.

She is not like the others. She aligns with gems, of course with fear, empathy, and joy—but she has no markings to speak of. Her ability to take away others' powers makes him uneasy. And yet, Raffaele cannot help feeling a bond with her, a comfort in knowing that she, too, can *feel* the world around her.

None of the three moons nor any stars are visible tonight;

only clouds blanket the sky. Raffaele offers Violetta his arm as they pick their way carefully down the stony path. A hint of charge lingers in the warm winds, prickling his skin. As they make their way around the edge of the estate, the shore comes into view, a line of white foam crashing into black space.

Now he senses what had troubled Violetta. Right along the shore where the sand turns cold and wet, the feeling is incredibly strong, as if all the strings in the world were pulled tight. The waves spray him with flecks of salt water. The night is so dark that they cannot make out any other details around them. Large, looming masses of rock lie nearby, nothing more than black silhouettes. Raffaele stares at them, feeling a sense of dread. There is a pungent scent in the air.

Something is wrong.

"There is death here," Violetta whispers, her hand quivering against Raffaele's arm. When he looks at her, he notices that her eyes seem haunted, the same look she has whenever she talks about Adelina.

Raffaele scans the horizon. Yes, something is very wrong, an unnatural energy permeating the air. There is so much of it, he cannot tell where it is coming from. His eyes settle on a dark patch far in the distance. He stares at it for a while.

A series of lightning streaks breaks through the sky, carving trails from the clouds to the sea. Violetta flinches, waiting for the thunderclap to follow, but there is none, and the silence raises the hairs on the back of Raffaele's neck. Finally,

after an eternity, a low rumble shakes the ground. His eyes travel down to the waves crashing along the shore, then stop again on the black silhouettes of rock.

The lightning flashes again. This time, the glow lights up the shore for a brief moment. Raffaele steps backward, taking in the sight.

The black silhouettes are not rocks at all. They are baliras, at least a dozen of them, beached and dead.

Violetta's hands fly to her mouth. For a moment, all Raffaele can do is stay where he is. Many sailors told stories about where baliras went when they died—some said they would go far out into the open ocean, where they would swim lower and lower until they sank to the depths of the Underworld. Others said they would leap out of the water and fly higher and higher, until they were swallowed up by the clouds. The occasional rib bone washed ashore, bleached white. But never had he seen a dead balira in the flesh before. Certainly not like this.

"Don't come closer," Raffaele whispers to Violetta. The smell in the air grows more pungent as he draws near, now unmistakably the smell of rotting flesh. As he reaches the first balira, he extends a hand out toward it. He hesitates, then places his fingers gently against its body.

The beast twitches once. This one is just an infant, and it is not dead yet.

Raffaele's throat tightens, and tears fill his eyes. Something terrible killed these creatures. He can still feel the poisonous

energy coursing through its veins, can sense its weakness as it takes another low, rasping gasp of air.

"Raffaele," Violetta calls out. When he looks over his shoulder, he sees her wading into the waves as they break against the beach. The hem of her dress is soaked, and she is quaking like a leaf. *Get out of there,* Raffaele wants to warn her.

"This feels like Adelina's energy," Violetta finally says.

Raffaele takes a hesitant step toward the ocean, then another. He walks forward until his slippers sink into wet sand. He sucks his breath in sharply.

The water is cold in a way that he has never felt before, cold like *death*. A thousand threads of energy tug at his feet as the water recedes, as if each one were barbed with tiny hooks, seeking a living being. It sends his skin crawling in the same way a rotting fruit filled with maggots would. The ocean is full of poison, deep and dark and vile. Beneath it churns a layer of energy that is furious and frightening, something he had only once felt in Adelina. He thinks of Enzo's strange distraction tonight, the faraway look in his half-alive eyes. The way he seemed drawn to the ocean. Raffaele remembers the storm that raged on the night when they'd brought Enzo back from the depths of the sea, where the edge of the living world ended and the world of the dead began.

Beside him, Violetta remains frozen in place as the water sways against her legs.

Raffaele takes a few more steps into the ocean, until the waves come up to his waist. The cold water numbs him. He

looks up again to where the silent lightning storm rages, and tears begin to spill down his cheeks.

Indeed, this feels like Adelina's energy. Like fear and fury. It is energy from another realm, threads from beneath the surface, an immortal place never meant to be disturbed. Raffaele trembles.

Something is poisoning the world.

Even now, decades later, I fear nothing so much as the open ocean at night, with darkness stretching around me in every direction.

—The Journals of Reda Harrakan, translated by Bianca Bercetto

Adelina Amouteru

A full week later, the wound in my arm still throbs when I move too quickly. A thick layer of bandages covers it. I wince as I make my way down the ramp to the Estenzian harbor, hoping I haven't broken open the skin again.

The harbor today is filled with the stench of rotting fish. I wrinkle my nose as soldiers lead us to a series of carriages awaiting our arrival. Beside me, Sergio walks with one hand resting permanently on the hilt of his sword. He leans toward me. "Your Majesty," he says. The title flows as naturally from him as if I were born to the throne. "My men have captured several citizens accused of trying to breach the palace gates. They're in the Inquisition Tower now, but I'd rather not take any chances."

I glance at him. "And what are they so unhappy about?"

"Giving up their land to the marked. Your new decree."

"And what are you planning to do with those prisoners?"

Sergio shrugs. He adjusts his cloak to wrap more snugly around his shoulders, then takes a long swig of water from his canteen. "Whatever you like. You're the queen."

I wonder whether he thinks differently of me than he did of the Night King of Merroutas. I'd like to believe Sergio respects me more than that. The Night King was weak, an enemy of the marked, a drunk, and a fool. I pay Sergio far more than that man ever did. Sergio's armor is lined with threads of gold, his cloak woven from the finest, heaviest silks in the world, embroidered with the initials of their makers.

The whispers laugh at me. *Watch your back, little wolf,* they say. *Enemies arise from unexpected places.*

I push stubbornly, in vain, against their words. Sergio will stay loyal to me, just as Magiano will. I have given them everything they could ever want.

But you can't *give them everything they want—they will always want more than they have.*

I remind myself to prepare another herbal drink once I'm inside the palace. My head has started to throb from their incessant noise, chattering away, echoing in my mind all throughout our journey home. "Have them publicly executed," I reply, trying to drown out the whispers with my voice. "Hanging, please. You know how I feel about burnings."

Sergio, as usual, doesn't bat an eye. The Night King had

commanded him to do much worse. "Consider it done, Your Majesty." He waits as I duck into the carriage and then lowers his face close to mine. "Stop by the dungeons when you arrive at the palace," he says.

"Why?" I reply.

A flicker of doubt crosses Sergio's face. "I've gotten word from the keeper that something is wrong with Teren."

A prickling feeling runs down my spine. Sergio has never liked me visiting Teren in the dungeons—so for him to tell me that I should go there now is surprising. The whispers instantly unearth an irrational thought. *He wants you to visit Teren because he wants you dead. Everyone wants you dead, Adelina, even a friend like Sergio. He's luring you there so that Teren can slit your throat.* They cackle, and for a moment I genuinely believe them. I hold my breath and force myself to think of something else.

Whatever's happened to Teren must be serious enough that Sergio wants me to see him. That's all.

"I'll have the carriages go around to the back gate," I say.

"And you should take a different route to the palace. A more discreet one."

I scowl. I'm not about to cower in my own alleys just because a few people have made the foolish decision to attack my gates. "No," I reply. "We've been through this. I will take my public route, and the people *will* see me in my carriage. They are not ruled by a coward queen."

Sergio utters an annoyed grunt, but doesn't argue with

me. He just bows again. "As you wish." Then he rides off to the front of our procession.

I peer outside the window in the hopes of seeing Magiano. He should be riding behind me, but he's not there. I continue looking as my carriage lurches forward and we gradually leave the pier behind.

Months have passed since I last set foot in Estenzia. It is early spring, and as we ride, I notice the familiar things first—the flowers blooming in clusters along windowsills, the vines hanging down thick and green along narrow side streets, bridges arching over canals, filled with people.

Then there are the changes. *My* changes. The marked, no longer called *malfettos*, own property and shops. Others make way for them as they pass through the crowds. I see two Inquisitors dragging an unmarked person through a plaza even as he struggles and cries. On another street, a group of marked children surround an unmarked one, throwing rocks, shoving him hard to the ground as he screams. Inquisitors standing nearby don't stop them, and I turn my gaze away in disinterest as well. How many rocks had once been thrown at me as a child; how many marked children had once been burned alive in the streets? How ironic to see these white-cloaked soldiers I once feared so much now obeying my every command.

We take a turn onto a small street, then lurch to a stop. Ahead, I hear a group of people shouting, their voices drawing close to my carriage. Protesters. My energy stirs.

A familiar voice drifts over to us from outside. An instant

later, something lands on the roof of the carriage with a thud. I lean out of the window and look up—just as a protester darts through the narrow street toward me.

Right away, Magiano's head appears over the roof of the carriage. I have no idea where he came from, but I realize he was what had landed on top. He casts me a quick look before turning his attention to the crowd. Then he hefts a knife in one hand and leaps down from the carriage directly in front of the first protester, putting himself between me and the mob.

"I think you're heading in the wrong direction," Magiano says to him, giving him a dangerous smile.

The protester wavers briefly at the sight of Magiano's dagger. Then he narrows his eyes and points a finger at me. "She's starving us to death!" he shouts. "This *demon, malfetto, false queen*—!"

I shift focus to the protester and his words falter at the sight of my face. Then I smile at him, reach for his threads of energy, and weave.

A burning sensation along your arms and legs, a feeling that turns into fire. You look down, and what do you see? Spiders, scorpions, spiny-legged monsters, seething and crawling all over your body. There are so many that you cannot see your skin anymore.

The man looks down at himself. He opens his mouth in a silent scream and staggers back.

They are pouring into your mouth, out through your eyes. They will eat you alive, from the outside in.

"Now, tell me again," I say as he finally finds his voice and shrieks. "What were you saying?"

The man collapses to the ground. His cries fill the air. Other protesters behind him pause at the sight of his writhing figure. I continue to weave, strengthening the illusion again and again until the man faints from the agony. Then my Inquisitors—white cloaks flying, blades drawn—descend on the rest of them, shoving those they catch to the ground. Ahead of us, I glimpse Sergio's heavy cloak and grim face, angrily shouting orders at his patrol.

You can finish him now, the whispers roar, urging me to stare at the man I'd attacked. *Come now, do it, you want to so badly.* They're dancing with glee in the air around me, their voices mixing together into one maelstrom. I close my eye, suddenly dizzy from their noise, and my sudden weakness only strengthens their shouts. *You want to, you know you want to.* A cold sweat breaks out on my arms. No, it's too soon since I killed in Dumor. Ever since I took Dante's life in that narrow alley not far from here, I've learned that the more I kill, the more my illusions grow, and the more they spiral out of my control as they feed on the strength of a dying man's terror. If I take another life now, I know I will spend tonight drowning in my nightmares, clawing helplessly at a wall of my own illusions.

I should have heeded Sergio's warning.

"Adelina." Magiano is calling my name. He's standing over the unconscious man, dagger still drawn, giving me a questioning look.

"Get him out of the street," I command. My voice comes

out weak and hoarse. "And have him sent to the Inquisition Tower."

Magiano doesn't hesitate. He drags the protestor to the side of the street, out of the way of the carriage, and then waves a hand at the two nearest Inquisitors. "You heard the queen," he calls out. As he passes my window, I overhear him mutter something to one of the Inquisition soldiers behind my carriage. "Keep a better eye on our path," he says, "or I'll make sure you are all tried for treason."

What if some of my own men are starting to slack on their responsibilities too? What if they want me dead? I turn back to the scene outside, refusing to show even a hint of insecurity, daring them to challenge me.

"That's better." Magiano's voice drifts over again from outside, and an instant later he's hopped through the window and seated himself right beside me in the carriage, bringing with him the scent of the wind. "I don't remember protests happening quite this often," he adds. His tone is lighthearted, but I recognize it as the one he takes on when he's concerned.

My side is pressed against his, and I find myself hoping that he stays in here with me for the rest of the ride. "When we reach the palace," I say softly, "have the Inquisitors brought to the tower for questioning. I don't want a rat in my midst, plotting behind my back."

Magiano watches me carefully. "It will be impossible to catch all the rats, my love," he says. His hand brushes against

mine. "Sooner or later, one will squeeze through the cracks. You need to be more careful."

What a funny thing to say. Perhaps he *is the rat.* The whispers dissolve into laughter.

"In good time," I reply, "we won't have to use violence to get our way. The people will eventually realize that the marked are here now, that we will remain in power. Then we can live in peace."

"Peace," Magiano replies, still lighthearted. He hops back up and crouches on the seat. "Of course."

I raise an eyebrow at him. "No one is forcing you to stay here, of course, in service to me. You are free to come and go as you wish. You're an Elite, after all. The greatest of mankind."

Magiano frowns. "No," he agrees. "No one is forcing me to stay."

There's another emotion buried in his words. I blush. I'm about to add something, but then he nods politely and hops through the window again. "Happy ride, Your Majesty," he calls. "I'll be in the baths, soaking off the dirt of this journey."

I'm tempted to get out of the carriage with him, and let him take us both away to the baths—but instead I slump back in my seat. There is a tightness in my chest now that I work to unknot. I'll find Magiano later, apologize to him for dismissing his companionship so carelessly, thank him for always watching me from a distance.

Perhaps it's not you he's protecting, the whispers taunt, *but*

his own fortune. Why hurt the queen who holds the strings of his purse? Why else does he stay?

Maybe they're right. The whispers burrow into my mind, digging their little claws in deeper, and the rest of the ride passes in silence. Finally, we reach the gates at the back of the palace, and the carriages roll into the royal grounds.

I have been the Queen of Kenettra for a year. And yet, entering the palace grounds still feels strange and surreal. This had once been where Enzo, as a child, had dueled with a young Teren in the courtyards, where Teren had watched the princess Giulietta from his hiding place in the trees. Enzo's steps had graced these paths, had been pointed at the throne room where he was meant to sit, what I had once wanted to help him achieve. Now he is gone, an abomination somewhere on the other side of the ocean. Even his sister has long passed into the Underworld, and Teren is my prisoner.

I am the one sitting in the throne room.

Alone. Just the way you like it. I have to force away the image of my sister's face, the tears I'd seen on her cheeks as she turned her back on me for the last time. I push aside a vision of Enzo and his look of utter hatred as we faced each other on the deck of Queen Maeve's ship. As if in response, the tether between us pulls taut for a moment, making me gasp.

Sometimes I wonder if it is Enzo trying to reach out through the miles separating us, attempting to control me. I do the same back. But he is too far away.

Sergio opens my carriage door, offering me his arm as I step down. Several Inquisitors are waiting to greet us, and

when they see me, they lower their heads. I pause for a moment before we enter the palace to look at each of them. "We've won a stunning victory. Go bathe, drink, and rest. I will tell your captains to clear your training schedules for today. Remember, you are a part of my personal guard now, and you will be afforded every luxury. If anyone fails to meet your expectations, report them to me, and I will see to their immediate removal."

Their eyes light up at that. I leave them before they can respond. Let them know me as their benefactor, the one who gave them everything they could ever desire. It should keep them loyal.

As the Inquisitors scatter, I walk with Sergio toward a small side entrance. He waves two of his former mercenaries over to follow me. We pass the front of the procession, and as we go, I see Magiano lounging near the back entrance of the palace, dressed as if ready to head for the baths, while one of the royal maids hands him his cloak. She's a girl I've seen talking to him on several occasions. Today, something she says is making him laugh. Magiano smiles and shakes his head at her before heading off in the direction of the baths.

They're mocking you behind your back, the whispers say. *You heard them laughing, didn't you? What makes you think your precious thief will stay by your side?* As they talk, the scene I'd just witnessed morphs in my memory so that, instead, I imagine seeing the maid run her hand through Magiano's braids, kissing his lips, and him responding by squeezing her arm,

44

murmuring a secret in her ear. My chest burns, filling with fire and pain.

Perhaps you should show them what you're capable of. They won't make a fool of you again.

"It's not real," I say under my breath. "It's not real." Gradually, the illusion fades, and the true scene replaces it again. My heart hammers in my chest as the whispers retreat, chuckling at me.

"The dungeon keeper tells me that they've prepared Teren for your visit today," Sergio says, jerking me out of my thoughts. I turn to him in relief. Based on his expression, he's saying this for the second time. "He's been cleaned, beard shaved off, given a new set of clothes."

"Good," I answer. Teren had killed several Inquisition guards over the past few months, those who had not been careful in his presence. Now they approach him very rarely, leaving him unkempt. "How is he now?"

"Calm," Sergio says. He pats the hilt at his side. "Weak."

Weak? We fall into silence again as we enter the palace and make our way down a poorly lit corridor. The ground slopes slightly until we reach a set of stairs winding into darkness, and here, Sergio takes the lead. I follow him, while other soldiers trail me. Our steps echo down into the depths.

"Rumor has it that the Daggers may be hiding in the Skylands," Sergio says after a while.

I look at him, but his eyes avoid mine. "Beldain?" I ask. "Is Queen Maeve planning to strike us again?"

"I've heard nothing." Sergio is quiet for another beat, and his face is drawn with a strange expression. "Although some say your sister may be in their company too."

Violetta. I grip the edges of my dress more tightly. Of course Sergio misses her—he has been making subtle remarks for months about where she might be. My pattern of conquests—Merroutas, Domacca, northern Tamoura, Dumor—is no coincidence. It is the order of countries where Sergio has heard that Violetta might be. "Send a scout and a balira in Beldain's direction," I finally say.

"Yes, Your Majesty," Sergio replies.

The original Inquisition Tower still stands, the very same one that Teren had once used to hold my sister captive, where I'd gone on several occasions to see him in my desperation. I was tempted to keep him in the same quarters—but the palace itself has a lower level of dungeons meant for the most important of prisoners, the ones to be kept close.

And I want Teren very, very close.

The dungeons are a cylinder spiraling into darkness, barely lit by slivers of light peeking through gratings from above. The farther down we go, the damper the stones and walls get. I wrap my cloak tighter around me as cold air prickles my skin. The steps turn narrower, and through their cracks grow strange mosses and weeds, plants that feed somehow on the dim light and trickling water. Survivors. I am reminded of my early days with the Dagger Society, the old cavern where we all used to train. We, as if there were still such a thing. I cast out the memory of Raffaele's gentle guidance, his smile.

The memory of Michel teaching me how to sculpt a rose out of thin air, of Gemma showing me her power with animals. Of Enzo, wiping a tear from my cheek. *Don't cry. You are stronger than that.*

He's luring you there so that Teren can slit your throat.

The memory of Enzo fades, claimed by the whispers, and morphs instead into the image of him confronting me on Maeve's ship, sword pointed straight ahead, wishing me dead. My heart ices over. *You are only a ghost,* I remind myself, pushing against the familiar tether between us with an illusion of ice, snow, cold. I hope he feels it, wherever he is. *You are already dead to me.*

A man is waiting for us on the lowest level, a marked soldier with a pale streak in his dark blond hair, grease glossy on his face, his Inquisition uniform stained and dirty with ash. He nods to Sergio and then bows low at me.

"Your Majesty," he says. Then he holds an arm out toward the dungeons and ushers us along.

The palace's cells are each their own space, with no bars and no windows. He leads us down a wide hall with iron doors lining either side of it, each one guarded by two Inquisitors. Some of the doors are spaced farther apart than others. When we near the end, we reach several that are spaced so far apart that I cannot see the next door from the one we've just passed. Finally, the dungeon keeper stops at the very last door on our right.

There are six Inquisitors outside this one, instead of two. They line up in formation when I approach, bow, and make

way for the keeper. He takes out one key while the senior Inquisitor takes out a second. Undoing this lock requires inserting two keys simultaneously.

Sergio and I exchange a brief glance. The last time I saw Teren was several months ago, before our expedition to conquer Dumor. I wonder how Teren looks now.

The lock squeaks, then clicks—and the door edges open. I enter behind the Inquisitors.

The chamber is large and circular, with a high ceiling, lit by eight torches along the walls. There is a moat in here, with dirty water fed down from the pipes of the bathhouse. Soldiers line the walls. The moat surrounds an island of stone, and upon this island lies a figure, chained by a dozen heavy links anchored at the very edges and guarded by two soldiers who rotate out once an hour, assigned to raise and lower a rope bridge between the island and the rest of the chamber. The figure stirs when he hears us gather at the far side of the moat. In the torchlight, his hair shines gold, and when he lifts his face in our direction, his eyes glint a familiar madness. Pale, pulsing, colorless. Even now, with our roles reversed, his stare sends a surge of energy through me, a mix of fear and hate and excitement.

Teren smiles at me. His voice echoes in the chamber, low and smoky. "Mi Adelinetta."

Maeve Jacqueline Kelly Corrigan

A letter from Raffaele should have arrived by dove today, but it didn't. Maeve wonders whether the bird has been killed in flight or delayed by storms. The seas *have* been strange lately. Whatever the reason, she didn't receive an answer yet on Lucent's current condition—so she stays in the training yard long after midnight, restlessly swinging her wooden practice sword.

A few of her guards are scattered around the yard's perimeter. Her brother Augustine is here too, helping her practice. He gives her a sympathetic look as she slowly swings her sword and stumbles in the dirt.

"You must be tired enough now to sleep," Augustine says as he gently nudges Maeve back a step and waits for her to switch her stance. He uses his sword to gesture at the

apartments. "Go, Your Majesty. You're no good to anyone out here like this."

Maeve shakes her head and scowls. She hefts her sword again. "I'll stay," she replies.

Augustine lunges at her. She blocks his attack, sidesteps, and swings her weapon high over her head. She brings it down at him and he stops it with his wooden blade. As Maeve grits her teeth, Augustine leans closer to her and frowns. "You need to go to Lucent," he says. "I'm tired of seeing you like this."

Maeve's eyes flash in irritation. "I'm not going to leave my country behind just to visit an old riding companion."

Augustine's lips tense into a line. "Oh, for the gods' sakes, Little Jac," he snaps. "We know Lucent wasn't just your riding companion." At her stunned expression, Augustine laughs. "You are good at many things, but you are horrible at keeping your love interests a secret."

Maeve's temper flares. She pushes Augustine away and swings her sword at him again. The wooden blade hits him squarely in his side before he can block her attack. He grunts at the hit and doubles over. Maeve seizes the opportunity, knocks him flat on his back, and shoves her knee against his chest. She presses the sword roughly against his neck and Augustine holds his hands up in defeat. "I'm not leaving my country," Maeve repeats through gritted teeth, "to visit an *old riding companion*. Not after our last battle. Adelina is on the move. She *will* come north."

Augustine pushes her sword away. "So are you just going to wait for her to arrive on our shores?" he argues back. "Word is that she has taken Dumor. She may have set her sights on Tamoura for now, but soon she *will* turn her attention to the Skylands."

Maeve sighs, lowering her sword. She hops back up and watches as Augustine struggles to his feet. "I can't leave," she repeats, quieter this time. "Tristan."

At the mention of their youngest brother's name, Augustine's mood softens. "I know."

"Did you see him yesterday?"

"Still the same, the doctors say. No change."

Maeve forces herself to lift her sword and concentrate on Augustine again. She needs the distraction. Tristan has not said a word for weeks now—the longest he has ever gone—and his gaze these days is always fixed toward the sea, pointed in some direction to the south. What little spark of light that was left in his eyes has disappeared entirely, leaving behind flat pools and a vacant, lifeless stare. Once, when she'd brought him out to the winter carnivals with her, he'd attacked her in a state of confusion. He'd done it halfheartedly, like some part of him knew he didn't want to, but even then, it had taken Augustine and another man to subdue him. Since then, he has not slept. He has instead stayed by his window, eyes turned to the sea.

The rumors about him swirl around Hadenbury. *Prince Tristan is mad. He attacked the queen, his own sister.*

Maeve charges Augustine again with her wooden sword, and the clash rings out across the yard. She'd tried reaching out to the Underworld last night, searching for clues. But the energy there was too strong, even for her, the darkness of it scalding her fingers, leaving a coating of ice on her heart. She knows, by some instinct of survival, that if she tried to use her power, it would kill her.

"We will have four more ships completed in just a few weeks," Maeve says, shifting subjects as she fends off Augustine's parry. "Our navy will recover fully by the end of the year. Then we can think about Adelina again."

"She doesn't have Enzo at her disposal anymore," Augustine reminds her. "He is with the Daggers in Tamoura. She'll be weaker."

There is a space between their words, where neither wants to mention the rumors of Adelina's descent into madness. "She might be assassinated before we even reach her," Maeve finally says. "One can hope."

Both of them look up at the sound of a gate opening. At first, Maeve thinks it is a messenger coming to bring her a parchment from Raffaele—and her spirits lift immediately. She starts walking toward the figure. "Augustine," she calls over her shoulder at her brother. "Fetch the torch on the fence. We have a message."

Then the figure takes a step into the moonlight, and she hesitates. Several of the guards along the wall move toward him too, although none of their swords are drawn. Maeve squints, trying to recognize him.

"Tristan?" she whispers.

It *seems* like Tristan. She can feel the tug between them, the faint tether that binds their two energies. Maeve frowns. *Something's not right.* His walk is strange and disjointed, and a sickening feeling rises in her stomach. Tristan has his own patrol of a dozen men that rotate around his cell, ensuring he stays safely where he can be watched. *How did he get out?*

As one guard reaches him, Tristan turns while one arm shoots out and grabs the man's neck, squeezing. The guard stiffens, shocked at the attack. Choking, he grabs for the sword at his side, but Tristan is squeezing his neck too tightly. The guard struggles desperately against his grasp. Maeve barely notices that she has already dropped her wooden sword and drawn her real blade.

Behind Tristan appear two guards, running breathless out to the yard. Maeve knows what happened before they even shout it. *Tristan has killed his guards.* She points her sword at her youngest brother. "Stand down!" she calls out.

Beside her, Augustine hops to his feet and draws his real sword too. Tristan doesn't make a sound—instead, he flings aside the man by the throat and then lunges at the next guard closest to him. He twists the man's arm around his back so hard that it breaks.

"Tristan!" Maeve shouts, breaking into a run toward him. "*Stop!*" She reaches out through their tether, seeking to control him. But somehow, this time, he resists her. His eyes swivel to her in a way that sends chills down her spine.

The darkness churning in him lashes out, shoving her power away, and Maeve feels the familiar touch of cold and death on her heart. The effect is so powerful that she freezes in place for a moment from the numbness. *This is not right.*

Maeve pushes forward and reaches Tristan before he can attack another guard. She hefts her sword, but the sight of his eyes frightens her. There is no white to be seen anywhere. Instead, his eyes are pools of blackness, completely devoid of life. She hesitates for a split second—and in that moment, Tristan bares his teeth as if they were fangs and lunges for her with hands outstretched.

Maeve manages to bring her sword up in time—the blade cuts deep into one of his hands. Tristan snarls and lunges at her again and again. He is shockingly strong. It is as if all the force of the Underworld has now crawled under his skin, aching to throw itself at her. The tether between them tugs painfully tight, and Maeve shudders.

When Tristan strikes again, Augustine appears between them and brings his sword up to protect his sister. Tristan growls—his arm moves in a blur of motion, grabbing the dagger tucked at Augustine's belt—and he turns on his older brother. Despite the younger's smaller frame, his attack knocks Augustine off balance. Both fall to the ground in a shower of dirt.

Maeve winces as the threads between her and Tristan pull taut again. The pain makes her light-headed. Through her blurry vision, she sees Augustine fighting desperately

to keep away Tristan's dagger. She reaches within, searching for the strings binding them that are hooked within her heart, the strings that keep Tristan alive and under her control. She hesitates again. A memory of Tristan, before his accident, before she brought him back, flashes in her mind—a smiling, laughing boy, the brother who could never seem to stop talking even when she would shove him lovingly away, the brother who liked to surprise her in the tall grasses and go on long hunts with her and Lucent.

This is not Tristan, she suddenly allows herself to think as she looks at the creature attacking Augustine.

Finally, Augustine manages to flip Tristan down to the ground. He takes his sword and aims it over his brother's heart. Tristan spits at him, but even then, Augustine hesitates. His sword trembles in midair.

Taking advantage of the moment, Tristan stabs up with his blade.

No. Maeve moves before she can even think. She lunges forward, shoving Augustine out of danger's way, and plunges her own sword straight into Tristan's chest.

Tristan lets out a terrible gasp. The dark pools of his eyes shrink away in an instant, leaving a wide-eyed, confused boy. He blinks twice, looks down at the blade protruding from his chest, and then follows it up to where Maeve stands above him, his stare settling on her for the first time.

Maeve reaches out instinctively for the tether that links them, but now, she senses it fading away. Tristan continues

to stare at her for what seems like forever. She feels as if she could read the look in his eyes. Her lips part in a silent sob.

Then, with a sigh, Tristan closes his eyes—the glimmer of light remaining in his soul, the imitation of a life that once was, finally flickers out—and he falls dead to the ground.

When the bugles sounded across the sea, still he ignored them.

When the cavalry reached the gates, still he slept.

When his people cried out, still he called for calm.

Even when the enemy swept his kingdom with fire

and gathered at his castle doors, he paced in his chamber,

refusing to believe it.

–The Second Fall of Persenople, *by Scholar Natanaele*

Adelina Amouteru

emories are funny things. My first recollection of Teren remains crystal clear even to this day—that shining white cloak, a silhouette washed in light by the sun on a brilliant blue day, the profile of a chiseled face, a slender tail of wheat-colored hair wrapped in gold hanging past his shoulders, his hands folded behind his back. How intimidating he looked. Even now, as I stare at this figure lying in chains, dressed like a prisoner, slivers of light now outlining the sinews of his muscles, I can't help but see that first image of him instead.

Sergio leads us forward to the moat. When he reaches it, he leans down to the water and pulls up a rope bridge anchored to the floor. He tosses it to the two soldiers on the island. One of the soldiers hooks the other end of the bridge

to two knobs on the island's floor, and Sergio steps onto the bridge. I follow him.

When we reach the island, Sergio and the other soldiers spread out to either side, giving me a clear path. I walk forward, stopping several paces from where Teren is chained.

"Hello," I say.

Teren stays crouching on the ground, his eyes fixed on me. He doesn't blink. Instead, he looks on as if he were drinking in the sight of me. His clothes have indeed been replaced by a clean set of robes, and his hair is tied back, his face smooth. He is thinner now, even though time has not worn down the chiseled look of his face or the hard lines of his muscles. He says nothing more. *Something is wrong with Teren.* I look him over, puzzled.

"You look well enough," I say. I tilt my head slightly at him. "Less filthy than when I last visited you. You've been eating and drinking." There were several weeks when he refused all food, when I thought he might intentionally starve himself to death. But he is still here.

He says nothing.

"I hear you've not been well," I continue. "Does the great Teren ever fall ill? I didn't think that was possible, so I came to see you with my own ey—"

Without warning, Teren lunges for me. His heavy chains do not slow him down. They pull taut just short of where I am, and for an instant, we stare into each other's faces, breaths apart. My past visits taught me where to stand safely,

but even so—my heart leaps into my throat. Behind me, I hear Sergio and the other soldiers draw their swords.

"Then have a good, long look, little *malfetto*," Teren growls. "Do you enjoy what you see?" He cocks his head in a taunting gesture. "What is it these days, Adelina? Queen of the Sealands?"

I tell myself to stay calm, to meet Teren's eyes steadily. "*Your* queen," I reply.

At that, pain flashes across his face. He searches my gaze, then takes a step back. The chains go slack. "You are not my queen," he grunts through his teeth.

Sergio sheathes his sword again and leans over to me. "Look," he whispers, nodding down at Teren's arms.

My focus flickers from Teren's eyes down to his wrists. Something catches my attention there, something deep and red. Dripping from his wrists and down his fingers is a trail of blood. It leaves a smattering of dots on the stone directly beneath.

Blood? I stare at it, trying to follow the trail. It looks like fresh blood, scarlet and wet. "Sergio," I say, "did he attack a guard? Why is there blood on his arm?"

Sergio gives me a grim look. "He's bleeding from the chains chafing at his wrist. From his *own* wounds."

From his own wounds? No. I shake my head. Teren is nearly invincible; his power ensures it is so. Any wound he received would stitch together before the blood had the chance to run. I cross my arms and look at him. "So it's true.

Something *has* been wrong with you." I nod at Teren's bleeding wrist. "When did this start?"

Teren studies my face again, as if trying to see how serious I am. Then he starts to laugh. It is a low rumble in his throat, one that grows until it shakes his shoulders. "Of course something's wrong with me. Something's wrong with *all of us.*" His lips settle into a wide grin that chills me to my bones. "You've known that for a long time, haven't you, little wolf?"

It has been more than a year since Queen Giulietta died, but I still remember her face well. I call on this memory now. Gradually, I weave an illusion of her deep, dark eyes and small, rosy mouth over my own, her smooth skin over my scarred face, her rich dark waves of hair over my sheet of silver. Teren's expression stiffens as he watches my illusion take shape, his body frozen in place.

"Yes," I reply. "I always knew."

Teren walks toward me until he can go no farther. I can feel his breath against my skin. "You don't deserve to wear her face," he whispers.

I smile bitterly. "Let's not forget who killed her. You destroy all that you touch."

"Well," he whispers back, returning my smile. "Then we have much in common." He takes in Giulietta's face. It is amazing, seeing his transformation. His eyes soften, turning moist, and it is as if I could see memories flitting through his mind, his days with the late queen, bowing to her commands, spending nights in her chambers, standing beside her throne, championing her. Until they turned on each other.

"Why are you here?" Teren asks. He straightens and pulls away from me again.

I glance at Sergio, then nod. "Your sword," I say.

Sergio steps forward. He draws his sword, the sound of the metal echoing in the chamber, and then heads toward Teren. Teren doesn't try to resist, but I see his muscles tense. He used to fight back during the early months of his imprisonment, his furious shouts ringing out through the dungeon, his chains rattling. Sergio had to strike Teren down over and over, with everything from rods to swords to whips, until Teren began to flinch at his approaching footsteps. It is cruel, some would think. But those are the thoughts of someone who has never known Teren's evil deeds.

Now he just waits as Sergio approaches him, grabs his arm, and makes a quick cut on his forearm. Blood gushes out, and I watch, waiting for the familiar sight of his flesh immediately stitching itself back together.

But . . . it doesn't. Not right away. Instead, Teren continues bleeding like any man would, the blood dripping down his arm to meet the wounds from the shackles at his wrists. Teren looks at the blood in awe, turning his arm this way and that. As we watch, the flesh slowly, gradually begins to heal itself, the wound turning smaller, the blood flow lighter, until the gash closes itself up again.

No wonder his wrists are still bleeding. The chafing is a constant reopening of those wounds. I frown at Teren, refusing to believe this. Raffaele's words — Violetta's words — come racing back from when I'd first heard them months ago, one

of the last things my sister said to me. *All of us, all Elites, are in danger.* Our powers are slowly tearing our mortal bodies apart.

No. That's all a lie. The whispers are upset now, hissing at me. I pass this anger along to the dungeon keeper as I snap at him. "I thought I told you to keep him in decent health. When did this start?"

The keeper bows his head low. His fear of me makes him tremble. "A few weeks ago, Your Majesty. I thought he had attacked someone too, but none of the guards seemed injured or complained of anything."

"This is a mistake," I say. "Impossible." But what Violetta had said to me so long ago keeps coming back: *We are doomed to be forever young.*

As Teren stares at me and laughs, I turn away. I cross the moat back to the other side of his cell and storm out, my men trailing behind me.

Raffaele Laurent Bessette

Some days after the storm, when Violetta had first alerted Raffaele to the strange energy in the ocean, the other Daggers follow him down to the shores. A small crowd has gathered near the balira corpses, whispering and muttering. Some children play near the bodies, daring one another to touch the rotting skin, squealing at the size of the creatures. The ocean continues to crash against the bodies, trying in vain to drag them back into the water.

"It's uncommon," Lucent tells Raffaele as they pick their way over the rocks toward the sand. "But not *unheard* of. Beldain has seen mass beachings before. It can be caused by anything—a warming or cooling of the water, a sparse year for migrating fish, a storm. Perhaps it's the same here. Just a temporary shift of the tides."

Raffaele folds his arms into his sleeves and looks on as the children run around the bodies. A simple storm or tide shift couldn't explain the energy he'd felt in the ocean last night, that had drawn Violetta out of bed and made him gasp. No, this was not caused by any natural phenomenon. There is poison seeping into the world. Somewhere, there is a crack, a break in the order of things.

The eerie energy lingers, but Raffaele has no way of explaining it to those who cannot sense it. His eyes stay fixed on the water. He hasn't slept, having spent the night at his writing desk, poring through what papers he still kept from his recordings, trying to solve the puzzle.

Lucent looks like she is trying hard not to show the ache in her bones. "Well, some of the villagers are saying there are reports of a similar event along the Domaccan shoreline." She finds a comfortable spot amongst the rocks and sits down. "Sounds like it's not just concentrated here."

Raffaele leaves Lucent's side and heads down to the edge of the water. He pushes back his sleeve and dips a canteen into the surf, letting it fill. The touch of the ocean makes his stomach churn just as much as it had the night of the storm. When the canteen is full, Raffaele hurries out of the water to shake off its poisonous touch.

"You're pale as a Beldish boy," Michel exclaims as Raffaele passes him.

Raffaele holds the canteen with both hands and starts making his way back toward the palace. "I'll be in my chambers," he replies.

When he returns to his quarters, he pours the contents of the canteen into a clear glass, then sets it on his desk so that it is drenched in light from the window. He opens the desk's drawers and removes a series of gemstones. These are the same gemstones he once used to test the other Daggers, that he had used on Enzo and Lucent, Michel and Gemma. On Violetta. On Adelina.

Raffaele lays the gems in a careful circle around the glass of ocean water. Then he steps back and observes the scene. He reaches out with threads of his energy, searching for a clue, coaxing the stones.

At first, nothing happens.

Then, slowly, *very* slowly, several of the gems begin to glow from within, lit by something other than the sunlight. Raffaele pulls on the energy strings as he would when testing a new Elite, his brow furrowed in concentration. Colors blink in and out of existence. The air shimmers.

Nightstone. Amber. Moonstone.

Raffaele stares at the three glowing stones. Nightstone, for the angel of Fear. Amber, for the angel of Fury. Moonstone, for Holy Moritas herself.

Whatever presence Raffaele felt in the ocean, it is this. The touch of the Underworld, the immortal energy of the goddess of Death and her daughters. Raffaele's frown deepens as he walks over to the desk and peers at the water in the glass. It is clear, shining with light, but behind that is the ghost of Death herself. It is no wonder that the energy feels so *wrong*, so out of place.

The Underworld is seeping into the living world.

Raffaele shakes his head. How can that be? The gods' realm does not touch the world of mankind—immortality has no place in the mortal realm. The only connection the gods' magic has to the living world is through gemstones, the sole, lingering remnants of where the gods' hands had touched the world as they created it.

And the Young Elites, Raffaele adds to himself, his heartbeat quickening. *And our own godlike powers.*

Even as he stands there, turning the mystery over and over in his mind, he finds himself looking in the direction of Enzo's chambers, where the ghost of his prince still lingers after having been pulled up from the Underworld. *After having been* torn *from the Underworld.*

A Young Elite, ripped from the immortal realm and dragged to the mortal.

Raffaele's eyes widen. Queen Maeve's gift, Tristan's resurrection, Enzo's . . . could it have caused all this?

He goes to his trunks and pulls out several books, stacking them in a precarious pile on his desk. His breathing has turned shallow. In his mind, the resurrection plays over and over again—the stormy night at the Estenzian arena, the appearance of Adelina disguised as Maeve, shrouded behind a hooded robe, the explosion of dark energy he'd felt in the arena's waters that came from somewhere beyond. He thinks of the lack of light in Enzo's eyes.

The goddess of Death had punished armies before, had

taken revenge on princes and kings who became too arrogant in the face of certain death. But what would happen if a Young Elite, a mortal body doomed to wield immortal powers, one of the most *powerful* Elites Raffaele had ever encountered, was taken from her domain? Would that tear the fabric separating the living and the dead?

Raffaele reads late into the night. He has ignored the others' knocks on his door all day, but now it is silent. Books strewn around him, volumes and volumes of myths and history, mathematics and science. Every time he flips a page, the candle on his desk flickers like it might go out. He is searching for a specific myth—the only reference to a time when the immortal realm touched the mortal that he's heard.

Finally, he finds it. Laetes. The angel of Joy. Raffaele slows down and reads it aloud, whispering the words as he goes.

"Laetes," he murmurs, "the angel of Joy, was the most precious and beloved child of the gods. So beloved was he that he became arrogant, thinking only himself worthy of praise. His brother Denarius, the angel of Greed, seethed with bitterness at this. One night, Denarius cast Laetes from the heavens, condemning him to walk the world as a man for one hundred years. The angel of Joy fell from the light of the heavens through the dark of night, into the mortal world. The shudder of his impact sent ripples throughout the land, but it would take more than a hundred years for the consequences of that to manifest. There is an imbalance in the world, the poison of the immortal touching the mortal."

Raffaele's voice trails off. He reads it again. *There is an imbalance in the world. The poison of the immortal touching the mortal.* His finger moves down the page, skimming the rest of the story.

". . . until Laetes could look up at the heavens from the place where they touched the earth, and step through once more with the blessing of each of the gods."

He thinks of the blood fever, the waves of plague that had birthed the Elites in the first place. *The blood fever.* Ripples throughout the land. Those plagues had been the consequence of immortality meeting mortality—they had been caused by Laetes's fall. He thinks of the Elites' powers. Then he thinks of Enzo, returning to the mortal world after having visited the immortal.

How had he not seen this before? How had he not made this connection until now? Until the poison in the ocean had given him this clue?

"Violetta," Raffaele mutters, rising from his chair. *She will understand—she felt the poison in the ocean first.* He throws on his outer robe, then hurries to the door. As he goes, he thinks back to when he had first tested Adelina's powers, how her alignments to the Underworld shattered the glass of his lantern and sent the papers on his desk flying.

This energy feels like Adelina's, Violetta had said when her feet touched the ocean's water.

If what he thinks is true, then they would not only have to face Adelina again . . . they would need her help.

When Raffaele turns the corner and enters the hall where

Violetta's room sits, he halts. Lucent and Michel are already standing outside her door. Raffaele slows in his steps. Even from a distance, he can sense a disturbance behind Violetta's door.

"What is it?" Raffaele asks the others.

"We heard a wailing," Lucent says. "It didn't sound like a normal human cry . . . Raffaele, it was the most haunting sound I've ever heard."

Raffaele turns his attention to Violetta's door. He can hear it now too, a low moan that makes his heart clench. It does not sound like Violetta at all. He glances at Michel, who shakes his head. "I don't want to see," he mutters, his voice soft. Raffaele recognizes the fear in his eyes, the wish to avoid the image of what he is hearing.

"Stay here," Raffaele says gently, putting a hand on Michel's shoulder. Then he nods at Lucent and steps into the room.

Violetta is awake—or she seems to be, at first glance. Her dark waves of hair are soaked with sweat, strands plastered against her forehead, and her arms are bare and pale against her nightgown, her hands desperately clutching her sheets. Her eyes are open, Raffaele notes, yet she is unaware that he and Lucent now stand beside her in her room.

But what holds his attention the most are the markings covering her arms.

This girl, the Elite who was once unmarked, now has markings that stretch all across her skin. They look like bruises, black and blue and red, irregular maps that criss-cross her arms and overlap one another. They stretch up to

her neck and disappear down her nightgown. Raffaele suppresses the gasp in his throat.

"She doesn't seem fully conscious," Lucent says. "She was fine yesterday—she was walking around, talking, smiling."

"She was tired," he replies, running a hand in the air over her body, thinking back to how weary her smile had seemed. The threads of her energy tangle, weaving and unweaving. "I should have sensed it last night."

But even he could never have guessed how drastically this could happen, how Violetta could go to bed an unmarked Elite and appear this morning as if she had been beaten. Was this triggered by her wading into the poisoned ocean? *It is all coming to pass.* The thought floods his mind even as he tries to ignore it. *It is the same phenomenon that is hollowing out Lucent's bones, that had killed Leo by turning his venomous power back on himself, and that will eventually happen to the rest of us. A side effect directly related to her power.* For Violetta, whose ability had once protected her from markings like the others', is now facing the opposite—her power has turned viciously on her.

Raffaele shakes his head as he studies her energy. *She will die. And it will happen sooner than for any of us.*

I have to tell Adelina. There is no other choice.

He straightens and takes a deep breath. When he speaks, his voice is calm and unwavering. "Bring me a quill and parchment. I need to send a dove."

And they say she loathed everyone in the whole wide world,
except for the boy from the bell tower.
–Lady of Dark Days, *by Dahntel*

Adelina Amouteru

It is only early afternoon, but a cold drizzle has settled over the city, bringing with it a layer of mist that dampens the light. Sergio has retired to his chambers, complaining of dizziness and thirst, his lips parched. I step out into the city streets alone, clad in a white hooded cloak shielding my hair from the elements. I'm completely hidden behind an illusion of invisibility. The rain dots my face with tiny pinpricks of ice, and I close my eye, savoring the feeling.

I've made it a habit to visit the bathhouse after my visits with Teren, so that I can wash away the flecks of his blood on my skin and cleanse myself of the memory of his presence. Even so, the look in his pale eyes lingers long after I leave his cell. Now I point my boots in the direction of the palace's bathhouse. I could reach it from the corridors within

the palace—but out here, the grounds are peaceful, and I can be alone with my thoughts under a gray sky.

A pair of men are standing across the bridge that leads to the palace's entrance, their eyes fixed on the main gates. They are whispering something to each other. I slow my steps, then turn to watch them. One is tall and blond, perhaps too blond to be Kenettran, while the other is short and dark-haired, with olive skin and a weak chin. Their clothes are damp in the drizzle, as if they've been standing outside for a long time.

What are they whispering? The words creep out of the shadows of my mind, their claws clicking. *Perhaps they are whispering about you. About how to kill you. Even your sweet thief warned you of rats that could slip through the cracks.*

I turn away from the path leading to the bathhouse and decide to follow the men. As I cross the bridge, still hidden behind my invisibility, they finish their conversation and continue on their way. My White Wolf banners, the new flags of the country, hang from windows and balconies, the white-and-silver cloth stained and soaked. Only a smattering of people walk the streets today, all huddled under cloaks and wide-brimmed hats, kicking up mud as they go. I watch them suspiciously, even as I trail behind the two men.

As I walk, the world around me takes on a glittering sheen. My whispers grow louder, and as they do, the faces of people I pass start to look distorted, as if the rain has blurred my vision and smeared wet streaks across their features. I blink, trying to focus. The energy in me lurches, and for a moment I wonder if Enzo is pulling on our tether from across the seas.

The two men I'm following are close enough now that bits of their conversation drift to me, and I quicken my steps, curious to hear what they have to say.

"—to send her troops back to Tamoura, but—"

"—that difficult? I'd hardly think she would care if—"

They *are* talking about me.

The blond man shakes his head, one hand held out as he explains something in obvious frustration. "—and that's it, isn't it? The Wolf couldn't care less whether the markets sold us rotting vegetables. I can't remember the taste of a fresh fig. Can you?"

The other man nods sympathetically. "Yesterday, my littlest daughter asked me why the fruit merchants have two piles of produce now—and why they hand the fresh food to *malfetto* buyers, the rotten food to us."

A cold, bitter smile twists my lips. Of course I had designed this law precisely to make sure that the unmarked suffered. After the ordinance first came into effect, I'd spent time walking the markets, relishing the sight of unmarked people grimacing at the rotten food they brought home, forcing it into their mouths out of hunger and desperation. How many years have we waited for our own fair treatment? How many of us have been pelted in the streets by blackened cabbage and meat filled with maggots? The memory of my own burning so long ago comes back to me, and along with it, the smell of the spoiled food that had once struck me. *Take back your rotting weapons*, I vow silently, *and fill your mouths with them. Eat it until you love it.*

The men continue on, oblivious that I'm listening to every word. If I revealed myself to them now, would they fall to their knees and beg forgiveness? I could execute them here, spill their blood right in the streets, for daring to use the word *malfetto*. I let myself indulge in the thought as we turn a corner and enter the Estenzian piazza where the annual horse races of the Tournament of Storms are held. The square is mostly empty this morning, painted gray by the clouds and rain.

"If I saw her right now," one of the men says, shaking water from his hood, "I'd shove that rotten food back in her mouth. Let her taste that for herself, and see if it's worth eating."

His companion lets out a bark of laughter.

So brave, when they think no one else is listening. I stop in the square, but before I let them go about their day, I open my mouth and speak.

"Careful. She is always watching."

Both of them hear me. They freeze in their steps and whirl around, their faces taut with fear. They search for who might have said it. I stay invisible in the center of the piazza, smiling. Their fear spikes, and as it does, I inhale deeply, relishing the spark of power behind their energy. I'm tempted to reach out and seize it. Instead, I just look on as the men turn pale as ghosts.

"Come on," the blond man whispers, his voice choking with terror. He has begun to tremble, although I doubt it's from the cold, and a hint of tears beads in his eyes. His face

blurs in my vision, smearing like the rest of the world, and for an instant, all I can see are streaks of black where his eyes should be, a slash of pink where his mouth once was. The two hurry off through the piazza.

I look around, amused by my little game. Rumors have spread throughout the city about how the White Wolf haunts the air, that she can see straight into your homes and into your souls. It has left a permanent sense of disquiet in the city's energy, a constant undercurrent of fear that keeps my belly full. Good. I want the unmarked to feel this perpetual unease under my rule, to know that I am always watching them. It will make any rebellions against me harder to organize. And it will make them understand the fear that the marked suffered for so long.

Other people pass me by, unaware of my presence. Their faces look like ruined paintings. I try to push past the blurriness, but a dull headache creeps in, and suddenly I feel exhausted. A patrol of my white-cloaked Inquisitors march by, their eyes searching for unmarked people who might be breaking my new laws. Their armor looks like an undulating wave in my vision. I grimace, clutching my head, and decide to return to the palace. The rain has soaked through my own cloak, and a warm bath sounds enticing.

By the time I arrive at the steps leading up to the bathhouse, the drizzle has turned into a steady rain. My bare feet create a faint slapping sound against the marble floor as I go inside. There, I finally drop my invisibility. Usually, two maidens are trailing behind me when I come here, but I just

want to sink myself into warm waters and let my mind wander away.

As I approach the bath hall, I hear a pair of voices drifting out from within. My steps slow for a moment. The bathhouse isn't empty, as I had thought. I should've sent a servant ahead of me to clear the halls. I hesitate a moment longer, then decide to continue on. After all, I am queen—I can always order whoever they are to leave.

The pool stretches out in a long rectangle from where I stand to the other side of the hall. A fog of warmth hangs in the air, and I can smell the moisture. At the other end of the pool come the voices I'd heard a moment earlier. As I slip off my damp robes and dip my toes into the warm water, I hear a low rumble of laughter that makes me pause. Suddenly, I recognize who it is—Magiano. He *did* say he was going to be at the baths.

He has his back turned to me, and it's difficult to see him clearly through the warm mist in the air. But it's unmistakably him. His brown back is bare and slick, his muscles gleaming, and his braids are piled high on his head in a knot. He leans casually over the edge of the pool, and standing nearby on the stones is the same maiden I'd seen with him by the palace. She is kneeling down, her hair falling over one shoulder, a shy smile on her face as she hands him a glass of spiced wine.

Ah, the whispers say, stirring. *And here we thought he was your plaything.*

Again, bitterness rises in my chest—and my illusions

weave an image before me once more. The maiden, no longer dressed, bathing with Magiano, water glistening on her
skin, him reaching for her, running his hands along the out-
line of her body. *Illusion.* I close my eye, take a deep breath,
and count in my head, trying to still my thoughts. It takes so
much more effort than it once did. I feel a violent urge to get
out of the pool, throw my clothes back on, and rush to my
chambers, to leave them here to whatever they want to do.
But I also feel an overwhelming need to hurt the maiden. My
pride pushes back. *You are the Kenettran queen. No one should
force you to leave.* So instead, I lift my chin and wade into the
water, letting the warmth envelop my body.

At the sound of my approach, the maiden glances in my
direction. Then she freezes as she recognizes me. I can tell
that her gaze goes immediately to the scarred side of my face.
A surge of fear comes from her, and I have to push down my
desire to frighten her even more, to taunt her with my power.
Instead, I just smile. She jumps to her feet and drops into a
bow.

"Your Majesty," she calls out.

At that, Magiano shifts slightly in my direction. He must
have sensed my energy the instant I entered the hall, I
realize—he must have known I was here. But he pretends to
be surprised. "Your Majesty," he says, echoing the maiden.
"I'm sorry, I didn't hear you enter."

I flick one hand at the maiden. She needs no second urging. She scurries off toward the closest door, not daring to
bid Magiano farewell.

Magiano watches her go, then turns to me. His gaze goes from my face to the water lapping around my bare shoulders.

"Do you wish to bathe alone, Your Majesty?" he asks. He makes a move to get out, and as he does, he rises halfway out of the pool. Water runs down his taut stomach.

I have never seen Magiano undressed before. My cheeks warm. I also notice, for the first time, his marking fully exposed. It's a dark red patch that runs along the length of his side, where Sunland priests had so long ago tried to cut off his marking, an attempt to fix him. The first time I saw a glimpse of that old scar, it was the night we sat together by the campfire, when Violetta was still with me. I remember Magiano's lips on mine, the silence surrounding the crackle of the fire.

"Stay," I reply. "I could use some company."

Magiano smiles, but there is a certain wariness in his eyes. "Just *some* company?" he teases. "Or mine?"

I shake my head once, trying to keep the smile off my own face as we both move to the edge of the pool. "Well," I say. "You're certainly better company than Teren."

"And how is our favorite madman doing?"

"He's . . . not healing like he used to. There are chafes on his wrists that are constantly bleeding."

At that, Magiano's carefree attitude shifts. "Are you sure?"

"I saw it myself."

Magiano is silent, even though I know he's thinking the same thing I am. Raffaele's prediction for us all.

"And how have you felt lately?" Magiano asks me quietly. "Your illusions?"

The whispers in my head murmur amongst themselves. *We aren't a weakness, Adelina. We are your strength. You shouldn't resist us so much.* I look away and concentrate on the water lapping around us. "I'm fine," I reply. "We will sail for Tamoura in a few weeks' time, and as always, I want you at my side."

"Invading the great empire of Tamoura already," Magiano replies. "Restless so soon? I've barely had the chance to unpack all of my possessions."

I can tell immediately that the lightness in his voice is not real. "You're not excited. I thought the great Magiano would be intrigued by all the gold that the Sunlands hold."

"I *am* intrigued by it," he says. "And, apparently, so are you. I only hesitate, my love, because of how soon it has been since we were in Dumor. Tamoura's not a weak nation, even after losing their northern territory to you. They are an empire, with three kings and a strong navy. Are your men rested enough for another invasion?"

"Tamoura will be my crown jewel," I reply. Then I frown at him. "You still pity Dumor, for what I did to them."

Magiano's smile finally drops away, and he gives me a serious look. "I pitied them for losing their country. But I do not pity them for looking down on the marked. The fire in you burns as fiercely as it did when I first met you. You'll make Dumor a better place."

"When did your heart turn so soft?" I ask him as I skim the surface of the water with my fingers, creating tiny ripples. "When I first met you, you were a hardened thief who delighted in taking others' belongings."

"I stole from vain noblemen and arrogant queens. Drunkards and fools."

"And do you miss that life?"

Magiano is silent. I can feel his nearness, the warmth of his skin barely brushing against mine. "I have everything I could ever want here, Adelina," he finally says. "You've handed me what feels like the world's riches, a palace, a life of luxury." He draws closer. "I get to be at your side. What more do I need?"

But I *have* taken something away from him. It is on the tip of his tongue, and I can hear it as surely as if he'd said it aloud. *Everyone needs a purpose, and I have taken away his. What can he do, now that he has been given everything?* There is no more thrill of the hunt, the excitement of the chase.

Magiano lifts one hand out of the water and touches my chin for a moment, tilting it up, leaving a droplet of water to run along my skin. "I'm looking forward to seeing you become Queen of the Sunlands," he says, his gaze wandering across my face.

What do you see now, Magiano? I wonder. When he first met me, I was a girl cast out by her friends, allied with her sister, intent on getting revenge on the Inquisition Axis. Now I *rule* the Inquisition. *What do you see when you stare at me? Is it the same girl you once kissed by a crackling fire?*

Gradually, an old, mischievous light appears in his eyes. I tremble as his lips brush against my ear, and I can't help but think about the submerged half of him, flushing at the knowledge that I, too, am naked below my shoulders. "I found a secret place," he whispers. His hand finds mine under the water, tugging on my wrist. "Come with me."

I'm unable to suppress a laugh. "Where are you taking me?" I say in a mock scolding voice.

"I'll beg your forgiveness later, Your Majesty," he teases back, flashing me a grin as he pulls us toward the far end of the pool. Here, the water branches into two narrower segments, each leading into a more private chamber. One of the private chambers has been sealed off for the past few months, though, as part of the archway had collapsed into the water and left it impassable. As we near the bend, I think Magiano is going to lead us into the still-open private chamber on the right. But he doesn't. Instead, he guides us to the left, toward the collapsed arch. We pause in front of it, a trail of water disturbed in our wake.

"Behold." Magiano spreads his arms in a gesture of pretend triumph. "Revel in its majesty."

I wrinkle my nose. "Are you trying to impress me with a collapsed archway?"

"No faith. No faith at all." He is back to his old self, and it sends a rare thread of joy through my heart. "Follow me," he murmurs. Then he takes a deep breath and dives down, grabbing my hand as he descends.

At first, I hesitate. There are still a few things I fear in life.

Fire. Death. And the last time I was submerged in water, in a canal in Merroutas when my illusions first betrayed me, I did not fare well. When I resist, Magiano resurfaces. "Don't be afraid," he says with a half smile. "You're with me." His hand tightens around my wrist, tugging me down again playfully. And this time, I feel safe enough to take a deep breath of my own and do as he says.

The water is warm, caressing my face, and as I go deeper, the world disappears into shades of light and muffled sound. Through the water I catch a glimpse of Magiano's bare body, gliding like a balira down toward the broken archway. Then I catch sight of what he wants me to see. At the very bottom, the archway hasn't completely blocked off the private chamber behind it. There is still a narrow entrance under the water, one that looks just wide enough for a person to swim through.

Magiano goes first. His movements send up a cloud of bubbles. I follow in his wake. The light in the water darkens, turning black, and for a moment, I feel a suffocating sense of fear. *What if I have entered the Underworld? What if I will never surface again?* The whispers in my head stir, chittering. *What if he is leading you in here so he can drown you?*

Then I feel Magiano's familiar hand close on my wrist again, pulling me up. I surface with a gasp. As I brush wet hair and water from my face, I look up to see a chamber lit only by the faint blue glow of moss on the walls.

Magiano watches me as I take in the sight. He turns in the small secret chamber, gesturing along the walls to where

the plants have started to grow. "Amazing, isn't it," he says, "how quickly life finds a place for itself when no one is around to keep it out?"

I stare in wonder at the moss's faint glow. "What is this?" I ask, reaching a hand out to the blue-green vegetation. It feels as velvet as the finest fur.

"Faery moss," Magiano replies, admiring the view along with me. "It thrives in damp caves in Merroutas too. Once it finds a good slit on the wall where it can seed, it spreads everywhere. They'll have their work cut out for them once they fix the archway and reopen this chamber." He grins. "Let's hope it takes them a long time."

I smile. The glow adds a hue of blue to the edge of Magiano's skin, softening his features. He drips water. I draw closer to him, suddenly bolder. "I suppose you come in here often, then," I say, half teasing. "Bringing your maids and admirers?"

Magiano frowns at that. He shakes his head. "You think I'm bedding every maid I speak to?" he says and shrugs. "Flattered, Your Majesty. But you are very wrong."

"So, what you're telling me is that you come to this secret space alone?"

He tilts his head in a flirtatious way. "What's wrong with a thief wanting a little private time now and then?" He comes closer. His breath warms my skin like the fog that hovers over the water. "Of course, here you are. I suppose I'm not alone, after all."

A blush rises on my cheeks as I become very aware of my

bare skin, both above and below the water. My energy stills, as it tends to around him, and I find myself aching for his touch. He leans down so that his lips are just a breath away from my own, and there we hover, suspended in time.

"Do you still remember the fire? Under the stars?" he asks, suddenly shy, and I feel innocent for the first time in a long while.

"I remember what we were doing," I reply with a small smile.

A laugh escapes his lips. Then his expression turns serious. "You asked me whether or not I miss my old life," he whispers, his voice now hoarse. "Do you know what I miss the most? That night."

My heart skips a beat, aching in sudden sadness. "And what about the girl you once sat beside, on that night? Do you miss her too?"

"She is still here," he answers. "That is why I stay."

Then he closes the distance between us, and his lips touch mine. Around us is nothing but the sound of water lapping gently against overgrown stone and the faint glow from the moss. His hand trails along my bare back, tracing the curve of my spine. He pulls me close so that our chests are pressed together. His kiss goes from my lips to my chin, and there he plants them lower and lower, creating a gentle path along my neck. I sigh, wanting nothing more in this moment than us, content with staying here forever. The tether tying me to Enzo fades in my mind, and for an instant I can forget that we are linked at all. Magiano's hands run down my back,

unwilling to let go. My breaths come in ragged gasps. Gradually, I notice that we have made our way to the edge of the pool, where he presses me tightly against the stone. One of his hands tangles in my hair, drawing me forward to him. His kisses return to my lips, more urgent now, and I fall into them eagerly. A low groan rumbles in his throat. I wonder, for a wild second, if he will take us further, and my heart pounds in my chest.

"Your Majesty," he whispers, breathless. A note of amusement creeps into his voice. "You'll ruin me." Then he pulls me to him, so that every inch of our bodies is pressed together. I lean against him, soaking in the luxury of the warm water. I don't want to ask him what he's thinking.

A faint voice rings out, muffled, from the other side of our hidden space. I ignore it as Magiano drowns me in another kiss. Through the haze of my thoughts, the voice comes floating over again.

"Your Majesty? Your Majesty!"

Water ripples against our bodies.

"Your Majesty," the voice continues, drawing nearer. Now I recognize it as one of the stewards who deliver my messages. "There is an urgent letter for you."

"She's not here," another voice complains. "The bathhouse is empty." The voice sighs. "She's probably off slitting some poor fool's throat."

The words break me out of my haze. I push away from Magiano right as his eyes open again. He glances toward the collapsed entrance too, then shoots me a questioning glance.

I straighten and give him a smile, unwilling to show him that the servant's remark has bothered me. Instead, I exhale and try to bring down the flush in my cheeks.

"You'd better go," Magiano whispers, his words echoing in the space. He nods toward the collapsed archway. "Far be it from me to interrupt something urgent."

"Magiano, I . . . ," I start to say. But the rest of the words don't want to come out, and I stop trying to force them. I take a deep breath before ducking under the warm water and swimming through the space that leads back out into the main bath hall.

I break through the surface with a loud splash. A yelp of surprise comes from somewhere in the chamber. As I wipe water away from my face, I see two messengers standing at the edge of the bath, their eyes wide, their fear hovering over them.

"Yes?" I say coolly, raising my brow at them.

This snaps the men out of their terrified stupor. They jump backward in unison and bend down in low bows. "Your Majesty, I—" one of them says, voice trembling. This is the one who had spoken about me with sarcastic disgust. "I—I—I—hope you had a lovely bath. I—"

His words fade into an incoherent jumble as Magiano comes up behind me, shaking water from his hair. If he weren't here, I might indulge myself in punishing this messenger for speaking about me so carelessly. The whispers stir, delighted at the fear emanating from the man. But I shake them off. He's lucky this time.

"You mentioned an urgent letter," I finally say, interrupting the messenger's distracted train of thought. "What is it?"

The second man, smaller and slighter, approaches the water. He presents a rolled parchment to me. I wade toward him and lift one hand out of the water to take it.

The letter's crimson wax seal bears the royal crest of Tamoura. I crack it open, unfurl the parchment . . . and freeze.

I know this handwriting. No one else can write in such an elegant script, with such careful flourish. Behind me, Magiano approaches and looks over my shoulder at the message. He whispers the first thought on my mind. "It's a trap," he says.

But I cannot speak. I only read the message again and again, wondering what it really means.

To Her Majesty of Kenettra,

Your sister is dying. You must come to Tamoura at once.

Raffaele Laurent Bessette

Where will you go, when the clock strikes twelve?
What will you do, when you face yourself?
How will you live, knowing what you've done?
How will you die, if your soul's already gone?
—*Excerpt of monologue from* Compasia & Eratosthenes,
as performed by Willem Denbury

Adelina Amouteru

omorrow, we set sail for the shores of Tamoura. So, to-night, the entire palace is alight with festivities in cele-bration of our upcoming invasion.

Long tables piled high with food sit in every hall of the palace, while the courtyards are bright with lanterns and dancing. I sit with Sergio in one of the gardens. In my hands is the strip of parchment from Raffaele, which I've played with so much now, I can hardly read the letters anymore. My stomach feels hollow and sick. I couldn't even finish my herbal drink, and now, with nothing to keep them at bay, the whispers have started murmuring incessantly in the back of my mind again.

Violetta is with the Daggers after all. Your enemies. What a traitor.

Why do you still care for her? Have you forgotten how she abandoned you?

Yes, she tried to wrench us away from you.

She's better off dead.

Beside me, Magiano's chair is empty. He has taken up his lute and is now sitting in the arched entranceway to the garden, playing a song he's composed just today. Below him, a crowd has gathered. Everyone is already drunk—they sway in their dances, stumbling all over, laughing uproariously. At the edges of my vision, an illusion of Violetta unfurls. I see her dying on the floor, blood spilling in a pool all around, while the other partygoers step over her body. I force my attention back to Magiano, hoping he can distract me.

Magiano is a sight to behold tonight. His silks are gold and white, and trinkets glimmer amongst his long braids, all of them pulled over one shoulder. He leans forward and flashes a brilliant smile down at the cheering people listening to his music; every now and then, he pauses in his playing to call for challenges. People shout the names of old folk songs at him, then cheer and clap when he takes them on. I blush as I remember the bathwater beading on his braids, his bare skin against mine in our secret pool, illuminated by the dim blue glow of faery moss. Perhaps he is thinking about it too.

Ignoring us won't change anything, Adelina. Your sister will still die. And you'll be happy about it, won't you?

The whispers push at my mind until I grimace, clutching my head.

"Your Majesty?"

Sergio's voice beside me sends the voices skittering to the recesses of my mind again. I relax a little in my seat and look over at him. He returns my look with obvious concern. "It's nothing," I say. "I'm thinking of Raffaele's letter." I hold it up to show Sergio.

He lets out a grunt of approval as he tears into a leg of roast hare. "Perhaps he's heard rumors of your split from her and wants to use it against you. Violetta might not even be with him."

A part of me still stirs at the thought of Raffaele—and instantly, I imagine him on the deck of Queen Maeve's ship, surrounded by flames, his forehead pressed against Enzo's, calming the prince, looking back at me with tragic, tear-filled eyes, shaking his head in despair. *If justice is what you seek, Adelina . . . you will not find it like this.*

"They are in Tamoura," I say a little too loudly, in an attempt to drown out the whispers. "No doubt working with the Golden Triad there. Their rulers must think using my sister against me will make me act carelessly."

"They're trying to trick you into a meeting," Sergio replies, although he casts me a careful glance that doesn't match his bold words. "To get you alone in a room. But what they'll get instead is an army." He throws back the rest of the drink in his cup, visibly reacting to how strong it is, and then clears some space on the table before us. He pulls out a wrinkled parchment and spreads it out. He has been carrying this with him everywhere lately, so I'm already familiar with it. It is his battle plan for Tamoura. "I've been digging up all

the maps I can find of the landscape around Alamour. Look: The city itself is surrounded by high walls, but if we can get up here"—he points to a strange outcropping of cliffs that meander along the eastern side of the city—"we can find a way to get over the walls."

"And how do we do that?" I ask, folding my arms. "Baliras can't fly that far inland, not in a Sunland desert. They'll suffocate in the dry air."

The instant I say it, I know the answer. I glance at Sergio, who gives me a sly smile as he pours himself a cup of water instead of wine. "I think I know someone who can bring us a good storm," he replies.

I give him a smile back. "It should work," I say, leaning forward in my seat to peer more closely at Sergio's calculations. I'm impressed with the way he has split up the rest of our men. "We'll surprise the Tamourans in their own home."

Sergio's eyes sweep once over the festivities, out of habit. I follow his gaze. Off in the corner, a path is being cut through the crowd, causing cheers and taunts to go up. The entertainment has arrived. "We'll do more than surprise them," Sergio replies. "We'll defeat them so soundly that their Golden Triad will soon be mopping your marble floors."

Our conversation pauses as the procession makes its way to the main clearing. It's led by two young Inquisitors who now gleefully shove forward several people with bound arms. They stumble and fall, then crouch into some resemblance of a bow in my direction. All around them, the crowd cheers. Wine spills out of goblets.

"Your Majesty!" one of the Inquisitors calls up to me. His hair shines in the light, revealing a glimmer of scarlet red against the black. "Found these four in the streets and brought them in for you. I overheard one using the word *malfetto*. Another was trying to pass as one of us with false markings."

At that, the crowd—all of whom are marked—starts to shout curses at the people tied up on the ground. I peer at them to get a closer look. One is an old man, while another is an aging woman. The third is a boy, barely out of childhood, while the fourth is a girl newly wedded, still wearing double bands around one of her fingers. I can tell the girl is the one who was trying to wear false markings—the color in her hair and against her skin looks disturbed, where an Inquisitor must have smeared his hand across it.

"Burn them all!" someone yells, and this is met with a thunderous cheer.

"Let's have some fun!" another shouts.

Over by the archway, Magiano's eyes meet my own. He isn't smiling anymore. *Their fear and hatred fill this place.* The whispers chitter again, fully awake now, and the terror wafting off the four prisoners fills my senses, feeding me. I take them in and feel little pity. After all, not much time has passed since they once stood by and watched as the marked were dragged through the streets and set ablaze, saw our families stoned to death by crowds of enthusiastic onlookers. We used to be the ones to sneak powders and potions from apothecaries, desperate to hide our markings. How quickly

our former enemies have tried to adopt our appearance—how eagerly they smear colors on themselves in an attempt to be more like us.

Why shouldn't we cheer their punishment now?

Beside me, Sergio has gone silent too. I look on as an Inquisitor lights a torch from one of the lanterns, then glances expectantly at me. So does everyone else. The noise fades as they wait for my command.

I am their queen. The *malfettos*, the malformed, the marked. I give them what they want, and they give me their loyalty. *It is what I want too.* My gaze turns to the trembling prisoners on the ground. I stop on the youngest, the boy. He stares back at me with vacant eyes. Beside him, the old man lifts his tear-stained face long enough for me to see the blinding hatred in them. *Demon queen,* I know he's thinking.

The whispers in my head build to a dull rumble. I bow my head and close my eye, trying in vain to shut them out. On another night, I would be more ruthless—in the past year I've ordered prisoners executed before me, so this would be nothing new. But tonight, my heart feels heavy with the weight of Raffaele's message. Visions of Violetta continue to crowd my thoughts.

One glance in Magiano's direction is enough. He gives me the subtlest shake of his head, and his words return to my mind, as if whispered in my ear. Perhaps he is drawing on my power. *Let the people love you a little, mi Adelinetta.*

"Release them," I hear myself saying as I rub my temples. "And get on with the celebrations."

The crowd's raucous cheers fade away as they gradually understand what I've said. The prisoners stare at me in stunned silence, as do my Inquisitors.

"Was I not clear?" I call out, my voice ringing in the chamber. The corners of the space turn dark, and a haunting wail whips through the air. The crowd lets loose a round of frightened gasps as they edge away from the encroaching blackness. My soldiers jump to action now, untying the ropes that bind the prisoners' arms and forcing them to their knees so that they can thank me. They sway, blinking away confusion, and I look on, wondering how my sister has the power to influence my decisions even when she's not here.

"Get out of my sight," I snap to the kneeling prisoners. "Before I change my mind."

They need no second bidding. The girl scrambles to her feet first, then rushes over to the old man and pulls him to his feet. The old woman follows. The boy lingers the longest, puzzling over my expression before he, too, hurries after the others. The crowd's eyes turn from me to them, and as the musicians try to strike up the songs again, scattered singing begins to puncture the awkward silence.

My focus shifts back up to the archway, but Magiano is no longer there.

His absence cuts through the rising tide of darkness in my chest, leaving me exhausted—in this moment, all I want is to get away from here and find him. I weave an illusion of invisibility around myself while the crowd tries to resume

celebrating. Only Sergio realizes that I've gone, although he doesn't call out to stop me.

I shake my head in disgust as I walk. All this dwelling on Violetta has turned me soft tonight.

I make my way out of the gardens and into a dark hall. There are crowds of new nobility here too, marked people to whom I'd handed aristocratic titles after stripping them from their unmarked masters. I push through them. One of the nobles spills her wine as I shove by. I rush down the hall until I come to a winding staircase guarded by Inquisitors, and then I head up to an empty floor. Finally, peace.

I stop and lean my head against the wall. The whispers whirl in a cloud around me, and their fury adds to the dizziness in my head. I try to steady myself. "Magiano," I call out, wondering if he might be nearby, but my voice just echoes down the hall.

You shouldn't have let them go, the whispers say. They always respond when no one else does.

"Why not?" I retort through gritted teeth.

The harmless grow up to become the bringers of wrath. You know this better than anyone, you fool.

"An old couple and a pair of children," I murmur with a sneer. "They can't hurt me." I close my eye, and in the darkness, the whispers lurch forward, flashing their naked grins at me.

Oh? How arrogant you've grown, little wolf. My anger flares at their use of my old nickname, and in response, the

whispers clap in delight. *Yes. That makes you furious, doesn't it? You* are *arrogant, my queen. Why, look. The boy has already come back for you.*

I open my eye again and glance around. There, standing in the hall right before me, is the boy with his grave eyes. He looks at me without a word.

My anger ignites again, and the ghosts of illusions flicker in the corner of my consciousness. "I thought I told you to get out."

The boy doesn't answer. Instead, he takes a step closer. Are those tears of blood coming from his eyes? *The blood fever.* My anger shifts to uncertainty. Then the boy emits a shriek and lunges at me with a knife.

I scream, stumble backward, and throw my arms instinctively across my face. Through my haze of thoughts, I see the boy vanish. He is replaced by a hulking beast. Black boils cover his hunched back, and his long claws click against the floor. He jerks toward me, his fangs stretching all the way around his head. The incarnation of my whispers.

What's the matter, Your Majesty? Afraid of your own halls?

He charges at me with arms outstretched, mouth extended. He is an illusion, just an illusion. He's not really there. Raffaele's note has distracted me, disturbing my energy, so I've lost control again. That's all this is. If only I stand still, he will disappear in a cloud of dust when he reaches me. He cannot hurt me.

But I can't make myself stop. I am in danger. I need to *run.* So I do. I run as the monster pursues me, his claws tearing

up the floor's stone. I can feel his hot breath on my back. The hall stretches endlessly before me, like a gaping mouth, and when I blink, arms tear out from each of the corridor's walls, reaching for me.

Wake up, I scream at myself as I run. *Wake up. Wake up!*

I stumble. I try to catch myself, but instead I fall to my hands and knees. The monster reaches me and I look up at him in horror.

But he is no longer a beast. I see my father's face, contorted into a picture of rage. He seizes my wrist and yanks me forward, dragging me along the floor. "Where have you put your sister, mi Adelinetta?" he asks in his eerie, quiet voice even as I try to pull free. "What have you done with her?"

She left me. It wasn't my fault. She left me behind, of her own free will.

"What did I do to end up with a daughter like you?" My father shakes his head. We round the corner and enter the cavernous space of our old family home's kitchen. Here, my father seizes a butcher knife from the counter. *No, don't, please.* "You open your mouth, and out spill lies. Who did you learn that from, hmm, Adelina? Was it from one of our stable boys? Or were you born this way?"

"I'm sorry." Tears spill down my cheek. "I'm so sorry. I'm not lying. I don't know where Violetta is—" *I know I am not a child trapped in my old home. I am in the Estenzian palace, and I am the queen. I want to return to the festivities. Why can't I wake up?*

My father glances down at me. He yanks my arm straight and slams my hand down on the floor. I'm crying so hard

that I nearly choke. He positions the butcher knife over my wrist, then brings it back high over his head. I squeeze my eye shut and wait for the blow.

Please let me wake up now, I beg.

The whispers chuckle at my plea. *As you wish, Your Majesty.*

"Your Majesty? *Adelina.*"

The hand clutching my arm suddenly loosens its grip. I look up to see that it belongs to Magiano. The kitchen is gone, and I am lying on the floor of the palace's hall again. Magiano pulls me to him as I continue to sob—even though his expression is concerned, he seems relieved to finally make eye contact with me. I hug him close and cling tightly. My body trembles against him.

"How do you always manage to find the worst hallway to lie down in?" Magiano says, his teasing only halfhearted. He brings his face down to my ear and murmurs something I can barely understand, over and over, until the whispers in my head fade into the shadows.

"I'm fine," I finally say, nodding against his shoulder.

He pulls away far enough to give me a skeptical look. "You weren't fine just a few moments ago."

I take a shuddering breath and wipe my hand across my face. "Why did you come up here, anyway? Did you hear me calling for you? Was it because of what happened outside?"

Magiano blinks. "You were calling for me?" he says, and then shakes his head. His mouth tightens into a thin line. "I'd hoped you would come looking for me." I search his face, wondering if he is still mocking me, but he seems serious

now. For the first time, I realize that there are Inquisitors behind him. There is an entire patrol with him, looking for me.

All of a sudden, I feel tired to my bones. Magiano sees me sag, and he ropes an arm behind me as I do, lifting me effortlessly. I let him. He mutters something to the Inquisitors, and they start to file out. I close my eye after that, content to let Magiano carry me back to my chambers.

Stock–

2 days' worth black bread

2 days' worth dried meat

6 days' worth water

Waste–

12 days' worth bread, infested

12 days' worth water, unfit to drink

—From the journal of an unknown soldier during the Battle for Cordonna Isle

Adelina Amouteru

It is for the best that we set sail for Tamoura the next day, under a brilliant blue sky.

The weeks at sea will force me to concentrate on our new mission, to forget about my loss of control over my illusions in the hallway last night. Magiano doesn't mention it again, either. We go about our business on the ship acting like all is fine; we have strategy meetings with Sergio as if no one remembers my incident. But I know that word of it has spread among my Inquisitors. Now and then, I see them murmuring in the shadows, eyeing me with wariness.

Our queen is going mad, they must be saying.

Sometimes I can't tell if my madness is what's conjuring these images, twisting my confidence. So I try to ignore them, as always. What does it matter if I'm mad? I have a

hundred ships. Twenty thousand soldiers. My Roses at my side. I am *queen*.

My new flag is silver and white, of course. In its center is a black, stylized symbol of a wolf, surrounded by flames. I am a creature who was meant to die in fire—but I didn't, and I want to be reminded of that every time I look at this image. With each passing day at sea, the silver-white flags seem to stand out more and more against the deep, strange gray of the ocean, like a flock of birds heading toward new nesting grounds. One week blends into the next, and then into a third, with stale winds slowing us down and the Falls of Laetes to maneuver around.

At the end of the third week, I stand on the deck of my ship and look back at the sea of ships behind us. Every single one of them flies my pennants. I smile at the sight. The nightmare within nightmares had visited me again last night, this time shifting so that I would wake over and over in my bed on board my ship. It is a relief that my army distracts me from the memory.

"We are nearing Tamouran shores," Sergio says as he comes to stand beside me. He is dressed in full armor this morning, with knives strapped to his chest and daggers crossed on his back, hilts poking out from the tops of both his boots. His hair is slicked back out of the way, and he looks restless, eager for action. "Do you want me to give the order to change pennants?"

I nod. "Do it." I, too, am dressed for war. My robes have been replaced with armor, and my hair is tied back in a tight

series of braids, a Kenettran hairstyle. I've left my Tamouran head wraps behind. It was a tempting thought, flying over Alamour looking like a Tamouran girl—but I want them to know what nation is coming for them.

"As you say, Your Majesty," Sergio replies.

I glance at him. A deep crease has formed between his brows. *Is he thinking about Violetta too?* "This time, we will succeed," I say. *At conquering Tamoura. At finding my sister.*

"We will," he echoes. He offers me a terse nod, his face expressionless.

The sky above us, startlingly blue when we first left Kenettra, is now a threatening gray. Black clouds streak the horizon in front of us. Sergio gathers his cloak more tightly about him, his eyes trained in concentration on the approaching storm. He has been working on this tempest ever since we set sail, and now it is strong enough that I can sense the sparks in the air, the prickle along my arms.

"Black seas," Sergio mutters, gesturing down at the dark waters. "A bad omen."

"Your Majesty!" Magiano's voice shouts at us from the crow's nest. We both look skyward. "We've sighted land!" His arm emerges from the side of the nest to point toward the horizon, and when I follow it, I see a sliver of gray land emerging underneath a dark sky. Even from this distance, the vague silhouette of a high wall can be seen, fortified by one side that is nothing more than a steep cliff.

An instant later, Magiano drops down next to us. I didn't even notice him making his way down the main masthead.

"That is Alamour, my love," he says, gesturing toward the cliff and wall.

The last time my forces set our sights on Tamoura, it was to conquer their northwestern territories. Now I am going to set foot in their capital. Thunder rolls across the ocean, and flashes of lightning make the clouds glow. I wrap my arms around myself and shudder. My mother told me stories of this place, from where my ancestors came, and how many times armies had failed to penetrate its walls.

But I will be different.

If Violetta were here, she would be trembling at the thunder. Is she doing so right now, somewhere in Tamoura?

Sergio rests his hand on the hilt of his sword. "I haven't heard their bugles sound. But if they haven't seen us yet, they will soon. Half of our fleet is going to sail into their western bay." He draws an invisible image in the air, gesturing at the city's two bays and the cliffs running along its northern border. "The west is their main harbor, difficult to enter because of the narrow passage in. The east is an easier bay to access, but full of sharp rocks. This is where the other half of our fleet—where *we* ourselves—will enter. We can sail in, but we can't dock. So we'll call our baliras instead." Sergio pauses to look at me. "I hope you feel rested, because we're going to need you to conjure one vast illusion of invisibility for us."

I nod. Even if the Tamourans can see a glimpse of our ships right now, they will not be expecting them to all vanish into thin air. Invisibility, despite all my mastery, is still the most difficult of my illusions—making myself invisible in a

city usually requires a great deal of concentration, painting over my appearance with whatever is around me, constantly, as I move. But out here in the open ocean, all I need to do is weave an illusion of repeating waves and sky over our ships. Even if I make a few mistakes, the Tamourans will be watching from far away. It should be easy to fool them. If I can weave invisibility across the entire fleet, they won't know where we are until we are upon them.

"And are the baliras ready?" I ask, stepping closer to the railing to look down at the ocean.

Sergio nods. "They're ready." But I sense an immediate unease in him and look up. When he sees my expression, he sighs and shakes his head. "The baliras have been restless all night. I'm not an expert in their behavior, but some of the other crew members tell me that they seem like they're ill. Something in the water, perhaps."

"Always knew the fish from this strait tasted funny," Magiano quips, but he barely says it like a joke. I study the baliras that skim the surface of the water as they swim. I can't tell how healthy they are, but Sergio's words frighten me.

"Will they be strong enough to carry us across the eastern bay?" I ask as one of them bursts through the waves with a haunting call.

Sergio crosses his arms. "They say the baliras will fly long enough to get us over the wall. I don't know if they'll survive a long battle, though."

"So we need to make it quick and clean," Magiano says.

"Essentially, yes."

Magiano raises an eyebrow at me. He doesn't say it, but I know he's wishing that we had someone like Gemma with us. Maybe we would have, once upon a time. But Gemma is dead. *She hated you, anyway,* add the whispers, and I harden my heart before I let myself think about her for much longer. The Daggers will be waiting for us, along with the Tamouran army. The thought of forcing them to their knees gives me some sense of satisfaction. *Finally,* the whispers sigh.

In unison, our silver-white pennants turn into black ones that blend with the darkening sky. Our war drums echo deep and rhythmic across the sea. The shores of Tamoura are growing closer, and I can see the towers of the capital. Ships have gathered in the harbor, some clustered at the narrow entrance, ready to stop us. But Sergio's storm is already doing its work. The ocean crashes hard against the harbor's rocks, sending white spray high in the air and rocking the Tamouran fleet.

The waves hit our own ships hard too, and as one smashes into our side, I careen toward the railing. My hands find it and latch on for safety. Behind me, Magiano makes a flying leap at the edge of the sail and lifts himself onto it in the blink of an eye. He pirouettes to the ladder steps, which lead up along the mainmast. "You're going to need a better view," he shouts. "Care to join me?"

He's right. I take his hand, and he pulls me to the first step. Slowly, I make my way up as the ship tosses. Blackness has nearly covered the entire sky, leaving only a sliver of blue over the capital, surrounded by churning storm clouds.

Fat drops of rain have started to pelt down on us. A roll of thunder shakes us. From here, I can see the entire expanse of the Tamouran coastline—the smaller bay off to one side of the city, and the wider bay that we are now sailing dangerously close to. The bay's mouth gapes before us, and the rocks lining it are sharp and jagged, like the jaws of a monster rising out of the ocean. Directly beyond it is a line of Tamouran warships, all facing our fleet and ready for battle. As we look on, a burst of cannon fire sparks from one of the ships. A warning shot.

I take in the ocean behind us. My Kenettran warships wait for our command.

Magiano gives me his perfect, sidelong smile. "Shall we, White Wolf?"

I turn back to the vast bay and the Tamouran ships, raise my hands, and draw on my energy. The whispers in my head awaken, thrilled with their freedom—and the energy all around me shimmers in a web of threads. I am darkness within, and my darkness reaches out, seeking the fear in the hearts of our enemy soldiers, the anxiety in the hearts of those in my own fleet. It grows in my chest until I can't hold it in anymore.

So I let it out   and weave.

The clouds over our fleet glow a faint blue. Then, a phantom creature bursts from the water, a figure of black smoke that morphs into the ghost of a white wolf, each of its fangs as large as one of our ships, its eyes glowing red against the storm. It hovers over our fleet with its glare trained on the

Tamouran ships. It lets out a roar right as another clap of thunder shatters the sky.

The Tamouran fleet fires a full volley of cannons at us—but I grin, because I can feel the sudden spike of terror in the hearts of their soldiers. To them, they are staring into the face of a demon.

I glance at Magiano. "Ready?" I ask.

He winks. Rain soaks us both now, coming down in sheets, and water drips from his high knot of braids. "Always ready for you, my love."

I blush a little, in spite of myself, and turn quickly away before he can see it. Then I shift my concentration away from my illusion. Magiano reaches out with his energy this time—he takes over the illusion of the white wolf, and as he holds it in place, I weave an enormous blanket of invisibility over all of our ships, morphing them into the image of black ocean and stormy skies. We vanish from sight in the churning waves.

The Tamouran ships continue firing, but now I can tell that they are aiming blindly, trained only in the direction of their last attack. We are close enough now to the bay's entrance that I can see the Tamouran soldiers running back and forth on the decks of the ships, their head wraps soaked in the rain. My heartbeat quickens in excitement at the sight of them. *I am coming for you all.*

I am coming for my sister.

Down below, Sergio's voice rings out, *"Fire!"*

Our cannons erupt in unison. They rip into the sides of the Tamouran ships, and distant smoke and screams fill the air.

They fire back, but they still cannot see us. Our ship reaches the bay's mouth, still shielded behind invisibility, and Sergio guides us in, narrowly avoiding the jagged rocks on either side.

Magiano suddenly seizes my wrist and yanks me down lower in the crow's nest. I duck instinctively with him. An instant later, I see what has caught his attention—baliras, dressed in silver armor, flying in our direction. It takes me a moment to recognize one of their riders. And the recognition only comes because of the flames that shoot out toward us.

Enzo.

The Daggers are here.

Our pennant catches fire for an instant, before the huge spray of waves crashes over us again and puts it out. But the glimpse of flames temporarily exposed where our ship is, and the Tamourans' cannons point in our direction. They explode, hurling cannonballs toward us.

I'm thrown against Magiano as one of their cannons rips into the side of our vessel. My concentration flickers, and my illusion wavers long enough to reveal our ships again, ghosts moving against the storm, before I quickly cover them up. Overhead, Enzo rains down another burst of fire. This time, it hits one of the ships behind us, and its forward sails erupt in flames.

Other enemy baliras start firing arrows at us. I grit my teeth and huddle against Magiano for warmth in the crow's nest, listening to the sound as they slice through the air. Our ship, as well as two others, has managed to make it inside

the bay, but we are not moving fast enough to repel the Tamouran fleet waiting for us. Enzo's bond tugs hard at my heart, and I can feel him reaching out for me as I call to him instinctively. He knows exactly where I am. Even now, I can see him circling back around, a rider separated from the others, hunting me down.

Bastard prince.

"I need to fly," I mutter to Magiano as I stagger to my feet. "We need to be airborne."

As soon as the words leave my mouth, a blast of wind hits us. His answer is lost as he grabs my waist and presses us both against the crow's nest, shielding our faces from the impact. It is such a strong gale that it threatens to lift us off our feet. Only Magiano's clinging to the crow's nest keeps us from being blown straight into the ocean. At the same time, a wave smashes against the ship behind us with a force far greater than the storm's waves.

"I see the Windwalker!" Magiano calls out to me. When I lift my head to look, he points at a balira that rushes past, coming close enough for me to see the coppery-blond curls streaming behind its rider. Lucent has someone else with her, and her posture is hunched, as if she is exhausted. But it doesn't stop her from glancing in our direction, and as she does, another blast of wind strikes us.

The impact hurls me off my feet. I collapse as another wave pummels the side of our ship, then stagger upright, blinking water from my vision. Magiano grabs my arm again and the world clears a little. Lucent's stunt has scattered all

my concentration, and now my cloak of invisibility has vanished entirely, leaving my ships fully exposed. I force back my frustration, reach out again, and weave.

Gradually, the ships disappear again into the storm. Off in the distance, Tamouran riders head in the direction of our second fleet as they close in on the capital's western border. My invisibility has thrown off the Tamouran line of ships defending the main bay, and as we look on, several of ours make it around the line, firing their cannons into the vulnerable sides of the closest enemy vessels.

Magiano guides us over to the side of the ship. He waves furiously at one of our passing baliras. "Ours!" he shouts at the soldier riding it.

The balira turns in our direction. It flies lower as it nears the ship, then dives to the surface of the water with an enormous splash. The wave rocks us. Magiano climbs on top of the nest's railing, steadies himself, and I follow him. As the balira swims right up next to the ship, we jump over the edge and onto its back. The original rider gets off, diving into the water and climbing up along the side of the hull.

Magiano pulls me to him on the balira's back. It is slick with rain, and I'm grateful for the strappings that give us secure footholds against its flesh. The balira stirs restlessly in the water. It turns sharply, then surges forward in preparation to fly.

As it does, a wave of ocean water soaks my legs. I suck in my breath.

Sergio had mentioned earlier that something in the water

110

seemed to be making the baliras sick. Now I know what he means. The ocean feels *wrong*. There is a poisonous presence here, a darkness that seems at once familiar and sickening. I shiver at the feeling and frown, trying to pinpoint what it is. I have sensed this darkness before in my nightmares. I know it. The whispers in my head stir, excited.

My thoughts scatter as the tether between Enzo and me suddenly pulls taut. I gasp. At the same time, Magiano yanks back on the balira's harness and launches us into the sky. He veers us sharply to the right, one of his arms locked tightly around my waist. I'm about to cry out when a burst of fire hits the space where we had been just a moment ago.

Enzo appears in the sky a short distance from us. His dark hair whips back from the wind and rain, soaked through, and I'm reminded instantly of the last battle between us, when I'd stared into the void of his eyes. My heart aches, even as I find myself hating him. I gasp again as his power pushes hard against mine, digging its claws in. The whispers snap at the threads as they threaten to turn me into a puppet.

Then Magiano strikes back at Enzo. He mimics the Reaper's energy, and I see strings of sparks flash from Magiano's hands and whip toward Enzo, bursting into lines of fire on impact. Enzo's balira jerks its head away from the flames, taking him farther from us, and the pressure against my energy lightens. I breathe again. Then I lash out at him.

Enzo cannot kill you without killing himself. He only wants to defeat you. I keep this thought close to me, and it gives me strength.

I pull us sharply around to face him. At the same time, I grasp our tether and flood it with my darkness, my threads hooking into his heart, drowning his energy. He shudders visibly, his eyes squeezing shut—he tugs hard on his own balira's reins, and the creature veers away from me. He begins to dive. His energy shoves against mine, hot and scorching, the fire burning at my blackness. I flinch. We fly lower and lower, until Enzo skims across the water. Rain beats down on my face, and I wipe desperately at my eye to clear my sight.

Through the tether, Enzo's energy rushes at me. The edges of my vision turn hazy, dimming for a moment, and a flash of shadowy silhouettes creep forward. *No.* I cannot afford to succumb to my illusions right now. Amid the chaos, I can sense Enzo's voice as if he were speaking directly to me.

You don't belong here, Adelina. Turn back.

His words send a surge of anger through me, and I push us to go faster. We are very close to the shore now, and several of our ships have broken through the Tamouran defense. The thought of victory dances in my mind. *I belong wherever I want. And I will take Tamoura, just as I took Kenettra from you.*

But Enzo's fire scorches my insides, wrapping around my own heart, closing it in a fist of his threads. Another layer of sweat breaks out all over me as my vision blurs even more. I can see myself reaching out and beginning to weave something in the air. *No. I cannot let him control me.*

You are mine, Adelina, Enzo growls. *Turn your powers against your own fleet.*

I cannot stop him. My hands lift, ready to do his bidding. Then I feel the world rip through me, and I toss my head back in agony. A cloak of invisibility snaps over the Tamouran fleet, hiding them from my own. At the same time, I cast a veil of imaginary pain and hurl it at my own riders in the air.

They shriek. I look on helplessly, unable to breathe through my surge of power, as my riders fall from their baliras. I struggle for air. The world becomes hazy. I force myself to focus on the tether. It is as if Enzo's own hands were tight around my heart, squeezing and squeezing until I am ready to burst. *I have to break his hold.*

A clear voice calls out above us. "Adelina! Stop!" Even before I can lift my head and see him, I know that it is Raffaele.

But he is not alone. In front of him on the balira's back is a small, delicate figure lying limply against the giant creature's hide. It's Violetta, her hair a dark streak of silk in the wind. Raffaele's arms are wrapped securely around her.

She is here. With them.

For a moment, everything around me disappears. All I can do is look on as Raffaele turns in my direction and opens his mouth to say something.

Something streaks past my vision. A white cloak. *One of my Inquisitors.* I have time only to glance to my side before I see one of my own soldiers on a balira, barreling toward us with a club raised. I don't have time to think—or even throw my arms up in defense. No one does. The Inquisitor swings his club and it catches me hard on the shoulder, the

force lifting me clear off my balira. The whispers in my head shriek. The world closes in, growing darker and darker, until I see nothing and hear only Magiano's shouts coming from somewhere far away.

Then, everything goes black.

Thus we agree, should the day ever come, my troops,
the Aristans, shall take possession of eastern Amadera to the
river's mouth, and your troops, the Salans, shall take possession
of western Amadera to the same. No blood will be shed.

—Treaty between the Aristans and Salans
before Amadera's Second Civil War, 770–776

Adelina Amouteru

I wake at the sound of clinking chains. It takes me another moment to realize that the chains are on my wrists. The world sharpens and blurs over and over again, so I can only tell that my surroundings are dark gray and silver, that the stone beneath me is cold and damp. For an instant, I am back in the Inquisition Tower's dungeons; my father has just died, and I am destined to burn at the stake. I can even hear his chuckle in the corner of the room, see a hazy mirage of him leaning against the wall there, the gash in his chest torn open and bleeding, his mouth twisted in a smile.

I try to shrink away from him, but my chains keep me from moving too far. A few mutters echo from a distance above me.

"She's waking up."

"Take her before the Triad. Be careful—those chains. Where's the Messenger? We need his help . . ."

They are speaking Tamouran; I can't understand the rest of what they're saying. The voices fade away, and a moment later, I feel the sensation of being lifted. The world lurches. I try to focus on something, anything, but my mind is too hazy. The whispers fill my head with nonsense, then scatter.

There is a hallway and stairs and the cool breeze of night. Nearby, a voice that I know all too well. Magiano. I turn, yearning for him, but I can't seem to pinpoint where he is. He sounds angry. His voice floats near and then far, until I don't hear him at all. *They're going to hurt him.* The thought sends every ounce of my energy roaring to the surface, and I snarl, lashing out blindly. *I will kill them if they do.* But my attack feels weak and uncoordinated. Shouts ring out around me, and the bonds on my arms tighten painfully. My strength dissolves again.

Where is everyone else? The thought comes to me and I try to hang on to it. Where is Sergio? My fleet? Where am I? *Am I lost in another of my nightmares?*

My memory of the battle comes crawling back, piece by piece. Enzo's power had overwhelmed mine. I was attacked by one of my own Inquisitors. This much I remember. The thought feels fuzzy, but it lingers long enough for me to process. *The Saccorists, the rebellion against me.*

A rat, the whispers say. *They always sneak through the cracks.*

The night changes to stairs again. We are outside, and soldiers—*enemy* soldiers—are leading me up steps. I lift my

head weakly. The stairs stretch endlessly to either side of us and seem to lead to the heavens. Towers loom above, candles burning gold at windowsills, and in front of us, a series of enormous archways soar across the stairs. I look higher to where the stairs give way to a grand, elaborately carved entrance, framed by pillars and covered with thousands of repeating circles and squares. There are words carved into six of the tallest pillars.

LOYALTY. LOVE. KNOWLEDGE. DILIGENCE. SACRIFICE. PIETY.

The words are Tamouran, but I recognize them. They are the famed six pillars of Tamoura.

Then I stumble on the steps, and someone hoists me higher. My head slumps.

The next time I wake, I am lying in the center of a vast, circular chamber. A low rumble of voices echoes all around me. Rows of candles line the edges of the room, and light comes from somewhere above me, enough to illuminate the entire space. A terrible pressure pushes against my chest—the familiar tether between Enzo and me feels tight, the energy in it pulsing and trembling. He must be in the room. My hands are still shackled and my head throbs, but this time the world sharpens enough for me to think straight. I push myself up to a sitting position.

I am in the middle of a circle drawn into the floor, the edges embellished by smaller circles. Three thrones sit along the perimeter, an equal distance from each other, all of them pointed in my direction. In each throne sits a tall figure dressed in the finest gold silks, his hair hidden behind

Tamouran wraps. *The Golden Triad.* I am in the Tamouran throne room, seated before their triplet kings.

I blink away the remnants of my hazy mind and glance quickly around the room. Soldiers stir and shift warily at my movement. Immediately, instinctively, I reach for my energy—the threads of fear and uncertainty in the chamber now call to me—and I lash out with a web of illusions. The chamber falls into sudden darkness, screams fill the air, and a whip of agony coils itself around the Tamouran soldiers closest to me. Several of them cry out. I bare my teeth, aiming next for the kings.

"Stay still, Adelina." It's Raffaele's voice.

I turn against the ground, until my chains don't let me move any farther, and search for him. He's standing next to one of the thrones, his hands folded into his sleeves. He looks grave, but his expression takes nothing away from his beauty. His hair is loose and straight tonight, black with sapphire strands that catch the candlelight. Just as I remember him. He returns my look calmly. The colors of his eyes shift in the light.

Beside him stand several archers, their crossbows pointed at me.

"Release your illusions," Raffaele says. "You are here at the mercy of King Valar, King Ema, and King Joza, the rulers of the great empire of Tamoura. Rise, withhold your powers, and address Their Majesties."

My temper surges, even though I know Raffaele is right. My powers are still only illusions—I will not be able to lunge

fast enough to keep those crossbows from hitting their target. I'll be dead within seconds. Thoughts flash through my mind. Why did Raffaele bring me here? Why hasn't he killed me yet? He could have let them unleash their arrows without warning me.

And the most pressing thought: If Violetta is here in Tamoura, why did he not use her ability against me? Why haven't they taken away my powers?

But what really stops me from attacking again is a shadowy figure standing several feet away from Raffaele, his eyes trained on me and his hands resting on the dagger hilts at his waist. When I meet Enzo's stare, the tether between us pulls so hard, I gasp. I have never felt our connection so strong, so *vicious*. He seems to feel it too—even from here, I can sense the tightening of his jaw, the shift of his muscles.

Enzo's eyes are as dark as I've ever seen them. They do not glitter with the sheen of life that eyes are meant to have. They are dull and deep, devoid of the scarlet fire that once used to fill them, hard with emptiness. He stares as if he hardly knows me. He doesn't say a word. I wince again as our tether pulls tighter, goes slack, and pulls again. Just like during our battle in the skies, he is trying to overwhelm my power. But I feel the pain in the tether too, intertwined with my own energy. Enzo was injured in battle, and I can tell.

I tense in anger. *How dare you try to control me.*

Slowly, I release my illusions on the soldiers and bring my energy close inside my chest, protecting it against Enzo's. Several of the soldiers collapse to their knees, still trembling

from phantom pain. Then I carefully stretch out both of my hands, so that Raffaele can see. If he is studying the shift of my energy right now, he will know that I'm not about to attack.

But I will not bow to a foreign power. My glare shifts to one of the kings, and I'm satisfied when he returns my stare. I'm tempted to look around at the rest of the chamber again, to meet the eyes of the other two kings, but that would require me turning around on the floor like a beggar. I will do no such thing here. "My fleet," I say instead, lifting my chin at the king. "My Roses."

"*Choursdaem,*" Raffaele says to the king. "*Rosaem.*"

The king says something to Raffaele in reply. Most of it is completely lost on me, but I do pick out the taunting lilt he adds to my name.

Raffaele bows his head to the king, then turns back to me. "The war rages even as we speak, Queen Adelina," he translates. "Our armies are sitting at a tenuous stalemate, because your forces know that you are in our captivity. Another of your Roses is also in our hands. Unharmed . . . for now."

Another captive. *It must be Magiano.* He was the only one riding with me, after all, and I'd heard his voice earlier. My energy flares again, and Raffaele shoots me a warning look. With great difficulty, I swallow and rein myself in. Magiano's life depends on how I act.

"It seems you were betrayed by one of your Inquisitors," Raffaele says.

One of my own. The fact that Raffaele had seen this happen

right before his eyes makes me blind with fury. "You planted a rebel in my midst," I snap. "Did you not?"

"I didn't need to," Raffaele replies. "You would have lost this battle."

"I don't believe you."

Raffaele's expression stays calm. "One of your men, attacking you. Is this uncommon?"

No. It is not uncommon. Previous attempts come blinking back into my memory, even as I try in vain to keep them away. *The rebels are everywhere.* I grit my teeth. I will have that traitor skinned alive.

The king speaks again as Raffaele translates. "What would you do, in our place?" The ghost of a smile appears on the Tamouran king's lips. "You would have us beheaded, I'm sure, and hold it up for our armies to see. I've heard that's what you do in other conquered cities. Perhaps we should do the same, dangling your body from the masts of our ships. That should end this war quickly enough."

My heartbeat quickens, but I refuse to let him see my fear. My mind spins. How will I break free from here? I look at Raffaele again. What deal have the Daggers struck with Tamoura?

And Violetta.

"Where is my sister?" I demand, anger shaking my voice.

Raffaele takes a step toward me. "She's resting."

He means she is not doing well. I scowl. "You're lying. I saw her riding with you in battle."

"She was in no shape to fight you," Raffaele answers. "I brought her with me solely so that you could see her."

Is the reason why Violetta has not yet taken my powers away because . . . she is too weak to do so? "You've lied so often, Messenger," I say with deliberate calm. "Why should you stop now?"

"For the gods' sakes, she doesn't deserve this," Michel mutters from the shadows. He looks different from what I remember—thinner, his cheeks hollow—and his eyes are fixed on me with a burning hatred. "Behead her and send it back to Kenettra. Toss the rest of her in the ocean for the fish. She's always belonged to the Underworld. Perhaps that will fix everything."

I frown, taken aback by such harsh words and that they come from the same boy who had once praised my illusion of a rose. He had been so fond of Gemma; any friendship he might have had with me ended the day I sent her falling from the skies. The girl I used to be stirs inside me, pushing past the dark queen to dwell on other memories. I realize I cannot recall the sound of Michel's laugh.

Raffaele doesn't take his eyes off me. To my surprise, the three rulers seem to be waiting for him to speak. After another brief moment of silence, he steps forward. "There are a thousand things we *could* do, with you here in our custody," he says. "But what we *will* do is let you go."

I blink once at him. "Let me go?" I echo, frowning in confusion.

Raffaele nods once.

This is his manipulation at work again. He never means exactly what he says. "What do you really want, Messenger?" I say sharply. "Speak plainly. We are at *war*. Surely you don't expect me to believe that you and the Tamourans are releasing me out of the kindness of your hearts."

In the silence, one of the kings turns to Raffaele and raises a bejeweled hand. "Well, Messenger," he says, his voice echoing in the chamber. "*Sa behaum.*" *Tell her.*

Raffaele walks closer. "Adelina," he begins slowly, "we are releasing you because we need your help."

Of everything I thought he might say, it was not *this*. I can only stare at him in disbelief. Then I start to laugh and the whispers join me. *You really must be going mad.*

Something about Raffaele's expression finally makes my laughter subside. "You're serious," I say, tilting my head in a mock imitation of his familiar gesture. "You must be desperate to think that I would work with you and the Daggers."

"You won't have much choice. Your sister's life depends on it, as do ours." He nods at me. "As does *yours*."

More lies. "Is this why you told me about her? Why you wanted me to see Violetta with you? So you can use her against me?" I shake my head at him. "Cruel, even for *you*."

"I took her in," Raffaele replies. "What did *you* do?"

As always, his words strike true. *This is what you wanted, Adelina,* the whispers coax me. *You wanted to find Violetta, for your own reasons. Now you have.*

Raffaele continues in the silence. "Your sister once took some documents of mine from the royal Beldish ship. Do you remember what they said?"

He's referring to the parchments Violetta had shown me on the day she left my side. That all Elites are doomed to die young, destroyed from within by our powers. As always, the thought of his theory chills me. I am reminded of Teren's stubborn wound, of Sergio's constant thirst. Of my own illusions, spiraling steadily out of my control. "Yes," I say. "And what do they have to do with me?"

Raffaele looks to each of the rulers in turn. They nod once in silence, giving him some sort of unspoken permission. As they do, Tamouran soldiers approach me from where they had been standing guard around the edges of the chamber. I stiffen as they draw nearer. Raffaele tilts his head at me, then starts walking to the chamber's entrance. "Come with me," he says.

Enzo shifts where he stands, as if he would accompany us too—but he stops as Raffaele shakes his head. "His power affects yours far too much," Raffaele says to me. "You need to stand alone for this."

Others follow in his wake. I'm pulled to my feet by soldiers, unchained from the floor, and guided along. We exit the chamber and enter a hallway, then leave the recesses of the palace and head down in the direction of the shoreline. The pressure on my chest eases, and I sag in relief as walls and hills come between the tether binding Enzo to me. It is a dark night; the only light comes from two slivers of moonlight I

can see peeking through the clouds. The storm Sergio had raged over the oceans has dispersed by now, but the scent of rain still hangs heavy in the air, and the grasses are wet and glistening. I crane my neck, searching. Somewhere out there on the waves are my ships and Sergio. I wonder what he's thinking. I wonder where Magiano has been taken.

We keep going until we finally hit the shoreline. Here, Raffaele comes over to us and murmurs something at the soldiers. They pull me forward toward the water. I have a sudden feeling that they intend to drown me in the ocean— that is what this whole ritual is about. I struggle for a moment, but it's no use.

I stagger forward. To my surprise, Raffaele comes to my side. We are standing on wet sand now, and I look on as the waves head toward us. The water and sea foam rush up the beach—I suck in my breath as cold water runs over my feet. Raffaele lets it rush across his legs too, soaking the bottom of his robes.

Instantly, I feel it again. I'd gotten only a quick flash of the ocean's strange darkness during the battle, and then I'd left it behind. But now, with the world around me quiet enough that I can concentrate, I can feel the death in the water. The ocean pulls away, then rushes forward again. Again, it soaks the bottom half of my legs. Again, I gasp at the cold energy swirling in the depths.

Raffaele looks at me, his eyes shining different colors in the night. "You, more than anyone, should be familiar with this energy."

I frown. The feeling turns my stomach, nauseating me with its wrongness—but at the same time, I realize that I look forward to each surge of the ocean, hoping for another dose of this dark energy. "Yes," I say automatically, almost against my will.

Raffaele nods. "Do you remember the day when I first tested your powers?" he asks. "I recall your alignments well. Ambition and passion, yes . . . but most of all, fear and fury. You remain the only person I've met birthed from both of the angels that guard the Underworld. Your energy is tied to the Underworld more than anyone I know."

This power I feel in the water—this is energy from the Underworld.

Raffaele's expression is grave. "The Elites exist *only* because of an imbalance between the mortal and immortal realms. The blood fevers themselves were ripples in our world caused by an ancient tear between those realms. Our existence defies the natural order, defies Death herself. Queen Maeve bringing Enzo back has only accelerated the process. There is a merging of the two realms that is slowly poisoning everything in our world."

I shudder. The water rushes forward again, and I close my eye, both repulsed by and drawn to the dark energy.

"The reason I persuaded the Tamouran royals to release you, on condition of a truce," Raffaele goes on, his eyes trained on the night's horizon, "is because we need your help to fix this. Tamoura is already feeling the effects along her

shores. If we do not do something soon, then not only will all Elites perish, but so will the world."

I stare out at the horizon, unwilling to let Raffaele be right. Of course it's ridiculous. "What do my alignments have to do with any of it?" I finally say.

Raffaele sighs and bows his head. "I think we had better take you to your sister."

I have tried every root, leaf, and medicine I know, but nothing
has worked on any of my patients. Only two have survived,
both with discolored hands. You mentioned a six-year-old boy
with scars on his face. Does he still live?

—Letter from Dtt. Marino Di Segna to Dtt. Siriano Baglio, 2 Juno, 1348

Adelina Amouteru

Violetta.

I hardly recognize her.

Her skin, once a rich, beautiful olive, looks ashen white—
and deep purple, bruise-like markings cover her arms and
legs. They even run up along her neck. Her eyes are sunken
with illness, and her body is much thinner than I remember. She stirs at the commotion of us entering her chamber. I
wonder if she can still sense our powers close by.

Raffaele walks to her side, then sits carefully at the edge of
her bed. After a while, I draw near too. Perhaps this isn't my
sister at all, but some girl they've mistaken as her. Violetta
does not have markings. She does not have pale skin. This
can't be her. I move closer until I am staring straight down
at her face, studying her features. Her hair is damp, her skin

dotted with sweat. Her chest rises and falls rapidly, as if she can't quite catch her breath.

Look what they've done, the whispers hiss, and I turn on Raffaele.

"You did this to her," I say in a low, ominous voice. My chains clink together. The soldiers that line the walls of Violetta's chamber draw their crossbows, the arrows clicking as they aim at me. "These bruises on her arms and legs"—I pause to glance again at the markings that scar her—"you had her beaten, didn't you? You *are* using her against me."

"You know that is not the truth," Raffaele replies. And even though I don't want to believe him, I can see in his eyes that he's right. I swallow, trying to push down my own fright and revulsion at her appearance.

"How long has Violetta looked like this?" I ask.

I'd hoped that Raffaele wouldn't be able to sense the shift in my energy, but he tilts his head at me in a subtle, familiar gesture, a slight frown on his lips. "When I wrote you that letter, the markings had appeared on her just the night before."

It's been barely more than a month since then. "It's impossible for her to have changed this quickly."

"Our powers affect each of us in different ways, often opposite that which gives us strength," Raffaele replies, remaining infuriatingly calm. "Violetta's abilities kept her immune from the blood fever's markings, just as Lucent's powers of flight made her light and strong. Now it has reversed. The meeting of the immortal world with our own is poisonous."

129

My stare returns to Violetta. She shifts, as if able to sense my gaze, and as I look on, her face turns on the pillow toward me. Her eyelids flutter. Then she opens her eyes for a moment, and they focus on me. I gape at the color of her irises. They are *gray*, as if the rich, dark colors that have always been there were now slowly fading away. She says nothing.

I feel a wave of disgust. Raffaele can't possibly feel pity for Violetta's condition—his compassion always comes with a price, a request. *Because we need your help,* he says. Just as he'd needed me when I was a member of the Dagger Society and then cast me out when I no longer suited him.

So why should I help a liar and a traitor? After everything the Daggers have put me through, does Raffaele honestly think I am going to fight for their lives just because he is using my dying sister against me? I am the White Wolf, Queen of the Sealands—but to Raffaele, I am merely *useful* again, and that has made him interested in me once more.

One of the other Daggers speaks before I can. It's Lucent, and she rubs her arms incessantly as if trying to stave away an ache. "This is preposterous," she mumbles. "The White Wolf is not going to help us, not even for her sister's sake. Even if she does, she'll betray us, as she always has. She's interested only in herself."

I glare at her, and she glares back. Only when Raffaele gives a firm nod to her does she look away, cross her arms, and let out a grunt. Raffaele turns back to me. "You know the myth of Laetes, yes? The angel of Joy?"

"Yes." The halls of the Fortunata Court had been adorned

with paintings of beautiful Laetes falling from the heavens. Teren once recited it to me, when I'd confronted him in the Inquisition Tower and taken Violetta from him. *Do you remember the story of Denarius casting Laetes from the heavens, condemning him to walk the world as a man until his death sent him back among the gods?* It makes me think of Magiano and his alignment to joy, that Magiano is probably somewhere down in the dungeons right now, where I can't reach him.

"The stars and the heavens move at a different pace than we do," he explains. "Something that happens to the gods will not be felt in our world for generations. Joy's fall to the mortal world tore the barriers between the immortal and the mortal. It was his fall that caused the ripples of blood fever that swept across the land. That birthed the Elites." Raffaele sighs. "The ever-shifting silver of your hair. The sapphire strands in mine. My eyes. These are lingering touches of the gods' hands on us, blessings from them. And it is the poison that is killing us."

The ghost of Teren's words comes back to me so strongly that I feel like I am standing once again in the Inquisition Tower, staring up into his ice-colored eyes. *You are an abomination. The only way to cure yourself of this guilt is to atone for it by saving your fellow abominations. We are not supposed to exist, Adelina. We were never meant to be.* And suddenly, I know why Raffaele needs my help. I know it before he can say it.

"You need my help to close the breach between our worlds."

"Everything is connected," Raffaele says, a phrase that

Enzo once said to me when he was alive. "We are connected to the point where Laetes fell, where immortality meets mortality. And in order to fix what has gone wrong, we need to seal the place that birthed us, with the alignments that we each bear."

We need to give back our powers.

"We are the children of the gods," Raffaele finishes, confirming my fear. "Only we can enter the immortal realm as mortals."

"And if I refuse?" I reply.

Raffaele's quiet nature has always both calmed and unnerved me. He lowers his eyes. "If you don't," he replies, "then in a matter of a few years, the poison of the immortal world will kill everything."

I look back down at my sister. Violetta's body, collapsing under the weight of her powers. Lucent's hollowing bones. Sergio's eternal thirst and exhaustion. Teren's never-healing wounds. *And me.* My worsening illusions, my nightmares within nightmares, the whispers in my head. Even now, they are chittering, chittering, chittering.

"No," I say. The voices hiss at my sister's body. *You owe her nothing,* they growl, stirring now and climbing out of their caves.

Raffaele watches me. "You are running out of time," he says. "She will not last long like this."

I glare at him. "And what makes you think I care if she dies?"

"You still love her. I can sense it in you."

"You always think you know everything."

"Well? Don't you?"

"No."

Raffaele narrows his eyes. "Then why come to Tamoura to find her? Why ask for her? Why hunt for her all over the world, as you conquer your new lands?"

At that, the whispers turn into shouts. *Because she doesn't get to turn her back on me.*

I lash out so suddenly with my illusions that the archers along the walls don't even have time to react. My powers wash across the others in a wave—*knives in your hearts, twisting, barbed, tearing*—barely within my control. I can even feel the pain of it myself, as if it had turned its head on me too and sought my own heart. Lucent gasps in agony, stumbling backward with wide eyes, while Raffaele clutches his chest with one hand, turning pale. The crossbows draw back.

"Quickly!" Raffaele manages to call out.

Something heavy hits me. *Not an arrow,* I manage to think before I'm knocked to the floor. All the air rushes out of me. I struggle to breathe, and in this instant, my powers flicker out, scattering from my grasp. *Someone has managed to throw a net,* I realize dizzily. No, it had dropped from the ceiling— Raffaele had guessed how I might react. Rough hands grab my arms and yank them painfully behind my back. I struggle to gather my power again and strike, but the whispers have grown so loud and disorienting that I cannot focus.

Leave this place and finish your conquest, the whispers snap. *Show him why he will regret what he's done to you.* Violetta stirs

restlessly in her bed, oblivious to our presence and lost in some nightmare of her own.

I hate you. I throw the thought at her, willing her to hear it. I think of how she had cowered in our childhood, unable to protect me, and how she had turned on me before leaving my side, trying to take away something that is mine by right. I try to hold these images in my head as Raffaele orders the Tamouran soldiers to take me away. I have become so good at remembering these moments during the past year, letting them strengthen me—recounting Violetta's failures in order to push my power to new heights.

But now, the images that flood my head are of a different sort. I see Violetta and me running through the tall grasses behind our old estate, hiding on summer afternoons in the shade of giant trees. There's Violetta wrapping her arms around me on a moonlit floor, holding me as I sobbed for Enzo. And Violetta curling up beside me during a thunderstorm, trembling. Her hands in my hair, braiding flowers between the locks.

I don't want to see these. Why can I not clear them from my vision?

If she dies, you lose yourself. This time it is not the voice of my whispers . . . it is my own voice. *If you do not go, you will die too.*

As the soldiers force me to my feet, Raffaele takes a step closer. "We were never meant to exist, Adelina," he says. "And we will never exist again. But we cannot take the entire

world with us." He meets my gaze. "No matter how it has wronged us."

Then he nods at the soldiers. I try to lash out again, this time with Raffaele in my sights, but something strikes the back of my head, and the world goes dark.

Raffaele Laurent Bessette

When Raffaele checks on Violetta again that evening, she is awake, her fever lowered somewhat. Even though she had been unconscious while Adelina was in the room, it seems as if the presence of her sister had offered Violetta some semblance of comfort, however small. Something that helped her fight back against the deterioration of her body.

It is the opposite effect that Adelina seems to have on Enzo. Raffaele had left the prince pacing restlessly in his chambers. The dark energy surrounding him had felt elevated by Adelina's nearness, agitated and ready to strike.

"She'll never agree," Lucent says to Raffaele as they and Michel look over the Tamouran ship at port, still bustling with sailors loading cargo. "And even if she does—how will we travel with the White Wolf? I can hardly stand being around her. Can you?"

"It's a shame I ever taught her how to focus her illusions," Michel says. "You heard what happened in Violetta's chamber. She attacked the soldiers and all but tried to kill *you*." He nods at Raffaele. "You said yourself that she is beyond help. What makes you think a voyage with her will work?"

"I don't," Raffaele concedes. "But we need her. None of us link with fury, and we will not be able to enter the immortal world without each of the gods' alignments—not if the legends are at all true."

"This could just be a waste of time," Lucent says. "You're placing your bets on a theory of something that, according to myth, happened hundreds of years ago."

"Your life depends on this, Lucent," Raffaele replies. "As much as any of ours. It is all we can do, and we have very little time to do it."

Michel sighs. "Then it depends on whether or not Adelina thinks *her* life depends on this too."

Raffaele shakes his head. "If Adelina refuses, we will have to force her hand. But that is a dangerous game to play."

Lucent looks ready to reply—but in that instant, a young guard hurries up to them. Clutched in his hand is a parchment, freshly arrived. "Messenger," he says, bobbing his head once at Raffaele before handing him the paper. "A new dove. This is from Beldain, from the queen."

Queen Maeve. Raffaele exchanges a look with Lucent and Michel, then unfurls the message. Lucent falls silent, and her eyes widen as she peers at the paper with the others.

Raffaele reads the message. Then he reads it again. His

hands tremble. When Lucent says something to him, he doesn't hear it—instead, it sounds like a muffled, underwater sound, coming from somewhere far away. All he can hear are the words written on the parchment, as clearly as if Maeve were standing with them and telling him herself.

My brother Tristan is dead.

Raffaele looks back toward the palace. A jolt of fear rushes through him. *No.*

"Enzo," he whispers.

And before the others can call him back, he turns toward the palace and runs.

Lost life by stab wound in sacrificing self for the sake of his child.

May he rest in the arms of Moritas,

adrift in the Underworld's eternal peace.

—Epitaph on gravestone of Tau Sekibo

Adelina Amouteru

I am alone in my dungeon cell. Illusions are useless if I have no one to affect but myself, and so I do nothing but curl up on the ground while soldiers stand on the other side of the wall, beyond my iron door. Out of my reach.

Unlike the dungeons of Estenzia, my cell is suspended high above the city in a maze of spiraling towers that funnel wind through their passages like maelstroms. A lone window sits high above me. Through it, weak slants of moonlight illuminate parts of the floor where I'm now huddled. I stay very still. The wind outside howls, taking on the tone of the whispers in my head. I try to rock myself to sleep. It has been far too many days since I last took my herbs to calm the whispers, so I can feel the madness creeping forward again, threatening to wrestle control from me.

I wish desperately that Magiano were with me.

Something creaks. *My prison door.* I raise my head to stare at it. The guards, they must be delivering my supper early. A sharp pain tugs on my chest. I frown as the door slowly opens—and then realize, somehow, at the last moment, that on the other side of the door are not the guards at all. It is Teren and his Inquisitors.

Impossible. He is my prisoner, trapped in Estenzia's dungeons.

My heart leaps into my throat. I scramble to my feet, stumble forward and attempt to close the door. But no matter how hard I throw myself against it, Teren edges in bit by bit, until I can see his mad eyes and blood-soaked wrists. When I look away and back at the interior of my dungeon cell, I see my sister's body lying in one corner, her face pale in death, lips drained of color, eyes staring vacantly at me.

I jerk awake. Outside, the wind is howling. I tremble against the stones of my prison floor—until I hear my door creak open again. Again, I rush toward it in an attempt to keep the Inquisitors out. Again, they push back. Again, I look away to see Violetta dead on the floor, eyes pointed at me. I jerk awake.

The nightmare repeats itself over and over.

Finally, I wake with a terrible gasp. The wind is still howling outside my prison door, but I can feel the cold floor beneath me with a solidity that tells me I must be awake. Even so, I can't be sure. I sit upright, trembling, as I look around my cell. *I am in Tamoura,* I remind myself. *Violetta is not in here with me. Teren is in Estenzia.* My breath fogs in the moonlit air.

After a while, I gather my knees up to my chin and try to stop shivering. In the corner of my vision, ghosts of clawed, hooved figures move in the shadows. I look out at the night sky through the barred window and try to picture my ships waiting for me out at sea.

Just agree to Raffaele's request. Agree to help the Daggers.

Indignation rises in my chest at the mere thought of caving to Raffaele's demands. But if I don't, I will stay helpless in this cell, waiting for Sergio to lead my army to storm the palace. If I simply say I will help them, they will have to agree to a truce and let me free. They'll free Magiano. The thought turns round and round in my head, gaining momentum.

Raffaele has betrayed you many times in the past. Why not use this as a chance to betray him? Agree. Just agree. Then you can strike them when they least expect it.

It seems too easy to be true, but it is my only way out of this prison. I look upward and try to gauge when the next rotation of soldiers will stand at my door.

The strings tug again, hard. A spike of pain shoots through me. I clutch my chest, frowning—this is what I'd felt in my dream, with the current yanking me down. But my nightmare has already ended. A sudden fear hits me, and I squeeze my eye tightly shut. *Perhaps I am still in one.*

The tug again. This time it hurts enough to make my body seize. I glance toward the door. *The pull is from Enzo.* Now I recognize the fire of his energy, his barbs in my heart as surely as mine are in his. *Something is wrong.* When the tug comes again, the door creaks . . . and then, it opens.

The guards are not waiting there. Instead, it is Enzo, swathed in shadows. My breath catches in my throat. His eyes are pools of black, completely devoid of any spark of life. His expression is nonexistent, his features seemingly carved from stone. My gaze darts down to his arms. They are exposed tonight, a mass of destroyed flesh. My heart freezes.

Did Raffaele send him here? He must have told the guards to step aside and let him in. I stare at him, unsure what to do next.

"Why are you here?" I whisper.

He says nothing in return. I can't even tell if he's heard me. Instead, he continues to walk forward. His gait seems off, although I can't quite put my finger on why it looks strange. There is something . . . unrealistic about it, something stiff and uneven, *inhuman*.

He is gripping daggers in both hands.

I must still be in a nightmare. Enzo narrows the black pools of his eyes. I try to push through our tether to read his thoughts, but this time I feel nothing except an all-consuming darkness. It is beyond even hatred or fury—it is not an emotion at all, but the *lack* of all emotion and life. It is Death herself, extending out through Enzo's vessel of a body and pulling me forward through the threads of energy that bind us. The touch feels ice cold. I shudder, pressing myself hard against the wall. But the cold claws of Enzo's changed energy continue to reach for me, drawing closer and closer— until they hook into me and pull tight.

My energy lurches. The whispers in my head burst free and roar in my ears. I cry out at the overwhelming sensation. The control I have over my energy starts to slip, and the whispers gradually take on Enzo's voice—and then, a new tone, one from the Underworld.

"What do you want?" I scramble backward against the floor, dragging my chains with me, until I can go no farther. Enzo approaches me until we are separated by nothing but his armor and my robes. His soulless eyes stare down at me as he sheathes his daggers. His hands clamp down on the chains that encircle my wrists and—in a moment that reminds me of the day he had rescued me from the stake—he heats the chains until they turn white-hot. They clatter to the floor. His lips curl.

"*You have something that is mine,*" Enzo murmurs, in a voice not his own. It resonates within my very core, and I immediately recognize it as the voice of Moritas, speaking through the Underworld.

She has come for Enzo. The tug between us pulls taut again, making me cry out in pain. *She will kill me in order to take him back.*

"Why don't you jump, little wolf?" he whispers.

And, suddenly, I feel a desire to step out of my cell, walk up the rampart, and fling myself from the tower. *No.* Panic flutters in my mind as my energy turns on me and Enzo gains control. An illusion wraps around me—I'm no longer on the top of this tower, but clutching the skeletal hands of the goddess of Death herself, hanging desperately on as I

float in the waters of the Underworld, trying not to drown. Cold hands pull at my ankles.

"You belong here," Moritas says, her featureless face leaning down to me. *You always have.*

"Don't let me go," I beg. The words come out silent to my ears. *Magiano!* I cry. This must be a nightmare, but I can't wake up. It can't possibly be real. Perhaps he will be nearby and save me from my illusion as he always does.

Magiano, help me! But he isn't here.

I blink, and now I am back in the prison tower, walking out of my cell's ajar door to stand on the wind-whipped steps outside. Enzo follows behind me as I continue forward. The hands of Death grasp my heart through our tether, and the ice of her touch burns me. Fires protected inside colored lanterns illuminate the path with spots of light. I squint in the darkness, then turn my face to where the stairs wind up and around my cell. I take a step forward, one after another. A narrow gap between the cells appears, where a thin rampart overlooks the night landscape and then the ocean beyond. I strain to see any sign of my ships, but it is too dark. The wind numbs my fingers. I approach the rampart and grip the ledge with both hands. The tether pushes me forward, urging me over the wall.

The whispers shriek over the wind. *Why don't you jump, little wolf?*

"Enzo!"

A clear voice cuts through my illusion—the Underworld wavers, then vanishes in a whirlwind of smoke. I'm back at

144

the tower, crouched on the edge of the ramparts. Enzo turns around to see Raffaele standing at the stairs behind us, a crossbow in his hands. He is pale, his face drawn with fear, his lips tightened into a determined line. The wind whips his hair into a furious river, and his pale robes stream behind him in waves of silk and velvet. Had he woken, too, at the strangeness of Enzo's energy? His eyes dart in my direction before returning to the prince.

Raffaele lifts the crossbow higher. He isn't aiming it at me.

"Enzo," he says again. His eyes shine wet in the night. "Leave her."

In the past, Enzo would have wavered. His eyes would clear, the pools of dull darkness making way again for those I know so well, dark and warm, slashed with bright scarlet. But even Raffaele's presence this time does nothing to clear the death from Enzo's gaze. I feel nothing of Enzo at all in our tether.

Before I can think anything else, Enzo turns away from me, reaches for a dagger, and lunges at Raffaele. The hands of Death loosen from my heart for an instant, and I recoil in horror from the rampart. Raffaele pauses for the briefest of moments—then he clenches his jaw and fires his crossbow. The arrow strikes Enzo in the chest. He staggers, but doesn't fall. Raffaele puts his arms up to defend himself, but his instant of hesitation has cost him. Enzo's strength is far beyond that of any human. He grabs Raffaele by the throat and slams him against the wall. Raffaele lets out a choked cry. Enzo's dagger flashes in the air.

I don't think—I just act. I reach out through our tether and yank the threads of Enzo's energy tight. Then I pull them toward me.

Enzo lets out a snarl of irritation that barely sounds human. He turns his black eyes to me again. A thousand thoughts whirl through my mind. The threads of his energy that I'm holding are so cold, they seem to burn through my consciousness, pulled so taut that they seem ready to break. I think back to the moment when Maeve had summoned him back from the Underworld, how she had tied him to me. Now the tension of the strings of his energy cut at my mind.

This is not him.

Raffaele reloads, tightens his grip on his crossbow, and fires at close range. This arrow hits Enzo in the back. He fires again. Another arrow. Enzo hunches, finally slowed by the attack, but the expression on his face doesn't change. His attention turns back to me and, again, I feel the hands of Moritas through our tether.

I am not yours yet, I think through the chaos, pushing defiantly against her. The darkness inside me crowds my chest, fighting Enzo's power—he shudders once at my touch. The steps around us turn black and are stained with illusions of blood, and the sky overhead takes on a scarlet tint.

But I cannot control him this time. Enzo's soulless eyes lock on mine—his daggers flash toward me.

Then, abruptly, he falls to one knee. His head bows. Behind him, Raffaele lowers his crossbow, and I see one final

arrow buried in Enzo's back, the one that has finally struck true. Blood drips on the stones beneath our feet. A low, labored gasp comes from him as his second knee falls, and the daggers clatter out of his hands. The tether between us trembles violently, and for an instant, I can feel the pain of his wounds as surely as if they were my own. I sink to the floor before him, unable to look away.

He is dying.

It doesn't matter anymore. The Enzo I once knew died a long time ago.

Enzo looks up at me. Suddenly, the blackness in his eyes seems to fade, replaced by the familiar warm brown of his irises, the red slashes, the glow of life. I see a hint of his old self there, fighting through the darkness of the Underworld to gaze at me one last time. It is the look he'd given me when we used to dance.

This is the real Enzo.

"Let me go," he whispers. It is *his* voice. It is the voice that once comforted me, gave me strength. And as I try to take in his words, the final tendrils of the tether linking us unravel from around my heart, freeing me.

Enzo collapses. As the last bit of my life and my light leaves him, he seems to turn gray, as if he could no longer contain the colors of the living world. He turns his head weakly in the direction of the ocean. The black pools in his eyes finally vanish, and a name drifts from his lips. He says it so quietly that I nearly miss it. It is not my name, but the name of another girl, one he had known and loved long ago.

Then, he closes his eyes and sinks to the floor. His body grows still. I know, without a doubt, that he is gone.

Raffaele says nothing. He stays against the wall, eyes fixed on Enzo. Then, he pulls Enzo's body to him and leans over his head. The silence goes on. I walk forward in a daze, coming to a kneel beside them. Now I am close enough to hear Raffaele's quiet crying. He doesn't pay me any attention; in fact, it is as if I were not even here.

After a long moment, he pulls away and lifts his jewel-toned eyes to me, the colors washed green and gold with tears. We stare at each other. I can see the confusion in his gaze as clearly as he must see the same in mine.

You didn't have to save me.

I am numb. I don't know what to do. The absence of my link to Enzo is a yawning chasm, a hollowness I first felt when Teren took Enzo's life in the Estenzian arena. How long had he been a part of my world? How had my life been before he stepped into it? All I can think is that I am losing him all over again, except that I already lost him.

I am not ready to die.

This realization strikes me hard. The terror I'd felt while crouching against the rampart makes me quake uncontrollably, haunting my senses. No, I am not ready to die, and there is only one way I can prevent that from happening.

As the sun starts to rise, I watch as Raffaele bends over Enzo's body, the two of us mourning the prince we both loved.

Dearest Mother, I am afraid, for there is something
he isn't telling me. It is not to do with our debt, I think,
nor his conversation with the king. But it leads him on
terrible midnight tantrums.

— *Letter from Ilena de la Meria to her mother, the Baroness of Ruby*

Adelina Amouteru

First, I have conditions.

I will go with Raffaele and the Daggers on their journey —*if* I can bring my own crew and my own ship. Sailing alone on a vessel with them is out of the question.

Magiano must be released, alive and unharmed.

Violetta stays with me.

These are my terms.

Tamoura agrees to stand with us in exchange for a truce. I am not finished with my conquests yet, although with Violetta back and our lives at stake —with *my* life at stake — my attention has shifted away from throwing my army at the Tamourans. It might be nice to have an ally for a change.

Raffaele and the Golden Triad agree to all of these terms. So, a day later, Tamouran soldiers move me from my cell to

the bathhouse, where two maids wash me and bind my hair in silks. Then I am taken to a real bedchamber in the palace, where I curl up in the bed and don't move again until the following afternoon. My hands stay chained, clutched near my chest, as if to fill the new gap there. Enzo had been tethered to me for so long, and the strength of that connection was so persistent that its absence now makes me dizzy, like I'm falling through the air.

In my drowsy, half-awake state, I can see a ghost of Enzo walking alongside us, an illusion that disappears the instant I try to focus on him. Enzo is gone, returned to the Underworld where he belongs. *When will Violetta join him?* the whispers ask me. *Or Magiano? When will* you?

Finally, days later, Raffaele arrives surrounded by soldiers. They release me. My wrists feel strangely light without chains weighing them down. We walk side by side through the palace corridors without saying a word. Something seems different in the energy between us now . . . whether it's a barrier lifted or a tension eased, I'm not sure. Make no mistake—we don't trust each other, not by any stretch of the imagination. Perhaps Raffaele is playing with my emotions, as he often has. I certainly wouldn't put it past him to do such a thing.

Of course he is, the whispers snap at me. *Don't be a fool. He will wait until your back is turned.*

But, for once, I have an easy time ignoring the whispers. There is something about shared grief that simplifies things,

that cuts through the discord. Even if Raffaele might be manipulating me, the change may be genuine. I remember what he had once told me.

Adelina, I loved him too.

And so had I.

I keep a fair distance between Raffaele and myself as we walk. He seems to do the same, and we don't look at each other as we make our way down the long steps of the Tamouran palace's main gates, where horses are waiting for us. From there, we ride underneath a cloudy sky that threatens more rain.

Several of my Kenettran ships have docked at the western bay of Alamour. There is a wide expanse of plains here, dotted with desert shrubs and low grasses, the sharp cut of rocks lining the horizon where the city begins. The rising sun paints a red haze across the landscape, making the sea's foam turn red and orange. By the shore, the banners of my ships flutter in the wind. I feel the burden in my chest lighten at the sight, and the whispers stir happily. I'm no longer a prisoner. I am a queen again.

The procession slows as we draw close. Now I can see my own troops lined up along the shore, waiting for us. The white robes of the Inquisitors look orange and cream in this early light too—and in front of them waits Sergio, still adorned in the dark red armor of the Roses. At the sight of me, they straighten.

Not many paces away from my own troops are Tamouran

soldiers, led by one of the three kings and flanked by Michel and Lucent. Then, I see Violetta. She is far from me, surrounded by a patrol of Tamouran soldiers. One of them, an enormous bearded man, carries her in his arms. She is awake this morning, and more alert than when I first saw her. Her eyes are trained on me.

I can't turn away from her gaze. *What is she thinking when she looks at me?* A strange surge of relief rises in my chest, followed quickly by a slash of anger. I'd spent the better part of a year leading my troops into other territories, imagining what it would be like to find Violetta hiding amongst strangers. Now I've found her, and she stares warily at me. She has the ability to wrench away the Daggers' powers, but she chooses not to. Dark markings travel along her neck, disappearing under her robes. The sight of them reminds me of what is happening to her, of why we are all standing here. It makes me shiver.

Violetta studies me. For an instant, I think she's going to reach out to my powers and yank them away, as she once did. I feel a sudden wave of panic—but then she looks away. She doesn't say a word.

I let out a small breath. *She's afraid of you,* the whispers say, but I look away too.

Then I notice Magiano. He had been shrouded under a heavy robe, waiting with the Tamourans—but now he sees me and swings down from the horse he'd been sitting on. A smile breaks unbidden onto my face, and I turn my own

horse instinctively in his direction. Beside me, Raffaele watches silently, no doubt sensing my emotions. But I don't care. Magiano is here. Even from a distance, I can see the upturn of his lips, the familiar joy on his face.

Our processions finally meet. Raffaele nods at the Tamouran troops, and they allow Magiano to step forward right as I swing down from my own saddle. I keep my hands folded in front of me as he approaches. We stop short of touching each other. Magiano looks tired, like all of us, but otherwise well. His long braids are loose today and blowing in the breeze.

"Well, Your Majesty," he says, the teasing lilt back in his voice. "It looks like they caught you."

"And you," I reply, unable to restrain my own smile.

Raffaele walks forward first, completely unprotected, and nods at Sergio. "Hello, Rainmaker," he says.

Sergio gives him a cold look. "A pleasure to see you again, Messenger."

Raffaele glances at us, then back at him. "The Tamourans have decided to release your queen. We have some things to discuss."

❦

That night, as our fleet remains docked, Raffaele joins Sergio, Magiano, Lucent, and me for a meeting in my royal quarters. "We are going to need to take this journey together," Raffaele tells us. His expression is dark, but his voice stays serene and calm. "But we cannot do that if we don't trust each other."

His face hardens again. "Trust will come slowly, for both sides. We give some; you give some."

"And who goes on this journey?" Magiano says, leaning forward as if to protect me. Lucent responds to his gesture with one of her own, turning herself toward Raffaele.

"Every Elite in the world aligns with the gods in some way," Raffaele replies, folding his hands behind him. Orange candlelight flickers against his robes. "The group of Elites who go with us must comprise all twelve of the gods. Missing even one alignment will not give us the combination of energy needed to reach beyond the mortal world—the touch of immortality could overwhelm us. It would be fatal."

The gemstones. The way Raffaele tested each of us. The memory flashes back to me—how he circled me slowly, watching my energy light up nightstone and amber, diamond and roseite and veritium. What had he found with my sister? He must have tested her by now too. He'd also tested Sergio long ago, when he was still a member of the Daggers. Who will go with us?

Raffaele looks at me. His eyes, jewel toned and bright, honey gold and emerald green, seem to see straight through me. "I remember yours quite vividly, Adelina," he says. "Fear and fury. Ambition. Passion. Wisdom. Five of the twelve." He nods at me. "Your sister also aligns with fear."

Fear. I am not at all surprised. Fear is indeed something Violetta and I have shared since we were children.

"In addition to that, she aligns with joy and empathy— with happiness and sensitivity."

Joy. Sensitivity. I think of Violetta's childish twirls, her ringing laughter, the way she used to carefully braid my hair. She is all of these things; I don't doubt Raffaele for a second. My heart aches as I think of her. Violetta is resting now in her own quarters on the ship. She still hasn't said a word to me.

"What are yours?" Sergio asks Raffaele, unable to keep his dislike out of his voice. "You've never mentioned them."

Raffaele gives him a slight bow of his head. "Wisdom," he replies. "And beauty." Of course. Sergio grunts, unwilling to acknowledge Raffaele's words as he continues. "Including Lucent's alignment to time, we comprise nine of the twelve gods. Sergio, your alignments already overlap these, as do Michel's. So we need to find others with the three remaining alignments, to death, war, and greed." He pauses to look at Magiano. "I would like to give you the same test that I gave the Daggers."

Magiano crosses his arms, suddenly indignant, but then he relents at a glance from me. Raffaele gestures to him. He reluctantly rises from the table and goes to stand in the middle of the floor. "I suppose you won't believe me if I just guessed my alignments for you," Magiano mutters.

Raffaele retrieves a satchel containing a series of raw, unpolished gemstones, just as he'd once done with me. He quietly places all twelve of the stones in a circle around Magiano. Magiano stands still, his body stiff. I can sense a note of fear over him, a cloud of wariness at Raffaele's intentions, but he doesn't move. When Raffaele finishes, he walks

around Magiano once, seeing which of the stones respond to his energy. After a while, three of the stones start to glow.

Diamond, a pale white. Prase quartz, a subtle green. And sapphire, a blue as deep as the ocean.

Raffaele starts to call on each of the gemstones in relation to Magiano, the way he had called forth memories from my past when he tested me. Was this why Magiano had such a penchant for sapphires, why he attempted to steal an entire treasury's worth of them in the past, why he wanted the Night King's pendant so badly?

Magiano shudders slightly as Raffaele accesses the first of his memories. I wonder what Raffaele sees, and for a moment, I wish I could see this glimpse into Magiano's past too. Magiano reacts to each of Raffaele's tests, but stays calm throughout the exercise. They finally reach the last stone, the pale green prase quartz.

Suddenly, Magiano jerks away and steps out of the circle. He is shaking all over—the tiny note of fear hovering over him has exploded into a shower of sparks, enough to stir my own power. Raffaele withdraws his hand.

"Get away from me," Magiano snaps at him.

I've never seen him so upset. He brushes past me without a glance, pushes past the table, and goes to stand before the porthole overlooking the midnight ocean. I frown, and my heart seizes for him. His reaction reminds me so much of when Raffaele finally called on fear and fury in me, unleashing a storm of energy and ugly memories. What had he unearthed in Magiano?

"Careful, Messenger," I say, narrowing my eyes at Raffaele. "Our alliance is not so solid that I wouldn't kill you for harming him."

In the silence that follows, Raffaele sighs and folds his arms again. He returns my look. "I cannot control how he responds to his alignments. Magiano aligns with joy and ambition. And greed. He needs to come with us, if he's willing." He doesn't mention anything more about the test, or Magiano's reaction to it.

I let out a short breath, relieved that I will have Magiano with me on this trip. I start to ask what Raffaele must have seen, then stop short. I'll approach Magiano about this later. Joy, ambition, greed. Ten of the twelve now.

"We need an alignment to Moritas and to Tristius," Raffaele replies. "To death, for the mortality of mankind, and to war, for the eternal savagery of the heart."

War and death. I know immediately that we won't find these traits in the Elites among us, if they don't already exist in me.

"Queen Maeve," Lucent says in a quiet voice, glancing sideways at Raffaele. "She will align with Moritas."

An uncomfortable silence. I can tell by everyone's expressions that we all know Lucent is right, even without Raffaele's test; Maeve, whose very power connects her to death itself, is undoubtedly a child of Moritas. But will she travel with our group, with *me*, who destroyed her fleet not too long ago?

"And war?" Raffaele answers. "What of that?"

Lucent shakes her head. "That, I don't know."

Suddenly, I realize something. It hits me so hard that it makes me gasp. Raffaele glances in my direction. "What is it?" he asks.

I know. I know with absolute, searing certainty the Elite who aligns with the final god. But he is no ally of mine—or of anyone else. And he is waiting in chains in Kenettra.

"Teren Santoro," I reply, turning back to Raffaele. "He will align with war."

Magiano

In the first memory, the boy was seven years old. When he asked his priest what his name was, the priest told him that he had no need for a name. He was the Boy of Mensah, one of the young *malfettos* chosen to live at the Mensah temple in Domacca, and this was the only name he would ever need.

He trailed after the priest and looked on as she showed him how to properly tie down and slaughter a goat at the altar in front of the temple. She was kind and patient with him, and praised him for wielding the knife correctly. He remembered looking longingly at the meat, wishing he could eat it to fill the hollows of his stomach. But the *malfettos* in the Domaccan temples had to be fed very little. It kept them awake and alert, making it so that their senses were always

on the prowl, searching for food. When he asked why this had to be, the priest told him gently that it was to strengthen his link to the gods, so that the priests could communicate through him.

In the second memory, the boy was nine years old, and the dark marking on his side now curved from the start of his ribs down to the bone of his hip. He had become friends with the Girl of Mensah, the second young *malfetto* in the temple, and the two of them played together when the priests weren't there. They would sneak out to the date orchards or startle the goats into a frenzy. She would toy with his long braids, tying them into elaborate designs.

One day, when they were both particularly hungry, they stole peaches from the fruit bowl left before one of the altars. Oh, how *good* they tasted! Ripe and fat and bursting with juices. They giggled and rolled around when the priests were otherwise occupied. After all, there were three altars, and they could rotate between them. It turned into a regular habit between the girl and the boy, and they became skilled at it—until the day they stole not one fruit each, but two. That night, the boy saw his priest murmuring about him to three other priests at the temple. Then she found him, dragged him out of his bed, and ordered the others to hold him down. He screamed when she murmured soft verses to him and dug a blade into the edge of his marking.

In the third memory, the boy was about to turn twelve years old. The girl found him and told him about Magiano, a fishing village along Domacca's Red River. She told him

about a boat there that left once a week for the Ember Isles, laden with a cargo of spices. *Will you meet me there? Tonight?* she had asked him. He nodded, eager to go with her. She gripped his hands and smiled, telling him, *No matter what happens, we look forward. Joy is out there, beyond these walls.*

That night, he wrapped some fruit and dates in a blanket and crept out of the temple. He was almost beyond the gates when he heard the girl's screams coming from near the altar. He turned back, desperate to save her—but it was too late. The Boy and Girl of Mensah had no need for names because they were to be sacrificed at the age of twelve, the holy number.

So the boy did the only thing he could. He fled the temple as the priests searched for him and did not stop running until he reached the village of Magiano. There, he huddled in the dark with the cargo until the boat came. As he sailed away into the dawn, he made himself two promises.

One: He would always have a name, and that name would be Magiano.

And two: No matter what happened, he would carry joy with him. Almost as if he were carrying *her*.

If one's ship can brave the stormy seas on the path
from the Ember Isles to the Skylands, he shall find himself
sailing in the calmest waters, so calm that he may be
in danger of stranding himself.
  —Excerpt from the journals of Captain Morrin Vora

Adelina Amouteru

The following mornings dawn gray as the last clouds from Sergio's storm linger. We sail for five days before we reach the Falls of Laetes that separate the Sunlands from the Sealands. Then we follow the chasm for another day until we reach the spot where the ocean comes back together, and here we finally sail around the edge. Baliras fly occasionally between the chasm's gaping mouth—as majestic as I remember them —but they also seem exhausted, their flight slower, the glow of their translucent bodies somehow dimmer. I peer at the water tumbling into the chasm. The water looks as strange as when we left, an eerie near-black color, as if the hues of life were being sucked from its depths.

Even though Violetta and I are on the same ship, and even

though Sergio visits her constantly every day . . . she never asks for me. I'm certainly not about to go to her myself, to give her the pleasure of turning me away. But every time Sergio comes out of her chambers, I'm there waiting, watching. Every time, he looks at me and shakes his head.

I can't sleep tonight. The silence of the open ocean is too loud, giving too much room to the whispers in my mind. I've swallowed two mugs of herbal drink, and still they chatter away, their voices pulling me out of my sleep over and over until I finally give up and leave my quarters.

I wander out onto the deck alone. Even the sailors tending to the masts are asleep at this hour, and the seas are so still that I can barely hear the ripple of waves bumping against the hull of our ship. Not far from us sails the Tamouran ship carrying Raffaele and the Daggers, where scattered torches now shine in the night. My gaze goes from their ship up to the sky. It is a clear night. Stars dot the darkness overhead, familiar constellations of the gods and angels, myths and legends from long ago, layers and layers so thick that the sky glitters with them. The ocean mirrors their light tonight, so that we are sailing through a sea of stars.

My eye settles on a constellation comprising a half circle and a long line. The Fall of Laetes. If what Raffaele has told us is true, then we will not last long in this world with our powers. No matter what happens, whether our journey succeeds or we perish along the way, I will leave this world powerless. The whispers in my head recoil violently at that

thought. My hands clench and unclench against the railing. I have to find a way to avoid such a fate—there must be a path that lets me live and preserves what makes me strong.

You can still turn your back on them. You can—

The sound of footsteps makes me whirl around. In the dim torchlight, I can make out Violetta approaching me, a heavy cloak wrapped around her shoulders. She looks gaunt and sickly, her eyes sunken, but she is standing on her own. She freezes at my movement. "Adelina," she says.

It is the first word I've heard from her since she left me months ago. Even her voice sounds different now—fragile and hoarse, like it might break at any moment. Hostile. Distant.

I stiffen and turn away from her. "You're awake," I mutter. After so long, these are the only words I can think of to say in return.

She doesn't answer right away. Instead, she gathers the cloak tighter around herself, approaches the railing, and looks up at the night sky. "Sergio said you came to Tamoura to find me."

I'm quiet for a long moment. "I went for many reasons. One of them happened to concern you, and a rumor that you were there."

"Why did you want to find me?" Violetta turns her face away from the sky and toward me. When I don't answer, she frowns. "Or did you remember me only after your invasion failed?"

The ice in her voice surprises me. I suppose it shouldn't.

"I wanted to tell you to return to Kenettra," I reply. "That it is safe for you there, and that what I did—"

"You wanted to *tell* me to return?" Violetta laughs a little and shakes her head. "I would have refused, had you found me under different circumstances."

The whispers tell me not to worry about her words, that they're meaningless. But the sting of them still pains me. "Look at you," I murmur. "Back to thinking about how noble you are."

"And what about you? Telling yourself you're improving these countries you march into—thinking you're doing something *good*—"

"I've never thought that," I snap, cutting her off. "I do it because I *want* to, because I *can*. That's what anyone *truly* means when they gain power and call it altruism, isn't it? I'm just not afraid to admit it." I sigh and look away again. I half expect Violetta to comment on my outburst, but she doesn't.

"Why did you want to find me?" Violetta asks again, her voice quiet.

I lean heavily against the railing, searching for an honest answer. "I sleep poorly when you're not around," I finally mutter, irritated. "There are . . . voices that distract me when I'm alone."

Violetta purses her lips. "It doesn't matter. Here I am, and here you are. Are you happy now?" She lets another beat of silence pass between us. "Raffaele told me that I've been delirious for weeks, and that I only woke up after you arrived."

She says it bitterly, like she doesn't want to admit it. But it makes me look at her again, studying her expression as I try to figure out what she really thinks. She doesn't say anything more, though. I wonder whether her words mean that she mourned my absence, that perhaps she would also lie awake at night, look to the side of her bed, and ponder why I wasn't there. I wonder whether her sleep is filled with nightmares.

I wait for her to leave my side and return to her quarters. But, for some reason, she decides to remain on the deck with me, both of us unwilling to apologize, each of us trying to decipher the hidden messages in the other's words, neither of us wanting to spend the night on our own. So we wait together, as we drift silently through the stars.

❦

By the time we reach the Estenzian harbor, my Kenettran fleet has surrounded our ships on both sides and my Inquisitors are guiding us into the port. Violetta is quiet this morning; she's returned to ignoring me, and I am satisfied to do the same. Magiano stays by me and frowns at the approaching harbor. Even though his stance is calm, I can feel the current of fear hidden underneath. He leans slightly toward me. "If Teren is not the one we need—"

"He is." I straighten my back and lift my head. This is the heart of my empire. I am a queen again here, and I will not be questioned.

"We'll have to watch another round of Raffaele conducting his tests." Magiano grimaces at this, and I wonder again what he must have revisited during his own test.

Clouds hang heavy over the city as we head to the palace. Even the air feels stifling today, something like a humid afternoon but darker, more insidious, the signs of a different kind of storm. The Daggers travel behind us, led by a patrol of Tamouran soldiers. They are uneasy too. *You can kill them all here*, the whispers tell me impatiently. *They are in your country, surrounded by your Inquisitors. Why don't you act, little wolf?*

I should. A part of me thrills at the thought of seeing the betrayal on Raffaele's face. But instead, I lead them onward to the palace and down toward the dungeons. As we near Teren's chamber, Raffaele seems to slow in his steps, as if the very air around us exhausts him. He must be able to sense Teren's dark whirlwind of energy, and its effect is weighing him down.

Beside him is Violetta. She seems tired from the time spent on the deck last night, because she cannot stand on her own this morning. Sergio carries her. He does so without much effort, while Violetta clings to him as if she might fall apart. At least she's awake. I force myself to look away from her.

When we reach the door to Teren's dungeon, Sergio waves away the guards posted on either side. "No," he tells them when they start to follow us in, as they normally would.

"We'll go alone." The guards exchange a hesitant look, but Sergio just gives them a grim nod. They bow their heads and don't challenge him.

We enter the chamber.

Sergio had sent word ahead of us that the Inquisitors posted inside the dungeon should leave today. So the chamber is empty, the sounds of the moat's water amplified by their absence. The only figure in here sits crouched in the center of the rocky island, his tattered prison robes spread around him in a circle. He looks up when we enter. The dark shadows under his eyes seem even deeper than I remember, giving him a haunted look. Dried blood covers his wrists in a ring, and when I look closer, I can see the brighter, wetter appearance of fresh blood as well.

"Are you sure you want to do this?" Magiano asks as we gather at the edge of the moat. "You can talk to him from here, can't you?"

"I can," I reply, even though both of us know the real answer. "But we cannot travel with someone who must be separated from us by chains and a moat."

Magiano doesn't argue. Instead, he gives my hand a subtle squeeze. His touch sends a spark of warmth through me.

Raffaele glances at Violetta. I look at my sister resting against Sergio's shoulders. She stirs, her face ashen pale, then lets Sergio help her step gingerly down. Her energy lurches as she draws closer to me, and a cloud of fear hovers over her. I can't tell whether her fear is because of Teren or

me—or us both. Still, she doesn't back away. She turns her attention to Teren's direction, closes her hand into a fist, and *pulls*.

Teren's eyes widen. He lets out a sharp gasp, then hunches over, his hands clawing at the rock beneath him. I recoil even as I watch this. I know the feeling well—it's as if the air has suddenly been sucked out of my lungs, and the threads that make up my body are pulled taut until they threaten to snap. Teren lets out a soft groan, then looks at us again with hatred in his eyes.

Violetta puts her arm down and takes a deep breath. She's shaking slightly; the lantern light in here highlights the trembling of her robes. *Does she even have enough strength to use her power?* "He's ready," she whispers.

Sergio affixes the rope bridge that will take us across the moat. Teren watches our approach, his eyes first on me, then on Raffaele. His stare lingers on Raffaele's face. I glance back at Raffaele, searching his expression for a reaction—but true to his consort training, he has resumed a calm state, his fear now a subtle undercurrent beneath a veil of steel. He meets Teren's gaze with his own level one. If he has noticed Teren's wrist wounds, it doesn't show.

"Well, Your Majesty," Teren says in his usual taunting tone, addressing me without withdrawing his eyes from Raffaele's face. A small smile plays on his lips, sending a chill down my spine. "You've brought a mutual enemy with you this time. Your tastes in torture seem to have evolved."

"He's even friendlier than I remember," Magiano mutters from the other side of the moat.

I say nothing. Instead, I wait until we have gathered a few feet away from him, settling at the safe distance that Teren can't reach in his chains.

Teren's eyes find me again. "Why is he here?" he asks in a low voice.

I turn back to Sergio and nod. "Unchain him."

Surprise flickers across Teren's face. He stiffens as Sergio walks over, one hand resting on his sword hilt, and bends down to Teren's wrists. Sergio twists a key in the shackles. They clatter one by one to the ground.

I brace myself. Teren lunged for me the last time I visited him in the dungeons—he may do so again now, even with his powers taken away. But instead, he just pushes himself to his feet and stares at me.

"What do you want now, little wolf?" he says.

At the shore across the moat, Magiano shifts. I can sense his unease, and my energy reaches for it. I let it strengthen me. I have lied to Teren before; I can do it again. "Haven't you always hated the existence of the Elites, Teren?" I ask. "Haven't you always hoped to see us destroyed, taken to the Underworld?"

Teren doesn't answer. He doesn't need to, of course—everyone knows his answers to these questions.

"Well," I reply, "I think the gods may grant your wish after all."

Teren's eerie smile vanishes. "Do not play games with the gods, Adelina," he says.

"Do you want to hear more?"

Teren sneers at me. He takes a step closer, close enough that if he wanted to, he could reach out and seize my throat. "Do I have a choice?"

"We can leave, of course. You can go back into your shackles. You can crouch here for all of eternity, never again seeing the light of day, never dying. That is a part of your power too, isn't it? Too strong, too invincible to die and end your own misery? What irony." I tilt my head at him. "So. Do you want to hear more?"

Teren continues to stare. "Always playing games," he finally says.

I glance at Raffaele. "You are going to have to trust us for a moment."

Teren laughs at that. He shakes his head. "What has trust ever meant to any of you?" But when Raffaele steps forward to place his gemstones in a wide circle around Teren, he doesn't react. He watches, noting each of the stones. When Raffaele finishes, he steps back and folds his arms. I crane my neck, too, suddenly curious. What memories will Raffaele see from Teren's past? What does he align with?

What if he does not align with what we need after all?

The chamber falls into silence. Raffaele furrows his brows in concentration as he studies each of the gemstones. As we look on in the darkness, three of the gems take on a subtle glow. One is white, which I instantly recognize as diamond, as ambition; then, a bold, brilliant blue; finally, a scarlet so intense that the gem looks like it is bleeding. I release my

breath. I recognize the blue glow—it is the same as one of my own alignments—the alignment to Sapientus, for wisdom and curiosity. But the scarlet . . .

When Raffaele reaches out, Teren stiffens, then gasps. His eyes become unfocused, as if he were reliving a memory—then he winces, squeezes his eyes shut, and turns away. I watch, fascinated, reminded of my own tests. I have never seen Teren vulnerable in this way before, his mind open to not only another person, but someone who is his enemy. Again and again, Raffaele reaches out, and again and again, Teren flinches and backs away from him. *Ambition. Wisdom. And . . .*

Suddenly, Teren lets out a snarl and lunges for Raffaele. Raffaele takes a quick step away just as Sergio steps between them. His sword is drawn before I can blink. He hits Teren hard in the chest with the hilt of the sword, then shoves him roughly back. Teren stumbles and falls to his knees. I wait, heart in my throat, as Teren stays there with his head down. He's breathing hard. He doesn't say anything.

Raffaele looks pale now. He nods, confirming what we already guessed. "Ruby," he says, his voice echoing in the dungeon. "For Tristius, son of Time and Death." His gaze wanders to me. "The angel of *War*."

I exhale again. Teren has the missing alignment we need.

"Why are you here?" Teren hisses. All hints of his taunting nature are gone now, replaced by raw anger. "What do you want? *What do you want?*"

I take a step toward him and bend down to his eye level. "Teren," I say softly. "There is something happening to the

world. To you, to me, to everyone here. The immortal Underworld is seeping into the real world, poisoning everything in it." I explain what Raffaele had told me, about the poison in the dark waters, the dying baliras, his wounds that now heal more slowly than they ever have before. "We believe we are the only ones who can stop it. The Elites. And you align with the immortal world in a way that we still need." Teren's head stays bowed, and somehow, a part of me aches in understanding. What had Raffaele forced up from his past? "I want you to come with us."

Teren lets out a broken laugh. He lifts his head, and my breath catches as his colorless eyes find mine, windows full of madness and tragedy. "We have an unpleasant history together, little wolf," he says. "What makes you think I have any desire to help you?"

"The last time we worked together, there was another standing in the way," I reply.

Teren leans forward. He is so close that I can feel his breath against my skin. "The one standing between us is you," he snaps. "We can only be enemies."

I suppress my hatred of him. "When we first met, you told me that I deserved to return to the waters of the Underworld. That all Elites are abominations, never meant to walk this world." I narrow my eye at him. "But tell me, Teren. If you are a demon, and I am a demon—abominations in the eyes of the gods—then why have the gods given me the Kenettran throne? Why do I rule the Sealands, Teren, and all armies fall before me? *Why*, Teren, do the gods keep rewarding me?"

Teren glares at me.

"You were born the son of a Lead Inquisitor," I say. "You have been taught all your life that you are lower than a dog, and you have believed it. Even the woman you once loved told you that you were nothing. She turned her back on you, in a way that makes me pale by comparison." Then I lift my head and look straight at him. "What if you are wrong? What if the gods sent you, and indeed the rest of us, not because we were never meant to be, but because we were *always* meant to be?"

"It's not possible," Teren replies calmly. But he does not answer my question.

"Is it possible that the gods created us in order to save the world, instead of destroy it?" I press, knowing the words that will weaken him. "Is it possible that they created us in order to undo something broken, so that we may one day sacrifice ourselves?"

Teren stays quiet. "So," he finally says, "you want me to join you in this quest to fix the break between worlds? Why would I do this?"

"Because we need you," I reply. "And you are still the strongest Elite I know."

Without warning, Teren lashes out and grabs my wrist with one of his hands. His grip is iron, painful, unyielding. I suck in my breath sharply at his touch. Sergio pulls his sword halfway from its sheath; Magiano utters a sharp warning. "I could kill you right now, Adelina," Teren whispers. "I could break every bone in your body, could crush

them into powder, and there is nothing your men can do to stop me. Let that prove to *you* that the gods are not on your side. You are still the same quivering little girl I tied to the stake that morning."

My hatred for Teren seethes, black and churning, rising above my fear and the pain in my wrist at his grip. Behind me, Magiano's energy stirs. I stare levelly back at Teren. "And yet, here I still stand before you. *Your queen.*"

My words have stirred doubt in him—there's a flicker in his eyes that I have never seen before. He is wondering whether I could possibly be right. And I *am* right, aren't I? The gods have blessed me. They've rid this world of the Kenettran king who despised us, then his queen who had used and manipulated us. The gods put on the throne a girl born to a father who wished her dead. They have spared my life again and again. They've given me everything.

And you pushed your sister away. You murdered a man you once loved. You are an empty vessel. Nothing. The gods have given you a power that is killing you.

"Teren, we are going to hand our powers back to the gods. We will fix the world by giving up our abomination. It is the only way, and it is the only mantra you have ever followed." I say it as if I were also trying to persuade myself to join this journey, that I do not fear the loss of my power, that I am not still attempting to cheat the inevitable. "I have no other reason to stand beside Raffaele. Nor you." I take a deep breath. "This is what you've always wanted."

Teren studies me for a moment. His expression shifts from

one extreme to the next, settling at last into a look I can't understand. There is a light there, behind his madness, a glimmer of something that lures him forward. *This is what you've always wanted, isn't it, Teren?* I think.

He releases me. Sergio loosens his grip on his sword, and the others in the chamber shift their stances. I relax, letting out my breath, trying to keep my composure. My heart hammers in my chest.

Teren gives me a slow smile. "We will see who is right, mi Adelinetta," he says.

Teren Santoro

Ｉn the first memory, Teren was seven years old.

He was in the uniform of an Inquisition Axis apprentice, a simple gray tunic and trousers, a student training to join the white cloaks that his father presided over. His hair was cut short and clean, and his eyes were still the color of the ocean. He's in one row with a dozen others, looking out at a crowd of young apprentices gathered in a courtyard of the palace, fenced in by tall statues of the twelve gods and angels. His father addressed them all. Teren stood tall, his head held high. He was the only son of the Lead Inquisitor of Kenettra, and that made him better than the others—so his father said, anyway.

"Our order has always existed to protect the Kenettran crown," his father was saying, "to protect the superiority of our people above all others, and to protect the purity of our

heritage. By pledging your lives to the Inquisition's order, you promise to forever dedicate yourselves to the royal family, and to guard the throne with your lives."

Teren felt his little chest swell with pride. The Inquisition Axis was the most esteemed army in the world—and his father led them. He hoped that, one day, he could look as regal as his father did in his Lead Inquisitor armor and cloak.

"We wage a noble war against those who are impure. Remember this, and go forth with it in your minds: Protect your country, at all costs, at whatever sacrifice."

Teren closed his eyes and took a deep breath, internalizing the words. *A noble war against those who are impure.*

"Teren Santoro." His father was calling his name now. "Come forward."

Teren needed no second calling. He immediately stepped out of his row and made his way forward. When he reached his father, the man nodded for him to kneel, handed him his first sword, and told him to look out into the crowd. Teren obeyed. The other apprentices, who were instead given wooden practice swords rather than Teren's steel one, followed his example and knelt. Teren bowed his head and closed his eyes as his father read out the Inquisition Axis oath.

He was pure. Superior. And he would follow in his father's footsteps.

Teren was eleven years old in the second memory.

The blood fever had swept through Kenettra earlier in the

year, so his eyes were no longer a pure ocean blue, but pale, so pale that they were inhuman, a complete lack of color. He stood with a bowed head and heavy heart before the funeral pyre upon which his father's body lay. The fire had spread now from the kindling to the late Lead Inquisitor's clothes. Teren stayed silent as the flames roared. His father had gotten sick only after Teren did—but while Teren had managed to survive, the blood fever had killed his father in only two days.

Teren knew it was his fault. It had to be. The gods did not make mistakes, and he knew he had to have been marked by the fever for a reason.

Later that night, Teren crept out of his chambers and fled down to the palace temple. There, in the dark recesses and pools of candlelight, he knelt before the gods and sobbed. The Inquisition Axis doctrine specifically taught that survivors of the blood fever were abominations, a punishment from the gods.

He was a demon now. What had he done? He whispered to the temple floor as he knelt. Before him loomed a statue of Holy Sapientus, the god of Wisdom. *Why my father? Why didn't you take me too?*

He knelt there for three days, until he was thirsty and starving. *How far I've fallen,* he thought to himself, over and over again until the thought seemed embedded in his very being. *I was once superior—and now I'm nothing. My father is dead because of me. Trash. Filth.*

Suddenly, in a fit of desperation, Teren grabbed the hilt of his sword and pulled it out. It was the same sword his father

had gifted him on the day he joined the Inquisition as an apprentice. He took the sword, placed its blade against one of his wrists, and slashed as hard as he could. He cried out at the jolt of pain. Blood bloomed instantly against his skin.

But, then . . . the wound closed. Teren *saw* it close, watched with his mouth agape as one side of the slashed flesh rejoined with the other, sealing shut. The pain disappeared.

Teren blinked at the sight. Then he tried slashing his wrist again.

Again, the wound bloomed with blood—before closing.

It can't be. Teren tried a few more times, gritting his teeth at the pain and then in horror as the pain faded almost instantly. He cut himself more and more frantically, trying to spill more of his blood. But he couldn't. Each time, the wound healed itself as surely as if it had never happened at all.

Finally, Teren flung the sword away. He collapsed at the feet of Sapientus, weeping. He couldn't even end his life. He was cursed forever by the blood fever.

He stayed in the temple for another day. Then another. A few friends, other young apprentices, came to check on him. He pushed them away, refusing to answer their questions. He didn't want to tell them the reason why he wouldn't speak to them—that it was because he was no longer an equal, but a dog who dared to talk to a man. He didn't want to speak because he was terrified of the horrible, secret power the blood fever had left with him.

The question haunted him every night he stayed in the temple. Why would the gods let him survive the blood fever

marked and disgraced, and then take away the ability for him to end his life? What did they want him here for? Why were they forcing him to stay?

On his last night in the temple, he drove his fist down against the ground in frustration. To his shock, the marble of the floor cracked beneath his knuckles, leaving a hundred jagged lines in the stone. Teren stared, frozen. He held his hand up to the moonlight, observing that his knuckles had healed over and left no mark or injury behind at all.

The gods had made him an abomination—and then given him near-invincibility and strength.

Perhaps they have punished me for a reason, Teren thought. He knelt quietly before Sapientus for the rest of that night, thinking. The next morning, he left the temple.

❦

Teren was sixteen in the third memory.

Though his father's legacy shielded him from punishment, he'd been kicked out of the Inquisition Axis for being an abomination—but that still didn't stop him from staying faithful to the crown, trying always to find some way or other to prove that he wanted to devote what little worth he had to serving the throne, to serving the gods.

So he scouted on his own, secretly helping the Inquisition root out *malfettos* without making himself known. He would follow those he suspected around the city, watching them talk and laugh with their families. Whenever he found a *malfetto*, he would creep to their door in the night and mark

it with the Inquisition's symbol. The Inquisitors didn't know he did this, but they must have been grateful for his secret spying.

Then, one afternoon, he stumbled across an apothecary.

It was a charming, small shop, run by a white-haired old man and his cheerful daughter, a beautiful Tamouran girl with a quick smile and infectious laugh. Teren would stop by several times a week to watch them taking orders from customers. Something seemed off to him about the girl. Her name was Daphne. Sometimes, Teren would see her run deliveries in the city. She would take so many winding paths that he'd always lose her in the busy streets. When she returned to the apothecary in the afternoons, Teren would wonder where she had disappeared to.

Until he heard a rumor about a group called the Dagger Society, a supposed team of demonic *malfettos* with frightening powers not of this world. Apparently, Daphne used her father's apothecary as a place where she would create pastes that would cover *malfetto* markings. She helped the Daggers and others paint over their markings. Teren thought that Daphne was the one responsible for keeping the Daggers hidden.

One night, Teren trailed Daphne as she left her father's apothecary and made her way toward the University of Estenzia. What was a girl doing out at an hour like this? She disappeared for a long time at the university, but Teren finally found her in a narrow alleyway. She was exchanging words with a hooded figure and handed him a small satchel.

Teren reported her immediately. Several days later, the Inquisition came to take Daphne away. They dragged her to the Inquisition Tower not far from the piers—and even though he couldn't see what happened to her, he knew what these soldiers did in the dungeons when they wanted to extract information from someone.

Daphne was supposed to burn at the stake. But she didn't live long enough to make it out of the dungeons.

Later, Teren was summoned by the king of Kenettra and the young queen, Giulietta. Teren knelt before their thrones as the king praised his loyalty for identifying a traitor in their midst. The king reinstated him in the Inquisition, telling the public that Teren did not have a marking after all. That he was not a *malfetto*.

In that moment, Teren knew. He knew why the gods had chosen to keep him alive, why they had taken away his choice of dying.

He was an abomination sent here to rid the world of abominations, to stop those demons from corrupting the kingdom of Kenettra. He was meant to atone for his sins by protecting all that was pure and good.

This was his reason to live.

This was his reason, and now the gods have given him a chance to prove it.

I am the wind, calm and fierce and deep.
I am the soul of life, the howl of storms, the breath of sleep.
—Imodenna the Great, *by Sir Elias Mandara*

Adelina Amouteru

When we board our ship, Teren is still wearing his chains. We trust him only to the extent he has agreed to accompany us, but we know that won't keep him from trying to attack us in our sleep. So he remains our captive, surrounded by guards at all times. As we sail from Estenzia's harbor, he is the only one who remains belowdecks, chained in his bunk. I stand at the bow of the ship and try not to think about his presence under our feet. Sailing beside us is Raffaele's Tamouran ship, gliding in unison through the waves. Magiano climbs up the mainmast and swings down with his usual ease. From the shore, I can still see Sergio on the pier with a troop of Inquisitors at his back, watching us go.

He'd kissed Violetta right before we left. It was the first time I'd ever seen him finally act on the subtle feelings he's

always expressed around my sister. Now Violetta is at the stern, her eyes trained on his speck on the pier. Sergio, with his mercenaries' help, is going to command the army while I'm gone. Still, I can't help but worry. What if he fails? What if I return to my hard-won empire only to find out that there had been an uprising—or that he's turned his back on me?

Everyone turns their back, the whispers sneer gleefully. Their poison caresses my thoughts. *Best if you turn yours first.*

"We sail northeast," Raffaele says the first night as we gather around the dining table. He had crossed over to our ship on a connected gangplank to meet with us. Violetta stays close beside him, while I try to keep as much distance between us as possible. "It will take several weeks if we follow the shortest route, as the northern terns migrate."

"How do you know where to go?" I ask. "You mentioned the origin of the Elites. Where is it?"

Raffaele runs a finger along the table, drawing an invisible line that represents the border of the Skylands and the sea, and then points to a spot far north of the shore. "Northern Amadera, deep in the ranges." He glances at each of us in turn. "The Dark of Night."

"Like in the myths?" Magiano says through a mouthful of dried meat. I've heard the tales before too, and now I raise an eyebrow at Raffaele.

Raffaele nods, strands of his silken hair slipping over his shoulder as he goes. "There are four places where the spirits still wander," he replies, quoting some ancient tome. "The snow-covered Dark of Night, the forgotten paradise of Sobri

Elan, the Glass Pillars of Dumon, and the human mind, that eternally mysterious realm where ghosts shall forever walk."

"They say the Dark of Night is a remnant of the gods," Lucent adds. "It is sacred land. Priests make pilgrimages there."

"If you study the chronology of the myths," Raffaele continues, "the first mentions of the Dark of Night coincide with the fall of Laetes from the heavens. It is known as a sacred place, yes." He nods at Lucent. "I believe it was created by the tear between the immortal world and the mortal. It is a place of eternal night, not meant for mortals. The priests you mentioned, Lucent, visit the lands around it. But they do not actually *enter* the Dark of Night. There are no tales of what is inside this place."

A land of myth, our destination based purely on Raffaele's predictions. "You believe it's the place where only Elites can enter," I reply.

Raffaele nods. "It is a land of gods."

"And will Queen Maeve meet us along the way?" Magiano asks. He is sitting beside me, his hand touching the edge of mine. "As soon as we enter the Skylands?"

Raffaele looks at him. "We will meet her at the passage between Beldain and Amadera."

"After our last confrontation?" Magiano makes a *tsk* sound. "Are you sure she'll want to join us? Hard to believe the Beldish queen will let us pass through her territory unharmed after we destroyed her entire fleet—let alone sit on a horse beside us for weeks."

"It is in Maeve's best interests to see us succeed," Raffaele replies coolly.

While Magiano shrugs, I stare at the map. Kenettra is a small nation in this view, as are the other Sealand nations. The Sunlands, including Domacca and Tamoura, seem to stretch endlessly. Even more vast than all of them is the sea, the great divide between the living world and the Underworld.

The extent of my own power suddenly feels insignificant. Our journey will fail, and we will pay for it with our lives.

❧

The next dawn, we sail into the dim light of a dark morning. The ocean has taken on an uneasy color of jet. From the porthole of my quarters, I can see clouds piling on top of one another until it looks as if there were never any such thing as the sky and hear a low growl of thunder echoing from somewhere far away. Had Sergio been on board, he could have told us about this oncoming storm—and done something about it. But this is not a storm of our choosing. This is something the gods have created.

My stomach sinks as the ship pitches on the waves. A tingle of fear runs down my spine and the whispers stir. *The Underworld is calling you home, Adelina.*

By the time I make it up the ladder and onto the top deck, the heavens have turned even darker. I look out onto the horizon to see that lightning streaks along the edge of the sky. Thunder continues to rumble. Magiano is helping two of the crew tie down barrels and secure the cannons. His robes are

coarse linens today, a heavy cloak wrapped tightly around a dark tunic, pants, and boots, and his braids are tied up in a high knot. "We are still ahead of the storm," he says when I approach him. "But its arms extend far. If we're lucky, we'll be able to sail around before the worst of it hits us."

I scan the horizon for any hint of land, but I see nothing except the churning of dark clouds. This tempest is different from the storm we'd faced while battling the Tamourans, where I could conjure images that struck terror into the soldiers we were fighting. But what use are illusions when the enemy we're facing is nature herself? From the water, I hear another echo of balira wails. There is a pod swimming some distance away from us, heading in the direction opposite the storm.

"Where is Violetta?" I ask. "Have you seen her this morning?"

"She hasn't come up here." Magiano nods back toward the ladder. "You should stay belowdecks too. I can take it from here. It may get violent."

Perhaps she's dead, the whispers cackle. *Good riddance. Now you can finally be free of her torment.*

Fat drops of rain have started to fall. I shake my head, trying to push away a blur of uncontrollable illusions, and turn around to head back down the ladder. As the air becomes heavier, the whispers grow louder, escalating until they shout in my ears. The fear of my crew hangs in the wind, feeding my energy until I feel like my chest might burst. In the corner of the ship, my father leans against the wooden

188

railing and stares at me with wild eyes. I swallow and look down. My illusions cannot overwhelm me now, not here.

The early raindrops turn into a torrent. From the crow's nest, one of our crew cries out, "Tie yourselves down!"

As I stumble toward the ladder leading below, I catch a glimpse of Raffaele's ship pitching against the waves, nearly lost in the spray. I can barely even stay on the ladder itself. On the lower level, lanterns swing in the narrow corridors and I think I hear shouting coming from the floor beneath me. I pause. The whispers in my head are restless—but this sounded real. Still, I can't bring myself to be sure about anything. I walk farther down the corridor until I reach my door. Here, everything seems muffled and distant, aside from the howl of the wind outside and the crash of ocean against wood.

I make it to Violetta's door, knock once, then step inside.

She stirs on her bed, but does not look up at me. One glance is all I need to know that she's feverish, her eyelids fluttering, her dark hair damp and matted against her head. Her markings stand out prominently along her neck and arms, blue and purple and black. She mutters something under her breath. Even in unconsciousness, she shifts uneasily when thunder rolls outside.

She is getting worse, I realize as I stand over her. Raffaele had thought that perhaps my nearness would slow her deterioration . . . but now she looks even frailer than when I first saw her in Tamoura. I look on for a moment as she turns in bed, her forehead slick with sweat, and then I sit down and brush her hand with my fingers.

What if she can't even make it to the origin, to help us complete our journey?

You're wasting your time here, say the whispers.

A loud thud shakes the floorboards. I startle and look back at the door. It sounded like it came not from above deck, but from our corridor. I wait to hear the passing of Inquisition boots, of a group of voices—but instead, the ship falls back into silence again.

I frown. For a moment, I want to ignore it, but then I rise and leave Violetta's side. I step back into the hall of swinging lanterns.

No one else is in the corridor.

I clutch my head and steady myself against the wall. Everything around me seems to be moving, and despite my attempts to concentrate, the walls blur into the floor and the floor blurs into the air, the lantern lights smearing together into faces and shapes. The whispers turn into screams. I press a hand against one ear, as if that might shut them out, but it only makes it worse, blocking out the sound of the crashing ocean and emphasizing my illusions gone mad.

Think of Magiano. I remember his hand on my wrist in that dark hallway at the palace, the light reflected against his skin in the bathhouse. Then I force my breathing to steady. One, two, three. The hooked claws in my mind still, if only for a moment, and the floor and walls sharpen again. The sound of waves and shouts of men return from above deck.

Then, another thud.

It comes from the deck below. Where we are keeping Teren.

A sense of dread creeps into my stomach. Something has happened—I can feel it. I hesitate for an instant, wondering if my illusions will spiral out of control again. The world seems steady enough, though, and the whispers have lowered into a rumble. I make my way toward the lower-deck ladder, then start heading down. The ship pitches violently, making me trip on the last rung. A muffled thunderclap sounds outside. The storm is quickly worsening.

The end of the corridor is pitch-black, and as the ship rolls, an extinguished lantern tumbles along the planks, its glass broken. I reach out tentatively with my power. There's fear here, the fear that comes with pain. As I walk closer, I realize that there are two shapes lying on the floor, one of them motionless, the other moaning softly. The guards stationed to watch Teren.

Teren's door is swung wide open.

My heart leaps into my throat in terror. *He is loose,* I think, right as a deafening clap of thunder shakes the ship. I whirl around and hurry toward the ladder. The back of my neck tingles, panic rising as I wonder whether Teren is hiding in the shadows. But I know he's no longer down here.

I climb up the ladder in a rush and run along the corridor of our other quarters. "Violetta?" I shout as I go. "Magiano! Teren is gone!"

No one answers. As the ship careens, making the lanterns along the walls swing wildly, I rush to the ladder leading

to the deck and start climbing. Where would Teren go, in a storm like this? We can't lose him. We need him on this journey. We—

I hear the *whoosh* of a blade through the air before I even see it. Something—fate, my instincts—saves me, and I duck at the last instant. A dagger buries deep into the wood of the ladder. I look back to see one of my Inquisitors charging at me, teeth bared. *A rebel.*

I throw my arms up and fling an illusion of invisibility over myself. I vanish from sight and dart out of his way. The Inquisitor stabs down at empty air, then blinks in confusion and whirls around. He is afraid now too, and his terror feeds my strength. "Show yourself, demon!" he shouts.

My heart pounds against my ribs. So—another rebel—just like the one who had attacked me during our battle. I grit my teeth and throw an illusion of pain at him. But my concentration flickers, and I shudder into existence for a fraction of an instant. It is enough for the Inquisitor to see me. He swings another dagger at me again, even as he howls in pain at my illusion.

I scramble past him and start climbing up the ladder. Had he been one of the guards I'd placed outside Teren's door? Had he released him, thinking Teren would kill me? Had he been loyal to Teren during his Lead Inquisitor days?

The man swings at me again. I react blindly, grabbing the dagger embedded in the wood, and then I whirl around and lash out at him. My blade strikes flesh. The man's eyes bulge,

and his mouth drops open. He stares at my scarred face for an instant, then collapses at my feet.

Another assassination attempt.

I clutch the dagger in one hand and struggle to the top deck. An icy wind blasts me with rain. I freeze and look up at the sky to see clouds hovering so low that they seem like they might touch the crow's nest, clouds so black and ominous that it feels like I am peering up into the gaping mouth of Death herself.

"Adelina!" a drenched Magiano shouts from near the bow of the ship, where he hangs on desperately to the rigging of the sails. He's pointing in the direction where Raffaele's ship must be. Frantic, I glance around the deck. It all looks like a blur—a mass of gray crew fighting the tempest, water everywhere. I whirl around, as if my would-be assassin is behind me.

"Teren!" I shout back at Magiano. "He's gone! He's—"

The moment the words leave my mouth, I spot him. Under the glow of a streak of lightning, I see Teren making his way toward Magiano. Teren's wrists are still bound in chains, and as he moves, they clatter noisily. A gasp escapes me. *No.* I shout again and prepare to strike with my energy, but a huge wave smacks the side of the ship and I stumble at the impact. A rope snaps loose from somewhere and hits Magiano viciously in his side—on his never-healing marking.

Magiano doubles over in agony and loses his footing. His hands grab for the rigging. I leap onto the deck right as

Teren reaches it. *Teren is going to kill him*. The thought speeds through me like lightning—and my powers well up, roaring to the surface as I face Teren.

But Teren seizes the rope—and swings it toward Magiano with all his strength. Despite his pain, Magiano manages to catch it. He swings back toward the mast and hits the spar with a soft thud—narrowly avoiding going overboard. He crumples on the deck, clutching his side.

I wipe water from my vision. Did Teren just save Magiano's life?

At the same time, another wave crashes against the deck, flooding it. It washes one of my Inquisitors into the sea. I stumble and fall on my knees. Before me, Teren loses his footing and tumbles. I rush forward. Somewhere in the gale, Magiano calls out to me. "Adelina—don't!" he yells.

The water sweeps Teren overboard. *We need him* is all I can think. *We need Teren if we want to live.* I reach the railing and look down to see Teren clinging to the side of the ship. His chains clack in the wind. He glances up and catches sight of me.

Let him drown, the whispers say. *Let the Underworld take him. Let him sink. He deserves it.*

I hesitate, trembling from the effort of listening to the voices. He *does* deserve it. For a moment, the thought crowds my mind and the whispers crow as if they've won. Teren's face shifts and moves, rippling with an illusion out of my control, shifting from a human face to that of an unrecognizable demon, the monster underneath his skin.

Then I remember why we are here. I reach down, close my hand tightly around his wrist, and pull as hard as I can. Teren climbs slowly, making his way up one step at a time. His eyes reflect the lightning and the torrential rain. *When he is back on board*, I think, *we will need to secure his quarters more strictly.*

"Look out!" someone shouts. I glance up just in time to see Magiano leap in my direction. But it's too late—an instant later, a wave hits the side of the ship like a battering ram and I'm flung free of the railing. All I see is a rush of black sky and ocean. Magiano is still standing along the deck, his arm outstretched toward me. Then he vanishes from sight as rain and ocean spray streak past. I look down to see the dark ocean rushing up at me.

The Underworld has come to claim you, the whispers scream.

Then I hit the water. And the ocean consumes me.

Said the man to the sun, "How I wish you could shine your light
on every day of my life!" Said the sun to the man, "But only
with the rain and the night could you recognize my light."

—*Domaccan poem, translated by Chevalle*

Adelina Amouteru

The world is deafening and silent. Light and dark. I think I see Caldora in the depths, her long, monstrous fins carving through the water. The thunder sounds muffled from underneath these black tides. I float for a while, unsure of where I am or whether I am even alive. The current tosses me, I am down, and my heartbeat thuds in my ears. I struggle to breathe.

I surface with a gasp. Rain and seawater pours into my open mouth. I choke, coughing, and search for the ship. It's behind me, looming. I try to swim in its direction, but another wave swallows me and I'm tossed over and over. I manage to pull myself up again, only to see the ship edging farther away.

"Magiano!" I cry out. "Violetta!"

But my voice is lost in the tempest. Another wave pounds me and I'm submerged in the depths once more.

I will not die here. Not like this. The thought becomes a drumbeat that fills me with rage, and the rage gives me strength. I force my limbs to keep churning, force my head above water one more time. The storm roars its fury overhead—lightning flashes between the clouds, and sheets of rain pummel me. I'm swallowed by another wave and every time I surface, the ship looks farther away. I start to lose feeling in my limbs. The energy of the Underworld seeps under my skin and down my throat. Monsters seem to swim in this sea, their massive black silhouettes framed by deep blue, which seems to extend down forever.

Will he miss me? I picture Magiano's face, contorted in fear as he watched me go overboard. Is he safe?

Will Violetta miss me?

Then, a hand. The fingers are rough, nails dig into my flesh, the grip so hard that I think my bones will break. I open my mouth to cry out, but the effort is soundless in the sea. Through the darkness, I catch a glimpse of wild, white, mad eyes and a flash of blond hair. *Teren.* It is Teren in the water, fighting upward alongside me, pulling me by the arm.

We break through the surface into the center of the storm. I gasp, choking on seawater—through a blurry haze of rain, I see our ship careening several dozen yards away. On the masts, Magiano is pointing for the others to search the waters for us. *I'm here.* I try to wave, but the sea swallows my arm.

"Not invincible after all, little wolf?" Teren shouts.

Illusions darken the world all around. I am struggling to breathe in the Inquisition Tower, and Teren has his sword pressed against my throat. *He's going to kill me; he's going to cut me open with his blade.* A wild surge of terror lodges in my throat—and I panic, struggling to get away from him.

Teren growls and only tightens his grip on my arm. I'm vaguely aware of the ocean surrounding us. Another wave crashes against our bodies, and seawater pours into my mouth. I splutter. *He's drowning you,* the whispers shriek. Anyone else would have lost his grip in a sea this fierce, but Teren—still imbued with his powers—manages to stay locked on me like a shackle.

"Let go of me," I choke out, clawing blindly at Teren. The sharp tang of blood suddenly fills my nostrils, and I realize that it is from his wrists, spreading a film of scarlet around us. Somewhere ahead, the silhouette of our ship looms. *We are getting closer.*

"I wish I could," Teren spits, dripping venom. "There's nothing I'd like to see more than you in the Underworld, Adelina."

His words spark my fury. *He never intended to finish this journey with you.* Teren grips my arm again so hard that I scream in pain. He is pulling us both toward the ship, his face set in grim determination.

Then I hear him shout, "But I won't."

But I won't. My fury wavers, turning into bewilderment.

We are very close to the hull of our ship now, so close that Magiano has caught sight of us. I can hear his shout over the wind, his arm pointing down to where we are. Teren waves back at them, and as the crew bustles along the deck, I feel a sudden lift from the water below. A whirlwind pushes it away, and for an instant, a crater forms in the sea around us. The wind urges us both upward. Startled, I glance in the direction of Raffaele's ship, which yaws behind our own. Lucent is up on the masts, arms pointed in our direction. The wind strengthens, and the world blurs as we are lifted up, up, up above the railing of our ship's deck, a funnel of sea-water raining onto the ship as we go.

Then we fall. I hit the deck hard enough to knock the breath from my lungs. Teren finally releases my arm, and I abruptly feel lighter without his iron grip on me. Inquisitors crowd around us. Magiano, still clutching his wounded side, shouts for blankets. In their midst, I see Violetta's face. Warm arms wrap around my cold neck, and I'm pulled forward, startled, into an embrace. Her hair drapes across my shoulder.

"I thought we lost you," she says, and I find myself wrapping my arms around her in return before I even realize what I am doing.

Beside me, Inquisitors surround Teren, forcing his arms behind his back again. He stares at me with the side of his face pressed against the ground. His lips are still twisted up into a crooked smile. His eyes pulse with something unstable.

I stare at him, trying to comprehend what he's done. *He saved Magiano from falling overboard. He saved* me. He is taking this mission seriously, however much he loathes us.

"Maybe next time," he says to me with that smile, "you won't be so lucky."

Laetes had not even a single coin to his name–but it did not matter. Such charm did he exude, such joy did he bring to every passerby he met that they invited him into their homes, fed him their bread and stew, and protected him from thieves and vagabonds, so that he passed through the border between Amadera and Beldain without harm.

–The Fall and Rise of Laetes, *by Étienne of Ariata*

Adelina Amouteru

The traitor Inquisitor turned out to be a new recruit from Dumor. After a tip from Teren and a brief hunt on board the ship, Magiano dragged every single member of our crew before me on the top deck, where they quivered and groveled at my feet. Magiano rarely has such a look of cold anger on his face—but he did then, the pupils of his eyes slitted so sharply that they looked like needles.

I could kill this crew, if I wanted. I could have their blood coating the deck of this ship by nightfall.

But I can't afford to do such a thing. There would not be enough people to guide the ship, nor protect us, if I rid myself of them all. So instead, I showed them the corpse of the would-be assassin. Then I ordered it tossed unceremoniously overboard.

"Let that be a reminder to those of you who still want to challenge me," I said, my head high. "Anyone else?"

Only silence greeted me, followed by the whispers in my head. They seemed amused.

It is only a matter of time, isn't it, Adelina, before they get you.

It is strange to see the ocean so calm tonight, when only hours earlier, our ships had nearly been devoured by the waves.

I sit huddled in a chair, blankets wrapped around me even after I'd taken as warm of a bath as I could, shivering with a mug of bitter tea. To my annoyance, my mind lingers on Violetta. After her sudden emotional display on the deck, she returned to her usual tense silence in my presence, although she did give me a concerned look before retiring to her quarters. I don't know what to make of it, but I'm too tired tonight to dwell on the thought. Now only Magiano lounges by the porthole nearby, while Teren crouches in his chair, quietly eating his supper.

He still has a set of chains between his wrists, along with two Inquisitors at his sides—but the chains don't do much to restrict his movements, allowing him instead to eat freely. His wrists are also bandaged with clean cloth and there's a blanket wrapped around him. He seems unharmed, for the most part, by our ordeal in the ocean. I suppose his powers have not yet abandoned him.

"Why did you save me?" I ask Teren, my voice breaking through the silence.

"Probably the same reason why that Dagger saved both of our lives. The Windwalker, was it?" Teren doesn't bother looking up from his plate as he speaks. It is his first proper, hot meal in a long time, and he seems to be savoring it.

"And what reason is that?"

"As you said, I am here only to carry out the gods' wishes. And I'll be damned if your foolish actions make this voyage pointless."

Let him keep you safe. My whispers are surprisingly calm tonight, perhaps subdued by the herbs Magiano mixed into my tea. I nod at Teren. "Remove his chains," I say to the Inquisitors standing beside him.

"Your Majesty?" one of them responds, blinking.

"Do I need to repeat myself?" I growl. The Inquisitor turns pale at my tone, then hurries to do my bidding. Teren eyes me as his chains fall away, landing with a heavy clang on the floor. Then he lets out a small laugh. The sound of it is familiar, and it scrapes against my memory.

"Trusting me," Teren murmurs, "is a dangerous game, mi Adelinetta."

"I'm doing more than that," I reply. "For the rest of this journey, *you* will be my personal guard."

At that, Teren's eyes flare with surprise and anger. "I'm not your lackey, Your *Majesty*."

"And I'm not Giulietta," I fire back. "You could have killed me on board the ship, when you first freed yourself. You could have drowned me in the ocean. But you didn't—and that makes you more trustworthy to me than even my own

crew. It's clear I can't rely on all of my men, and for once, we have the same goals. So, for the rest of this journey, you *will* be my personal guard. It is in both of our personal interests."

The mention of Giulietta, as always, seems to hit Teren hard. He winces, then turns back to his food. "As you wish, Your Majesty," he replies. "I suppose we'll see how well we do together."

I take a deep breath. "This will all be over soon," I say. "And your duty to the gods will be complete."

Teren puts his plate down. We exchange a long stare.

Finally, he rises from his seat and faces one of the Inquisitors. The man swallows hard as Teren seizes the sheath of his sword and pulls it off the belt. Teren glances at Magiano, then at me. "I'll need a weapon," he mutters, hoisting the sword in the air before he steps out of the cabin.

I do not realize how tense his unchained presence made me until he is out of the room; I relax my shoulders in his absence.

"I'll keep an eye on him," Magiano says, walking over and offering his hand for support as I rise. "One heroic act doesn't make a man trustworthy. What if he decides to turn his blade on you?"

I follow Magiano out of the main cabin and turn down the corridor to our quarters. "You can't watch me all the time," I say wearily. "Teren will be better than leaving me at the mercy of any other rebels who might be on board."

Magiano tightens his lips, but doesn't argue. His eyes search my face, pausing for a heartbeat on my scars. His

braids are tied up in a thick mess, ruffled from exhaustion, and light from the corridor's lanterns highlights the gold glint in his eyes. "You aren't well tonight," he says softly.

Before I can respond, the whispers hiss again, fighting against the herbal tea, and I rub my temples in an attempt to soothe my headache.

Magiano takes my hand and leads me inside my quarters. "Come," he says. I follow him to the bed, where I gingerly sit down, while he goes to the writing desk, lights a candle, and prepares me another mug of tea. Outside my porthole, a strange wailing echoes across the ocean. I sit still in bed for a while and listen to it. It is a low, lingering sound, like a ghost's whisper on the wind, and as I continue to listen, I feel it coming from right beneath the waves. My energy trembles at the call, even as something about it sounds familiar, even beckoning, to my ears. This is a sound from the Underworld.

The shadows in the corners of my quarters seem to bend and shift, even as Magiano stands barely a few feet away. I must be hallucinating again, my illusions twisting out of my control. The shadows change into shapes with claws and teeth, tiny empty sockets for eyes, and as I look on, the shapes sharpen until their faces take on the characteristics of people long gone. They struggle to crawl out of the shadows and into the moonlight that paints the floors. I sink deeper into bed, try to ignore the sound outside, and pull my blankets up to my chin. I have to find a way to regain control over the threads of my energy. I practice taking deep breaths—in and out.

The wail outside fades, then strengthens, then fades again. After a while, I can barely hear it anymore. The shadows against the walls lose their threatening shapes, settling into flat darkness.

"Adelina." Magiano's whisper. I hadn't even noticed him approach and sit on the corner of my bed. He holds a mug out to me.

I take it in relief. "Did you hear the wailing?" I ask.

He leans over and carefully peers out of the porthole, his hand supporting his marked side. If the moons were new tonight, the ocean would be a black mass, reflecting nothing but a sky full of stars. But tonight the storm clouds have cleared and the water is brightly lit, and as we look on, I can see the rolls of water pushed up by a pod of baliras swimming by.

"I've never heard them wail like that before," I say as they pass.

"I heard them several nights ago," Magiano replies. "Raffaele told me he heard it, too, when he came on board our ship. It is the sound of a dying balira, poisoned by this water."

His words tug at my heart. I look out the porthole again to catch a sight of the last ones swimming by, until nothing but triangles of ripples drift in their wake. *Let them die,* the whispers say. *When it is all done, you can turn your back on them. On everyone. Escape with your powers. You can't give them up.*

Yes, I could do this. I'll wait until we've reached the border of Amadera and Beldain, and begin the trek northward. Then Magiano and I can return to Kenettra. I shake my head, frowning, and sip more of the herbal drink. Would Violetta

return with me? Could I leave without her? Will I abandon the others? I stay very still, focusing my thoughts on
following through with this plan. I imagine sailing back to
my country and returning to my throne. I force myself to be
happy about it.

I picture Raffaele and Lucent, who saved my life, and then
Teren, who has turned against every belief he holds in order
to do what he thinks is right.

Magiano looks at me. His side is pressed against mine, his
skin warm and full of life.

"I'm afraid," I finally whisper to him. "Every day, I wake
up wondering whether or not this will be the last day I get
to live in reality." I look at him. "Last night, my nightmare
returned. It went on for longer than it ever has. Even now,
when you were standing so close by, I could see the shadows
in the corner reaching their claws toward me. Even at this
very moment, my illusions are growing stronger, evolving
completely out of my reach." I pause as the whispers scold
me for speaking against them.

*This boy will betray you, just like all the others. He is here for
the pouch of gold you give him. He'll disappear the instant you
reach land, gone to search for better companions.*

"Good thing we're going to find a way to fix this, then,"
Magiano replies, his eyes turned down at me. His words
sound like they should be teasing, but his voice is grave, his
face serious. "It won't be like this forever."

No response comes to my lips. After a while, I rest my
hand upon his. "You're still in pain."

"Just my old wound acting up again, " he replies quickly. "But I'm declining slower than you are, my love. I can endure this."

"Let me see," I murmur gently. "Maybe you need to wrap it."

Magiano pulls away at first, but when I give him a pointed look, he sighs and relents. He shifts a little so that his back is turned to me, and then he reaches up and pulls his shirt over his head, exposing his torso. My gaze goes straight to the massive mark on his side. It stretches from the small of his back to the side of his upper chest. I bite my lip. Tonight, it looks swollen, red and angry from the mast's strike.

"Perhaps Raffaele can have a look at it tomorrow," I say, frowning at the sight. My thoughts turn to the priests from Magiano's childhood, the ones who made this wound by trying to cut off the marking on his skin. The image makes my temper boil.

"I'm all right. Don't worry."

I meet his gaze. He looks vulnerable and gentle, his pupils round and dark. "Magiano, I . . . ," I start to say, then pause, unsure. Even after our moments of shared kisses, our encounter in the bathhouse, I've never confessed my feelings to him. *Don't, foolish girl. He'll only use it against you.* But I decide to push on. "We might not return from this voyage. None of us. We might all lay down our lives when we reach the end, and not ever know whether our sacrifice changed anything for the better."

"It *will* be for the better," Magiano replies. "We cannot just die, not without trying. Not without fighting."

"Do you really believe that?" I ask. "Why are we doing this, anyway? To preserve my own life, and yours—but what has the world ever done for us in order to deserve our sacrifice?"

Magiano's brows furrow for a moment, then he leans in closer. "We exist because this world exists. It's a responsibility of ours, whether or not anyone will remember it." He nods at me. "And they will. Because we will return and make sure of it."

He is close enough now that I can feel his breath against my lips. "You are so full of light," I say after a moment. "You align with joy, and I with fear and fury. If you could see into my thoughts, you would surely turn away. So why would you stay with me, even if we return to Kenettra and resume our lives?"

"You paint me as a saint," he murmurs. "But I aligned with greed solely to prevent that."

Even now, he can make my lips twitch with a smile. "I'm serious, Magiano."

"As am I. None of us are saints. I have seen your darkness, yes, and know your struggle. I won't deny it." He touches my chin with one hand. At this gesture, the whispers seem to settle, pushed away where I can't hear them. "But you are also passionate and ambitious and loyal. You are a thousand things, mi Adelinetta, not just one. Do not reduce yourself to that."

I look down, unsure how to feel.

"None of us are saints," Magiano repeats. "We can all do better."

We can all do better. I lean toward him. Every bone in my body yearns to keep this boy safe, always. "Magiano . . . ," I start to say. "I don't want to leave this world having never been with you."

Magiano blinks once. He searches my face, as if trying to understand the true meaning of my words. "I'm with you right now," he whispers.

"No," I say quietly, bringing my lips up to his. "Not yet."

Magiano smiles. He doesn't say anything. Instead, he leans forward and closes the gap between us, pressing his lips to mine. The light in his energy floods my insides, chasing away the dark shadows and replacing them with warmth. I can hardly breathe. I gasp as he touches my back and pulls me more tightly to him. His movement makes me lose my balance, and I topple backward into bed, bringing him with me. Magiano tumbles forward on top of me. His kisses continue, trailing the hollow of my throat. His fingers tug at the strings on my bodice and they loosen. He pulls it up over my head and tosses it to the foot of the bed. My skin is bare against his, and I realize that I'm trembling.

Magiano pauses for a moment to look at me, searching for a sign of my emotions. I study his face in the darkness. "Stay with me," I whisper. "Tonight. Please." The words said aloud suddenly frighten me, and I pull away, wondering whether I should have opened myself up to him like this. But

the thought of sleeping alone, surrounded by my illusions, is too much to bear.

He touches my hair with one hand, brushes the strands away, stares at the left side of my face. He kisses the scar gently. His lips touch my forehead, then my mouth. And then, as if he understands me better than anyone in the world, he whispers, "It will make this night a little less dark."

That night, he dreamt of a place full of pillars, silver-white, reaching up to the sky. And that morning, his enemy's soldiers broke through the inner gates.

—Excerpt from The Requiem of Gods, *Vol. XVII, translated by Chevalle*

Adelina Amouteru

Afterward, no whispers lurk in my mind. My energy is very quiet. I have no nightmares. Stirring when the pale light of dawn creeps into my quarters through the porthole, I half expect last night to be nothing more than an illusion . . . but Magiano is still here, his soft brown skin pressed against mine, his breathing gentle and rhythmic in sleep.

I stretch against him, a genuine smile on my lips. The air is chilly, and I wish I could stay nestled forever under these thick blankets. Memories from last night still linger, Magiano's hot breath against my neck, his whispers of my name, his sharp inhale. When I first met him that evening in Merroutas, he seemed like a mysterious, invincible figure, a wild boy with a mess of hair and a quicksilver smile. Now, he seems quiet. Vulnerable. His fingers stay entwined with

mine, hanging on firmly even in sleep. I study his long lashes. For a moment, I wonder what he had seen in the memories Raffaele unearthed during his test.

❧❀❧

Every day, we head farther north. Every day, the air turns colder. Soon, I have to put on a heavier cloak and sturdier boots each time I go above deck. Magiano seems uncomfortable here, in this colder climate. His blood is thinner than mine, and his Sunland heritage shows in his deep scowl.

This morning, as we see the first hints of land on the horizon, he joins me on the deck with two cloaks fastened tightly around his neck. His arm brushes against mine.

"Why can't the origin of the Elites be in a tropical paradise?" he complains.

Even now, looking out at this bleak, dark ocean, I have to smile at his words. He has shared my quarters every night since our first together, and as a result, the whispers have become quieter over the past few weeks. But now that we draw closer to the Skylands, the voices have returned with a vengeance. "We shall reach Beldain today, at least. I'll be happy to be on solid land again."

Magiano grunts. I wonder which poor soldier he stole the second cloak from. "Small victories," he agrees.

Nearby stands Teren, who watches the approaching land without a word. He has caused us no trouble for the weeks he's gone without his chains and, true to his appointment, has stayed near me, a hand always on the hilt of his sword.

The new white bandages around his wrists look red again, though. His wounds are stubborn.

A rumble of voices behind me grabs my attention. Violetta talks in low whispers to Raffaele as they sit together on stacks of cargo, pointing at the strip of land growing before our eyes. I watch them over my shoulder. Raffaele joined us shortly after my accident overboard and has been with us since then. Violetta has gradually eased around me, ever since that night, but she still keeps her distance and confides in Raffaele more often than she does with me. She leans heavily against him and trembles, her lips dry and cracked. Her voice is weaker than it has ever been, and her cheeks are hollow now, the result of her poor appetite. The sight sends my energy churning darkly, not in anger but in sorrow.

I wish it were me she turns to for comfort.

"You said the Beldish would meet us here with troops of their own," I call to Raffaele. "I see no Beldish flags on any of the ships on the horizon." I pause to nod toward the nearing port again. "Any word from Queen Maeve?"

"She will be here," Raffaele replies. Like Magiano, he has an air of unhappiness about him, and pulls his heavy cloak tighter. He must not have enjoyed spending weeks in Beldain the last time he fled here. "But we have to move quickly out of this city."

"Which city is this?"

"Laida, one of Amadera's most populous port cities." Raffaele gathers his black hair into a thick rope across one

shoulder. "Rumor has it the Saccorists have a base here and may be waiting for you."

I smile bitterly at him, then weave an illusion of his face across my own. Raffaele's expression flickers in surprise for a moment before settling back into its pool of calm. "They may have a hard time finding me," I reply.

Raffaele gives me a tight smile in return. "Do not underestimate your enemies, Your Majesty," he says.

I raise an eyebrow at him. With my anger stirring, the whispers awaken. *Ah, yes. You know that better than anyone, don't you?* "Is that a threat, Raffaele?"

My words bring on a stubborn silence between us. Raffaele shakes his head, then gives me a grave look. "You are looking for conflict in the wrong places, Your Majesty," he replies.

I don't answer. Instead, I turn back to the sea and try to control my emotions. Beside me, Magiano presses a hand against my arm. *Steady*, he seems to be saying. But even he cannot keep the whispers at bay forever.

Perhaps I'm getting worse, just like Violetta.

The port is crowded with ships from every city and nation, and their flags form a rainbow of colors on the bay, reflected in the waters. Our own flags are hidden beneath an illusion mimicking an Amaderan crest, and to my relief, no one seems to pay us any mind. As our two ships dock, I take a deep breath and look out at the bustling piers. The salt of the sea and the odor of blood and fish hang thick in the air. Gulls circle the sky above us, diving for entrails tossed into the water. Groups of

men with heavy beards carry what look like sharp hammers swung over their backs and loops of rope around their shoulders. Women in fur pelts and coarse skirts huddle along the multiple piers, cooking stews over small fires. They hold out bowls in one hand and a single Amaderan silver in the other, shouting in a strange tongue I can't begin to understand. The people here are large and sturdily built, so pale that freckles stand out starkly on their skin. Only Lucent blends in completely, while Teren seems passable with his pale eyes and blond hair. Even though my Inquisitors and companions are not dressed in Kenettran silks, we attract a few stares for our more slender figures and darker complexions.

You are in enemy land, the whispers remind me. *Do you remember the tales of Amadera's civil wars? When the Aristan people conquered the Salans, they took everything with them: their jewels; their honor; and their children, sometimes straight from the womb. What will they do to you, when they find out who you are?*

Raffaele claims that Maeve will meet us here, but there is still no sign of the Beldish queen and her men. As we unload some of our supplies onto a waiting horse, I gradually weave differences into my appearance—lightening my skin, dotting the bridge of my nose with freckles, curling my hair, hiding my scars. Snapping at Raffaele doesn't mean I don't take his words to heart. If the Saccorists are here, then they will find a way to seek us out in town. When I finish with myself, I work on altering the appearances of Magiano, Raffaele, and Violetta.

"Leave the others," Magiano says quietly to me as we

prepare to leave the piers behind. He subtly gestures to where our Inquisitors and Tamouran soldiers wait. "We'll go on from here to find Queen Maeve."

He's right, of course—having a patrol of soldiers behind us attracts far too much attention, even at a bustling port city. I nod my agreement. "We go alone," I reply.

But as we move forward with the Daggers, I find myself fearing the open air at my back. The whispers only feed my paranoia, sending black silhouettes flickering in and out of the crowd. *You are hunted here, little wolf. What does it feel like to be prey?* Only the knowledge that Teren walks next to me reminds me that he is, at least, ready to defend me. Magiano is close too.

I grit my teeth and follow Raffaele. Let them come. I have slit throats before, and I can do it again.

Violetta is too weak to walk for long, so the first stop we make is to purchase a horse for her. She rests against its back with her eyes closed. I lighten her hair until the illusion of it looks red. She is sickly enough now that her skin is almost as pale as a Skylander's. She doesn't stir as we make our way deeper into the city.

Magiano sniffs the air as we pass tall buildings of limestone, their windows tiny and shrouded with curtains. "Do you smell that?" he says.

I do. It smells like cooking eggs, as well as something tangy and sour, like a shredded plant I'd once eaten at the ports in Dalia, Kenettra. My stomach rumbles. Suddenly I'm tired of the weeks of dried meat and stale bread on board the

ship. "It smells like breakfast," I reply, turning in the direction of the scents. "Something we could use a bit more of."

Magiano smiles at me. As he does, his face suddenly changes into a different one—it is my father's, dark and grinning, the harsh lines of his wrinkles deep and prominent. I gasp, then turn away and shut my eye. *Not now,* I scold myself as my energy flares in fear. I cannot lose control of my illusions in the middle of this crowded street.

"Are you all right?" Magiano whispers. When I gather the courage to look at him again, he has returned to being himself.

My heart beats weakly within my chest. I straighten my shoulders and try to forget the images. "Don't worry," I say. "I'm just impatient to find the Beldish."

Nearby, Violetta frowns in concern, but she doesn't say anything. Raffaele slows to fall into step beside me. He nods in the direction where the city eventually ends. "Your illusions," he says. "Disguising us. It is exhausting you, isn't it?"

The energy in my chest strains as we continue to move through the city. I wish there were not so many people here; the constant shifts of their movement and colors and shapes make it difficult for me to keep the illusion over myself and the others. "I'll be fine," I mutter at Raffaele.

"We are close enough to the origin that I can feel its slight pull. Remember, everything is connected to everything else." He shakes his head and frowns. "Its energy will disturb all of ours. Be careful."

Only now do I see that there is a certain strain in Raffaele's

face too, as if he were drained from more than just our journey. I look around, wondering who else is feeling the effects. Magiano seems to be doing well enough, aside from his sour mood, but Violetta's face looks exhausted, and Lucent is uncharacteristically silent.

As we go, I continue to blink away bits and pieces of illusions. The sky seems to darken, and a weight hangs over the city. Masked faces appear and vanish from narrow alleys that we pass, the glint of silver reminding me of how the Daggers once looked. The whispers stir, appearing in the corners of the streets and the shadows of overhangings.

Why don't you abandon this journey, Adelina? they say. *Return to Kenettra. Go back and rule your empire.*

I look away and try to keep my concentration ahead of me. *It is a good idea.* I shake the thought from my mind. We are all tired, and the sooner we can have a good night's rest, the stronger we will feel in the morning. Perhaps Maeve will meet us by then.

But what if she doesn't meet us at all? What if she sends troops to attack us instead? What if she has no interest in joining us on this journey? Raffaele must believe her on good faith, that she will come because she loves Lucent, but that is all. I look to my side, where Lucent walks in silence. What if this is Maeve's way of seeking revenge for what I did to her navy, to withdraw herself, making our journey worthless?

This is what I would do, if I were her. So why doesn't she choose it too?

We turn off the main road and down a narrow path with

steps, heading around the side of a hill toward the tavern. As we pass by a small intersecting alley, the masked faces appear and vanish. Beside me, Magiano frowns, stiffens, and cranes his neck down the alley for another look.

"Did you see something?" I ask.

Magiano nods, his eyes still lingering on the alley we passed. "A flash of silver," he says after a moment. "Like a mask." He meets my stare. My stomach twists.

It wasn't just an illusion of my own creation.

Suddenly, Raffaele halts. Ahead of us are several people standing there, blocking our path. Even though my illusions remain in place, they seem to recognize that we do not belong. Their leader steps forward from the crowd. This man doesn't look like he is from the Skylands—his skin is light brown, and his eyes are deep and dark. He hoists a knife in one hand. "So," he says. "A foreign troupe heading through our territory."

The whispers grow louder in my head. "We want no trouble, sir," I manage to say, keeping my chin up and voice calm, working to keep the illusions I've woven over our faces steady.

The man nods at me. "Where are you from?"

Kill him. It has been so long. It will be so easy. The voices are persuasive. I could wrap him in agony right now, make him believe I am ripping his heart out of his chest. But I cannot afford to do it here, not without knowing if there are more of them beyond this narrow street, and not with Violetta so sick.

Magiano saves me from responding by flashing the man a smile full of white teeth. "From a much friendlier place than this town, I can tell you that," he proclaims. "Do you greet all the foreigners passing through with knives? That must take up an awful lot of your time."

The man's scowl deepens, even as he looks at us in doubt. Raffaele joins Magiano at his side. "We have a friend who is very ill," he says, nodding up to Violetta. "Can you tell us where the nearest inn might be?"

The man stays silent. More of his men have come behind us now, people whom I'd taken as fishmongers and passersby, gathering on the steps to block the way we came. There is fear in the air, sharp and dark, calling to me—and I hunger to call back, to grasp the threads draped around us and weave. My illusion over my appearance wavers, only for an instant.

The man narrows his eyes at me. "They said you'd be in disguise, White Wolf. We know you are Queen Adelina of Kenettra."

I blink in mock surprise. "What?" I reply, keeping my voice surprised. "We're from Dumor to—"

The man interrupts me with a bark of laughter. "Dumor," he replies. "You mean one of your puppet states."

Magiano unsheathes two of his own weapons. His pupils have narrowed into sharp slits, and his body is tense. Near Raffaele, Teren stands tall with his sword half drawn, ready to move. For the first time, I'm grateful to have him with us.

There is no point in dragging this out. I've had enough. "Let us pass," I say, pushing myself forward. My anger is starting

to rise, and that energy becomes my defense. "And we will spare the lives of your men."

The group stirs. The leader draws a second knife from his belt. Beneath his brave exterior, I can sense the tides of terror. He is afraid to die today. "For the Sealands," he whispers. "For the Sunlands."

Then he gives a nod, and his men lunge at us from both sides.

Magiano moves so quickly, I barely see him jump into the fray. His daggers flash silver in the light. Ahead of us, Teren sets upon two of the first men with a snarl of fury, unleashing his pent-up rage on them. He cuts them down easily.

"Move!" Raffaele snaps, rushing us forward. We dart ahead as Teren opens a pocket for us. But the narrow street continues filling with more people, forcing us to a stop again. How many of them are here? They must have been waiting for our arrival for months. Violetta's horse rears in the midst of the chaos, lets out a squeal, and throws her from its back. Lucent catches her—just barely—with a curtain of wind. Violetta falls on the steps, and instinctively, I push her behind me and force her against the wall. She is awake now, her body shaking like a leaf.

One of the men lunges at her, but Lucent lashes out with her sword, cutting the other man in the stomach. Ahead of us, Teren cuts the path clear even as more come. Blades catch him, slicing his flesh, but he seems oblivious to his injuries, his body slowly, laboriously trying to heal itself with each attack. It's even clearer now—he heals noticeably slower

than I remember. Behind us, Magiano leaps up against the wall of the building and twists in midair, slashing one man neatly across the throat and another in his chest. The smell of blood and fear fills my senses, and I feel the voices feeding on the darkness, growing louder with each passing moment, strengthening me even as they veer me farther from what I can control. I stumble forward, trying to stave off the rush of illusions that threaten to overwhelm me. Our attackers' smiles turn skeletal, their forms monstrous. Their hands extend like claws toward us, as if they were dead trees in a forest, and suddenly I am struggling through their grasp, trying to breathe. *Keep moving. This isn't real.* I tell myself this over and over again. Teren continues moving us forward through the fight, and behind us, Magiano keeps them back. I try to concentrate on them. We have to find a way out of this street.

Then, ahead of us, Raffaele stumbles. He grimaces in pain, then falls to his knees.

Lucent rushes to his side. As I look on, she grabs his arm and tries to help him to his feet—but he winces, clutches his head, and stumbles again. There he kneels, crouching in pain, his hair spilling past his shoulders in a black sheet.

His fear is a blanket over him, and my energy lunges for it. I glance around us. There is far too much chaos here for me to make all of us disappear behind a curtain of invisibility, and I want to save my power—but I can already see two of the attackers eyeing Raffaele in his weakened state. If I don't hide him now, he won't make it out of this fight.

I focus my energy on Raffaele. Then I weave invisibility

across him. He vanishes. I rush over to him and Lucent as blades flash all around us. When I reach them, I wrap one of Raffaele's arms around my shoulder and help her lift him. Magiano looks in our direction from where he's fending off an attacker.

A few steps ahead, Teren suddenly jerks backward as a team of attackers charge at once. One of them manages to get past Teren. We're invisible now, but even though the attacker can't see us, he swings his blade in an arc toward us. I only have time to get a glimpse of his silver mask.

An arrow sings through the air from the rooftops. It hits our attacker straight through his throat. He freezes in mid-movement, stunned, and then he drops his weapon and reaches up to clutch in vain at his neck. As I look on, he falls backward onto the steps.

More arrows cut through the air from the roofs. Every single one of them finds its mark. I search the rooftops until I catch sight of a blur of armor darting by. Behind us, Magiano lets out a whoop of laughter—in a flash, he has leapt onto one of the signs dangling in front of a door and swung forward, flinging a dagger down at the attackers.

As I look up to see another figure dart by on the roofs, I finally glimpse a tall young woman with braids woven high on her head, the strands half black and half blond, crouched with one elbow resting on her knee. She has a bow stretched back and pointed down in the direction of one of our attackers. She lets the arrow fly.

The Beldish queen has finally arrived.

More and more of her soldiers appear on the roofs. The Saccorists, now recognizing the crest of her men, start to break apart in their confusion. Several of Maeve's guards appear at the end of the street. The sight of them seems to be the last straw for the Saccorists. Someone shouts an order to retreat, and the remaining attackers scatter immediately, dropping their weapons and making a run for it. Teren continues to fight, but the battle is already over. The attackers melt away as quickly as they appeared, until all that's left in the street are the fallen.

I lift the illusion from all of us. My own strength leaves me, and suddenly Raffaele feels overwhelmingly heavy. Magiano hurries to our side and takes Raffaele's limp body in his arms. My attention turns to Violetta. She is still crouched against the wall where I left her, curled into a tight ball and looking as if she were concentrating on staying conscious. I walk over, then extend a hand to her.

Violetta turns up her face to me. Some of the lingering fear and distance in her eyes that had so defined our last few weeks together has faded, replaced by a familiar glimmer. It is a light I remember from when she used to walk at my side through Merroutas, when we were the only company we needed in the world.

The whispers still haunt the air around me, but I refuse to listen to them, pushing them aside. Violetta takes my hand and I help her to her feet. She leans against me, barely able to

stand. "Teren," I say as he approaches us. There are slashes in his tunic and smears of blood on his armor, but otherwise he seems unharmed. He gives Violetta a cold look, then hoists her effortlessly onto his back without a word.

"We have an encampment," Maeve calls down to us from the roofs. She has heavy black powder rimming her eyes, and a streak of gold war paint on her cheeks. "You all look like you could use a rest."

I see Maeve searching for me from her perch, and when our eyes lock, we stare for a long moment. I stiffen—there is an air of uncertainty hovering around her at my presence. I think back to the last time we set eyes on each other, when she had watched me call on Enzo's power to destroy a devastating number of her fleet. Even now, I can envision the flames roaring all around us.

She straightens and nods in the direction of the city's outskirts. "My men will lead us there." Then she disappears over the edge of the roof.

Adelina Amouteru

Queen Maeve is thinner than I remember, and her face has become harder in the months since we last met. The Elite who aligns with death. With my weary demeanor, sunken cheeks, and hard gaze, I imagine she thinks the same when she looks at me. She and her battalion traveled over the Karra Mountains, the crooked range of long-dead volcanoes that divides Beldain from Amadera, and set up an encampment of sheepskin tents here on the outskirts of Laida, where humanity ends and a horizon rimmed completely by ice-capped mountains begins. Torches light the snow in patches between the camp's tents. The air has turned cold and cruel, cutting straight through my riding gear. As evening washes the bleak landscape in blues and purples, the Beldish queen makes her way through puddles of slush from her tent to ours, flanked by her soldiers.

I wonder what she has gone through since we faced each other on the seas, and what the state of her navy might be. A part of me calculates whether it will be worth invading Beldain in the future or not. No doubt she wants to do the same to Kenettra—but we both bite our tongues now as she nears. She gives me a stiff nod of greeting.

"We leave at dawn," she tells me. "If your sister does not wake by then, carry her."

I return her nod, even though my whispers hiss. This is the closest we will come to civility. "We'll be ready."

Maeve walks past me without acknowledging my words. I turn and watch her disappear inside our tent. *Show her what you can do, and then she will respect you.* The Queen of Beldain and I may be forced allies for now, but there will be a time after this when we will all return to our sides, and our enemy state.

Behind her soldiers walks Magiano. When he sees me, he removes his cloak and wraps it around my shoulders. I relax as it blocks the bite of the wind; the lingering warmth from Magiano feels soothing against my body. "I can't talk him into getting inside a tent," he says, gesturing over his shoulder as ice crystals flake from his braids. Some distance from the tents, where the land fades off into the blackness of the mountains, I can see a lone blond figure kneeling in the wind, his head down in prayer. Teren.

I put a hand on Magiano's arm. "Let him stay," I reply. "He will talk to the gods until he feels comforted." But my stare lingers on Teren for a moment longer. Does he, like Raffaele,

228

now feel the pull of the Elites' origin calling from somewhere deep in the mountains? I can sense a pulse in the back of my mind now, a knot of power and energy lying somewhere beyond what I can see.

Magiano sighs in exasperation. "I've told Maeve's men to keep an eye on him," he says. "Let's not have come all this way only to lose him to frostbite." Then he turns and walks alongside me as we head back into our tent.

It's warm inside. Lucent sits in one corner, grimacing as she wraps her arm in a hot cloth. She has injured her wrist again during the battle, but when she notices me looking, she quickly glances away. Nearby, Raffaele rises from his chair and bows his head in Maeve's direction. Maeve stands near the tent's entrance, her body turned subconsciously toward Lucent, her eyes on Violetta's bed.

Even in the lantern light, Violetta still looks deathly pale. Her eyelids flutter now and then, as if she were lost in a nightmare, and a sheen of sweat covers her forehead. Her dark waves of hair fan out across the cloak folded under her head.

"Snow is coming from the north," Maeve says, breaking the silence. "The longer we stay here, the more we'll risk having our routes cut off. The snow breakers are already heading up to the ranges."

"Snow breakers?" Magiano asks.

"Men who are sent up to the snow packs. They break up the snow into small, controlled avalanches in order to prevent larger ones. You probably saw them in town, with their

ice picks." Maeve nods at Raffaele. "Messenger." At the mention of his name, her stony face softens a touch. I'm surprised at the twinge of envy I feel, that Raffaele can so easily draw others to him. "Are you well now?"

"Better," Raffaele replies.

"What happened?" I ask. "We saw you freeze—you crumpled to your knees."

Raffaele's jewel-toned eyes catch the light, glinting a dozen different shades of green and gold. "The energy around me was overwhelming," he explains. "The world became a blur. I couldn't think, and I couldn't breathe."

The feeling overwhelmed him. Raffaele's power is to sense each and every thread in the world, everything that connects with everything else. This must be how Raffaele's powers are deteriorating, the equivalent of my spontaneous, out-of-control illusions, of Violetta's vicious markings, and Lucent's fragile bones. Unless we can succeed in our mission, his power will be his undoing, like the rest of us.

I can tell by the look on Raffaele's face that he is thinking the same thoughts that I am, but he just gives Maeve a tired smile. "Not to worry. I'm well enough."

"It seems you stumbled across our traveling band at exactly the right time," Magiano says to Maeve.

In the silence that follows, Lucent pushes herself to her feet, wincing as she goes, and heads for the tent flap. "We should all get some rest, then," she mutters. She hesitates a step as she passes Maeve. A flicker of expression—something lonely, longing—crosses her face, but nothing more than that,

and before Maeve can react, Lucent ducks out of the tent and disappears.

Maeve watches her go, then follows. Her soldiers leave in her wake.

Raffaele meets my gaze and sits back down in his chair. "Your sister is growing weaker," he says. "Our nearness to the origin of Laetes's fall has intensified our connections to the gods, and it is ravaging our bodies. She will not last much longer."

I stare at Violetta's face. She furrows her brows, as if aware of my presence near her, and I find myself thinking of when we once lay side by side on identical beds, struck down by the blood fever. Somehow, it never has left us.

I glance at Magiano, then Raffaele. "Give me a moment alone with her," I say.

I'm grateful to Magiano for his silence. He squeezes my hand once, then turns away and steps out of the tent.

Raffaele stares at me, doubt on his face. *He doesn't trust you alone with her. That is what you inspire, little wolf, a cloud of suspicion.* Perhaps that's what the expression is—or perhaps it is guilt, some lingering hint of regret for all that has happened between us, all that could have been avoided. Whatever it means, it disappears in the next breath. He tightens the clasp of his cloak and folds his hands into his sleeves, then moves toward the tent flap. Before he can step out, he turns back to me.

"Let yourself rest," he says. "You will need it, mi Adelinetta."
Mi Adelinetta.

My breath catches; the whispers go still. The memory rushes to me, clear as crystal, of an afternoon long ago, when I sat with him by an Estenzian canal and listened to him sing. With the memory comes a rush of wistful joy, followed by unbearable sadness. I hadn't realized how much I missed that day. I want to tell him to wait, but he has already left. His voice seems to linger in the air, though, words I haven't heard from him in years . . . and somewhere, deep in my chest, stirs the presence of a girl buried long ago.

On the bed, Violetta lets out a soft moan and shifts, breaking through the turmoil of my thoughts. I lean closer to her. She takes a deep, rasping breath, and then her eyes flutter open.

I hold Violetta's hand, weaving my fingers with hers. Her skin is scalding to the touch, darkened by overlapping markings, and through it I can feel the bond of blood between us, strengthened by our Elite powers. Her eyes search the room, confused, and then wander up to my face. "Adelina," she whispers.

"I'm here—" I start to reply, but she interrupts me and closes her eyes.

"You're making a mistake, Adelina," she says, her head now turned to her side. I blink, trying to understand what she means—until I realize that she is talking in a feverish state, and perhaps not even aware of where she is.

"I want to turn back," she whispers. "But your Inquisitors— they are searching everywhere for me. They have their swords drawn. I think you may have ordered them to kill me when

they find me." Her voice cracks with dryness, hoarse and weak. "I want to help you. You're making a mistake, Adelina." She sighs. "I made a mistake too."

Now I understand. She is telling me what happened after she fled the palace, after my illusions had overwhelmed me and she had turned on me—after *I* had turned on *her*. A lump rises in my throat. I take a seat in Raffaele's chair, then lean toward her again.

"I told my soldiers to bring you back," I murmur. "Unharmed. I searched for you for weeks, but you had already left me behind."

Violetta's breathing sounds shallow and uneven. "Took a ship bound for Tamoura, at first light," she whispers. Her hand tightens around mine.

"Why did you go to the Daggers?" I sound bitter now, and my illusions spark, painting a scene around me of the days after Violetta had first left my side. How I sat on my throne, clutching my head, refusing trays of supper from servants. How I conjured blackness over the skies of Kenettra, blocking out the sun for days. How I'd burned parchments in the fire after my Inquisition patrols would write me, one after another, that they could not find her. "How could you?"

"I followed the energy of other Elites across the sea," Violetta murmurs in a trance. Sweat drips down the side of her face as she shifts uneasily again. "I followed Raffaele, and I found him. He found me. Oh, Adelina . . ." She trails off for a moment. "I thought he could help you. I begged him on my knees, with my face pressed to the ground." Her

lashes are wet now, barely holding tears back. Beneath her lids, her eyes move restlessly. "I begged him every day, even as we heard you sent your new navy to invade Merroutas."

My hand clenches harder around Violetta's. *Merroutas*, I'd ordered my men. *Domacca. Tamoura. Dumor. Cross the seas, drag the unmarked from their beds, bring them out into the streets before me.* My fury seethed, day after day. "I couldn't find you," I snap, irritated at the tears that spring to my eye. "Why didn't you send me a dove? Why didn't you let me know?"

Violetta is silent for a long moment, lost in her fever world. Her eyes open again, vacant and gray, bleeding color, and find me. "Raffaele says you are lost forever. That you are beyond help. I think he's wrong, but he sheds tears for you and shakes his head. I'm trying to convince him." Her whispers turn urgent. "I think I'll try again tomorrow."

I reach up and angrily wipe my tears away. "I don't understand you," I whisper back. "Why do you have to keep trying?"

Violetta's lips tremble with effort. "You cannot harden your heart to the future just because of your past. You cannot use cruelty against yourself to justify cruelty to others." Her gray eyes slide downward, away from my face, until her gaze rests on the lantern burning low near the tent flap. "It is hard. I know you are trying."

All my life, I have tried to protect you.

The room blurs behind my curtain of tears. "I'm sorry," I whisper. My words float in the air, quiet and lingering. Before me, Violetta sighs, and her eyelids drift closed again.

She murmurs something else, but it is too quiet for me to hear. I squeeze her hand, unsure what I am holding on for, hoping she will wake and recognize me not in a fever dream, not in a nightmare, but here at her side. I stay long after her breathing turns even. Finally, when the lantern has burned so low that the tent is all but shrouded in darkness, I put my head down against her bed and listen to the wind howl until sleep finally, mercifully, claims me.

Maeve Jacqueline Kelly Corrigan

Maeve hears Lucent calling for her, but not until she reaches the entrance of her tent does Lucent finally catch up. Maeve turns around to face her former companion. In front of her tent, the queen's personal guards place their hands on their swords' hilts, their eyes following Lucent's movements.

Maeve hesitates at the sight of Lucent's grave eyes. They had ended their relationship a year ago, right along the white cliffs of Kenettra. She should let it be; after all, Lucent had told her then that she would not agree to Maeve's wishes. *I cannot be your mistress,* she said. So why does Lucent look so desperate to speak to her now?

"Yes?" Maeve says coolly. The girl looks ill, and the sight of her wan skin and aching limbs twists Maeve's heart.

Lucent hesitates, suddenly unsure of what to say. She runs a hand through her reddish-blond curls, then gives Maeve a hurried bow. "Are you well?" she finally asks, her voice faltering.

"Are *you*?" Maeve asks in return. "You look terrible, Lucent. Raffaele mentioned in his last letter that you were . . . suffering."

Lucent shakes her head, as if her own health were not important. "I heard what happened," she replies. "Tristan. Your brother." She bows her head again, and the silence drags on.

Tristan. This was why Lucent is here. The weakness of her voice cracks Maeve's resolve, and she finds herself softening toward Lucent in spite of herself. How she has missed Lucent's presence, how quickly they had been separated again after the last battle against Adelina. She turns her head and nods once at her guards. With a clatter of armor, they step away and leave the two alone.

"He was never meant to stay this long," Maeve replies after a while. She shakes away the image of her brother's dead eyes, the mindless nature of his attack. It wasn't him, of course. "He was already in the Underworld."

Lucent winces and looks away.

"You still blame yourself," Maeve continues, gentler now. "Even after all this time."

Lucent says nothing, but Maeve knows what must be going through her head. It is the memory of the day Tristan had died, when the three of them had decided to go hunting together in the winter woods.

Tristan had shied away from the lake. He'd always been afraid of the water.

Maeve closes her eyes, and for an instant, she relives it again—Lucent, gangly and laughing, dragging Tristan forward through the brush to see the deer she had tracked for them; Tristan, staring at the deer that had made it halfway across the frozen lake; Maeve, kneeling into a silent crouch, lifting her bow to her line of sight. They had been too far away from the creature. *One of us will have to get closer,* Maeve had suggested. And Lucent had goaded and encouraged Tristan.

You should go.

They'd played on the ice often, never with incident. So, finally, Tristan grabbed his bow and arrow and crawled out onto the frozen lake on his elbows and stomach. They toyed with death a thousand times, but that day would have a different outcome. There was a hairline crack in the ice at a fateful spot. Perhaps the deer's hooves were the cause, perhaps the weight of the creature made the ice unstable, or perhaps the winter was not cold enough, had not frozen the lake solidly. Perhaps it was the thousand times they'd cheated death, all returning for them.

They heard the crack of the ice an instant before Tristan fell through. It'd been just enough time for him to look back at them as he plunged into the water below their feet.

"It was my fault," Maeve tells her. She reaches up, about to lift Lucent's chin, then stops herself. Instead, she gives Lucent a sad smile. "I brought him back." She looks down. "I cannot reach the Underworld any longer. The touch of it has

leaked into the mortal world, its harsh presence like ice on my heart. My power will kill me, if I choose to use it again. Perhaps," she adds in a low voice, "part of all this is my punishment for defying the goddess of Death."

Lucent studies her for a long moment. Has it really been so long since they were young? Maeve wonders whether this will be the final journey they take together, whether Raffaele's predictions will all come to pass, that they will enter the mountain paths and never return.

At last, Lucent bows. "If we must all go," she says, eyes turned down, "then I'm honored to go with you, Your Majesty." Then she turns to leave.

Maeve reaches out and grabs Lucent's arm. "Stay," she says.

Lucent freezes. Her eyes widen at the queen. Maeve can feel the heat rising to her cheeks, but she doesn't look away. "Please," she adds, quieter. "Just this time. Just this once."

For a moment, it seems Lucent might turn away. The two remain fixed in place, neither willing to move first.

Then Lucent takes a step toward the queen. "Just this once," she echoes.

All my wealth, power, territories, military might . . .

none of it matters now. She has gone, and with her shall I go.

—*Final letter of King Delamore to his general*

Adelina Amouteru

ray clouds blanket the skies the next morning, clear warnings of snow, stretching as far as the horizon. As Maeve leads two riders out ahead to check our path, I sit with Magiano, chewing on strips of dried meat and hard bread. Around a nearby fire, Raffaele sits with his cloak gathered tightly about him, talking in low voices with Lucent. Teren sits alone, ignoring us all.

Magiano is in a dark mood, no doubt brought on by the cold and gloom. Without his joy, I find myself fending off the whispers in my head more than ever, struggling to stay sane. *You will lose yourselves in the snow and wilds*, they are saying. *You will never return.* Beside me, Violetta lies unconscious, shivering uncontrollably, under a pile of furs and blankets. Hard as it is to see her like this, I am glad that she is

shivering. It tells me that she is still alive. I reach out and rest my hand on the furs.

"At this rate," Magiano mutters, pulling me out of the depths of my thoughts, "we won't see blue sky again until we leave this place." He turns his eyes to the sky and utters a loud, mournful sigh. "What I wouldn't give for a little Merroutas warmth and gaiety."

Maeve and her riders return as we are finishing our breakfast. "The paths are covered with ice," she says as we load our packs onto our horses. She catches Lucent's eyes for a moment, and something unspoken passes between them. "But they are otherwise clear. The snow breakers have already been through." I notice the queen touch Lucent's boot briefly before heading to her own mount. There is a new closeness between them.

Nearby, Magiano and Raffaele help me secure Violetta on a stretcher behind two of Maeve's horses. She stirs restlessly as we go, murmuring something that I can't understand. Her markings look darker now, almost black, as if Moritas were slowly claiming her body for the Underworld. I grit my teeth at the sight.

Magiano watches me as I stand beside Violetta's stretcher. "She'll make it," he says, placing a hand on my arm, but I can hear the doubt in his voice.

As we near the paths that lead into the first mountains, the narrowness of the valleys starts to funnel the wind, so it

bites our cheeks and cuts through every gap in our clothing. I tie my hood down tight over my head and try to pull my cloak higher to cover the lower half of my face. Even then, my breath freezes against the cloth, creating a patch of white frost. With the wind come the whispers, howling against my ears with every blast. Their words are such a jumble, I can't understand what they're saying, but they send my heart racing until my shoulders sag from exhaustion. Now and then, I think I see dark silhouettes standing in the crevices of the mountains, watching us with sightless eyes. I can only see them in the edges of my vision—when I turn my head, they vanish.

Magiano continues to frown at the sky. "Is it just me, or is the sky turning darker?" He nods up at the clouds. "The clouds aren't growing any thicker—it just seems as if the day were passing more rapidly than it should."

I glance up too. He's right. What should be the light of a midday sun hidden behind clouds looks instead like the sun is already setting. The shadows in the valley deepen as we go, stretching around us in muted shapes as the mountain ranges around us turn steeper. The path beneath our horses' hooves crunches with frost and ice.

I lose track of how many hours we travel in this strange twilight. We all stay quiet. I ride behind Violetta's stretcher so I can keep her in my sights. Now and then, her eyes open, gray and uneasy, but they never seem to focus on anything or anyone. It is as if she has already gone somewhere else.

She's still here, I tell myself. But the whispers in my

mind now sound like they are the wind, drowning out my thoughts, and my exhaustion and worry settle into a frenetic beating in my heart. This must be the way the origin's pull is affecting me.

That night, a night that seems to fall prematurely, we stop in a hollow that shelters us partly from the elements. The wind is furious in this narrow pass, making it impossible for us to pitch a proper camp. Our horses are listless too, huddled together for warmth close to the fire we've built.

"The early twilight will come more frequently in the days ahead," Raffaele says as we all gather around him. He draws one curved line through the dirt with a stick, then notes several spots along it, including our location. "We are getting closer." He points to a spot at the top of the path, nestled between two mountains. "The Dark of Night."

Raffaele speaks with calm and grace, as he always does, but even his voice seems to carry underneath it a current of doubt. My hand lingers on top of the furs blanketing Violetta, who stirs uneasily in her fevered sleep. We are headed toward a realm known only in legends and folktales. What will happen when we arrive?

"The laws of our world may bend and stretch there," Raffaele says after a moment. "Things may not be as they appear. We'll need to be careful." At this, he glances my way. "I feel the pull of this place. Can you?"

I nod. Around me, the others do the same. My gaze wanders to where Teren sits a short distance away, his cloak undone, seemingly oblivious to the cold. He is methodically

sharpening his sword and knives. My whispers are growing stronger, while an air of darkness seems to hover around Magiano. Violetta is fading, and Raffaele's senses are being overwhelmed by threads of energy from every direction. What must Teren feel here, so close to the origin? Will this journey drive him even closer to madness?

Before we settle in to rest for the night, I ask Maeve to set up extra sentries around Teren. Even then, I still find myself waking at odd hours and looking in Teren's direction, wondering whether I will see him snap.

The dawn never seems to arrive the next morning. Instead, the world lightens only into the dim twilight we'd experienced the day before, leaving the landscape frightening in its darkness. A light snow has started to fall, sprinkling a coating of white all around us. Magiano sleeps pressed next to me, one arm draped over my shoulders. My whispers are loud this morning, restless and roaring and without end. When I look behind us, I see nothing but the trail of our footprints leading off into the lonely mountains. I see the same up ahead. In my periphery, illusions of dark silhouettes continue to hover, my own ghosts that refuse to leave me alone.

I shake fresh snow from my hair, then rise carefully so as not to wake Magiano. I stretch my sore limbs. Only a few sentries posted by Maeve are also awake, standing some distance away, their attention fixed on the bleak terrain surrounding us. I look around at the scene, realizing that, if I wanted to, I could eliminate them all in this moment of weakness.

Do it.

The whispers are so strong this morning that I almost follow their orders. I scowl, shake my head, and press my hands to my temples. Why are they suddenly so insistent? We must be edging very close to the Dark of Night. Trying to ignore them, I rub my hands and decide to wander in a circle around the camp. Teren's not in his sleeping area—this sends a note of panic through me before I notice him standing several paces past the sentries, his face tilted at the heavens in prayer. I watch him for a short time, then head to where Violetta is asleep.

When I reach her cot, I kneel beside her. Her dark hair is frozen into clumps, and her pallid skin looks almost frosted. It's far too cold here for her to handle; we'll need to find extra furs. She can have mine before we need to stop again, but even then, I'm not sure if that will be enough.

"Violetta," I whisper, gently touching her shoulder.

She doesn't stir.

I hesitate, then remove one of my gloves and touch her cheek with the back of my hand. Her skin is ice cold. No warm breaths come from her.

The whispers surround me, but I force them violently away. Surely she's breathing—this must be an illusion. I'm creating a nightmare for myself again. I will wake over and over until Magiano rouses me from this dream. I shake her again, this time harder. "Violetta," I say, louder. My voice catches Raffaele's attention nearby. He sits up and looks in

my direction. Then his eyes go to Violetta. The immediate expression on his face confirms my worst fears.

No. It's impossible—I'd fallen asleep last night seeing the rhythmic rise and fall of her chest. She had been murmuring something I couldn't understand. Beads of sweat dotted her brow, and her skin was hot to the touch. This is not real. I shake her again, my hands clutching her shoulders hard. "Violetta!" I shout. This time, the others all startle awake and the sentries look over at me, but I don't care. I keep shaking her until I feel someone's hands on me, forcing me to stop. It's Raffaele. He kneels at my side, his eyes on Violetta's still form. The sadness on his face shatters my heart all over again.

"Can you revive her?" I ask him.

"I will try," Raffaele murmurs, but the way he says it tells me what I desperately don't want to hear.

Everything will be all right. I will wake from this, as many times as I have to, until I return to reality. The illusion will disappear, as it always does, and I will spend another morning with Violetta.

Now Maeve rises too, as well as Lucent and Magiano, and heads over to me. "Your Majesty," I say to her. It is the first time I've addressed her properly. "You align with Moritas. You can call her back, if needed." I look at Raffaele. "Wake her," I say angrily, my voice a command now.

"Adelina," Magiano whispers.

Raffaele's hand tightens on Violetta's cold shoulder. He reaches up and cups her cheek in his palm. I wonder if he is working his magic on her, the gentle tug of his energy on her

heartstrings, perhaps stirring her with his calming touch. I crouch as he hovers there, my stare fixed on Violetta's face, waiting for her gray eyes to flutter open.

"Adelina," Magiano says again. His hand touches mine, and he squeezes it tightly.

Maeve shakes her head. "She's gone," she says quietly, bowing her head.

"Then bring her back," I snap. The darkness in me rises up from the depths of my chest. "I have *seen* you do it."

Maeve looks at me with cold eyes. "I cannot."

"Lies," I hiss. "We need her. We cannot enter the Dark of Night without her. I—"

I glance to my side, where Teren still has his face pointed up to the heavens. He is the only one of us all who has not gathered here in a circle. The whispers, already a chaotic din, now explode into a whirlwind around me. *Him,* they say, their voices merging with my own voice. *Teren killed her. He is the only explanation—you knew he could not be trusted.*

"You," I say, the word trembling out of me with all the rage and blackness in my heart. Teren lowers his head and turns to meet my gaze. "This is *your* doing." In this moment, I do not see a former prisoner of mine. I do not see the man who saved me from drowning in the rough seas. All I see is the Lead Inquisitor who had once laughed at me with his poisonous white eyes, who had stolen Violetta from me and used her against me. The whispers repeat Teren's old threats, words he once spat at me with a blade pressed to my throat. *You have three days.* His taunting voice echoes across time. *If*

*you go back on your word, I will shoot an arrow through your
sister's neck and out the back of her skull.*

He killed her when we were all asleep. Raffaele had
warned that we might behave differently here, that our powers might be unstable. Teren has always wanted Violetta
dead so that he can hurt me. The entire world around me
now turns scarlet with my fury. *It was him.*

Teren looks at me, his expression blank.

"Adelina." Magiano's voice rings out again, but he sounds
far away.

The dark energy in me bursts free.

I fling an illusion of pain at Teren. *Your skin ripped away,
your heart pulled from your chest, your eyes bleeding from their
sockets. I will destroy you.* The others seem to vanish from
my sight—all I can see before me is Teren crumpling to his
knees from my onslaught. I rush toward him. The mountain
path we are on turns black and crimson; demonic silhouettes
rise from the snow, their fangs bared. I tighten the illusion
around Teren in fury and pull a dagger from my belt. Then
I lunge at him.

Teren bares his teeth—his sword is in his hands before
I can blink. He swings it at me in a shining arc. I whirl to
one side and tighten my fist at him. He lets out a shriek of
pain as my illusion covers him in a net. I strike at him with
my dagger, but his hand shoots up to grab my wrist. His
strength, even in agony, nearly breaks my bones. I wince and
thrash out of his grasp—my dagger clatters to the ground. I

can hardly see straight through my illusions anymore. I am surrounded by silhouettes and night, white cloaks and fire.

Then a boy with golden eyes and dark braids stands before me. Between us. His pupils are narrowed into black slits, and his jaw is clenched with resolve. He walks toward me without fear.

"Adelina, stop!" he says.

"*Get—out—of my way.*" I lash out at him with my illusions—but he narrows his eyes, raises his arm, and flings my illusions out of his way. They dissipate in a cloud of smoke around him. He continues toward me.

"Adelina, *stop.*"

It is Magiano. Magiano. Stop. The name is a small light, but it is there, and I cling to it in the maelstrom around me. I falter as he reaches me and pulls me into a rough embrace.

"He didn't kill her," Magiano is whispering. "Stop. Stop." His hand cradles the back of my head.

My strength leaves me in a rush. The world around us lightens, the silhouettes of demons vanish. Teren crouches before me on one knee, leaning heavily against his sword, breathing hard. His pale eyes are fixed on mine. I look away from him and concentrate on Magiano's arms holding me tight. *Teren didn't kill her.*

But she is gone. It is too late.

I start to cry. My tears freeze on my face. In my exhaustion, I step away from Magiano and stagger back to where Violetta's body lies on the cold ground. The others watch in

silence as I fall to my knees. I gather my sister into my arms, brushing her stiff hair from her face, repeating her name over and over until it becomes a constant loop in my mind. A note of anguish escapes me in between sobs. I see a vision of the night I'd first run away from our home, when we touched our foreheads together. I do this now, resting my forehead on hers, and I rock her back and forth, begging her once again, in vain, not to leave me.

It is the holiest of places, where the stars shine against rock and the twilight never ends. Be wary, for pilgrims may be so drawn to its power that they may lose themselves entirely.

–Charted Paths of the Karra Mountains, *various authors*

Adelina Amouteru

ad Violetta died in Kenettra, we would have buried her ashes in the maze of catacombs extending underneath the city. But out here, on the cold paths of the Karra Mountains, without enough wood to create a funeral pyre and the ground too frozen to dig, we can only cover her beneath a mound of stones, turned in the direction of our homeland. Before we do so, I lay her cloak over her body and bend to touch her hair—how luscious and dark her locks once were, how much I'd envied them when we were young—now it looks faded, as if its light had gone from this world along with my sister.

We should have moved faster. I should have argued less with Raffaele when negotiating in Tamoura. *I should have been kinder.* The whispers haunt me with these words, and this time, I don't stop them.

The others stand beside me, hands folded into sleeves. Even Teren stands here, his face vacant. No doubt he does not grieve my sister, but to my surprise, he does not say it aloud. He seems lost in his own world, making silent prayers to the gods. Raffaele's head is bowed in grief, and his eyes are moist with tears.

"What do we do now, Messenger?" Maeve murmurs, her hand resting on the hilt of her sword. It is the question on all of our minds. "We've lost her. Is all this futile?"

Raffaele doesn't answer right away. Perhaps, for once, he *doesn't* know the answer. Instead, he just continues to stare at the mound of stones, wisps of his hair blowing across his face. The question is numb in my own mind. I let the whispers swirl in circles around me, their presence so familiar now.

It is your fault. It is always your fault.

"We continue on," Raffaele finally replies. And none of us says anything different. It is simply too late to turn back now, even if it may not even be possible to step inside our destination, when we have come so far.

I should have listened to Violetta, all those months ago. When she had tried to take away my powers, I should have let her. Perhaps she would still be alive, if I'd done so. Perhaps we could have acted sooner, somehow. Perhaps we would have had more time together. The guilt sits like a weight in my chest.

I should have listened, but it doesn't matter anymore. None of this seems to matter anymore.

As the soldiers begin to pile more stones at her feet, I take out a knife sheathed at my belt, reach out, and cut a length of Violetta's locks. The warmth of my hand melts the ice on the strands. I entwine it with a length of my own silver hair, taking in for a moment the contrast, thinking back on the lazy afternoons when she used to weave my braids. *I love you, Adelina,* she used to tell me. The dried tears on my face crack when I move.

We stay for as long as we can, until finally Maeve commands us forward. I look back and try to hold Violetta's grave marker in my sights, until she disappears around a bend.

One morning blurs into another. The twilight becomes darker each day, and the snow turns steady. No one crosses our path. It is as if we were traveling at the edge of the world. Our travel settles into long silences, where none of us feel in the mood to speak. Even Magiano rides quietly by my side, his expression dark. The energy of this terrain pulls us forward, calling to us. I see illusions at night and during the twilight days, see them chased away only by the light of our fires. Sometimes, the ghost of Violetta walks alongside my horse. Her dark hair doesn't move in the wind, and her boots leave no prints in the snow. She never looks my way. Our path turns narrow, branching a dozen different ways every few hours, each leading deep into yet another set of mountains. Without Raffaele's guidance, I have no doubt that we would lose ourselves out here in the cold.

Then, one day, we halt in front of a yawning cave.

It is an ominous entrance, its mouth lined with jagged rock, leading into complete and utter darkness. Still, we never would have found this place without the pull of its energy. Here, I can feel the tangible presence of the pulsing power that calls to us, the strength of it like a thousand threads tugging against every muscle in my body.

"We have to go alone," Maeve says as she trots up beside us. "My men, they cannot follow us this way." She nods to our horses, some of which have thin trickles of blood dripping from their nostrils. Their suffering gets worse the closer they get to the entrance. My own stallion refuses to take another step forward. I look back at Maeve's troops. They also hang back. I'd never thought about how an energy powerful enough to affect each of the Young Elites might end up affecting common men, but now I can see it on their faces. Some have a sheen of cold sweat on their skin, while others look pale and weak. They have come as far as they can. If they enter this cave with us, they will die.

Maeve swings off her horse and nods at one of her soldiers. "Take them back with you," she says.

The soldier hesitates. Behind him, the others shift too. "You will be left in a frozen wasteland, Your Majesty," he replies, glancing around at us. "You—you are the Queen of Beldain. How will you make it back?"

Maeve fixes him with a hard stare. "We will find our own way," she says. "If you join us, you will not survive. This is not a request. This is a command."

Even then, the soldier lingers a moment longer. I find

myself looking on in longing and envy, bitterness and grief. Would any of my soldiers in Kenettra be so loyal to me? Would they follow me out of love, if I did not use fear against them?

Finally, he nods and bows his head. "Yes, Your Majesty." He places one hand over his chest, then kneels in the snow before her. "We will wait for you at the bottom of the pass. We will not leave until we see you return. Do not ask us to leave you entirely, Your Majesty."

Maeve nods. Her hard composure cracks, the only moment I've ever seen it do so. She suddenly seems very young. "Very well," she replies.

The soldier stands and shouts an order to the troops. They salute their queen before turning their horses around, making their way down the path that we'd originally come. I stand in silence, watching them go. Would my soldiers ever salute me in honor?

When the sound of hooves fades to a dull rumble, Maeve returns to join us at the entrance of the cave. No matter how hard I try to stare into it, I can't see anything except black— it is as if there were nothingness on the other side, and we would fall into it if we enter. Raffaele stands at the edge and closes his eyes. He takes a deep breath, then shudders. He doesn't need to speak for me to know what he is going to say. I can feel the pull. We *all* can.

The Dark of Night is at the end of this cave.

Teren draws his sword and a long knife, while Lucent and Magiano do the same. I stand close to Magiano as we start to

walk in. Violetta's absence is a gaping void beside me. If she were here, I would tell her to stay close. She would give me a quiet nod. But she isn't here.

So I turn to face the darkness without her, and walk in. I am too afraid to wonder whether we will be able to walk out.

I can see nothing, at first, and it makes me hesitate with every step I take. Our footsteps echo in the darkness, coupled with the sound of metal occasionally scraping against stone. The others must be using their swords as a guide along the edge of the cave. The air is bitterly cold in here and smells of something ancient, salt and stone and wind. I gulp over and over again, trying to keep myself from thinking that the walls are caving in on us. If only I could see—*if only I could see*. My old fear of blindness now flares to life, taking on a shape of its own in this darkness, and I think I can see the eyes of monsters in here, their stares fixed on me.

You will never get out of here, the whispers chant, pleased at my rising terror. *You will live in darkness forever, just as you deserve.*

I jump when a hand, warm and callused, touches mine. "You're all right." Magiano's voice comes out of the darkness like a beacon, and I turn toward him. *You're all right. You're all right.* I force the whispers in my head to repeat this, and slowly, the mantra gives me the strength to take one step after another.

After what seems like forever, my vision finally starts to adjust. I can see the subtle grooves of stone in the cave's ceiling, looming several feet above us, and from inside the grooves comes a faint ice-blue glow. Slowly, as more of the

cave comes into focus, I can see the glow emanating from nearly every crevice in the ceiling. My steps slow as I try to get a better look at it.

The light comes from millions of tiny, dangling beads of ice. They shimmer and twinkle, pulsing in a pattern, and they seem to gleam the strongest where we pass. For a moment, I forget my fear and just stand there, unable to tear my gaze away from their beauty.

"Ice faeries," Raffaele says, his voice echoing to us from somewhere in front. "Tiny creatures of the north. They must have awoken at the ripple of our movement in the air. I have seen them described in the accounts of priests on their pilgrimages here. This is the place that travelers worship as the Dark of Night, but they go no farther."

The glow lights our way, leading us along a trail painted by stardust.

Minutes pass. Hours. At some point, I feel the faint bite of a cold breeze against my face. We must be nearing the cave's exit. I tense, wondering what lies on the other side. Beside me, Violetta's ghost walks in and out of the shadows, faded and gray. The wind turns steady, until we round a curve in the cavern and find ourselves looking at an exit.

I suck in my breath at the glittering world of snow beyond it.

I have heard the myths about this place, the Dark of Night. But I am standing in front of it now, staring into an untouched, magical world. This is the entrance connecting our world with the gods. And we cannot enter without Violetta's alignment, her link to empathy.

Raffaele stands at the entrance and reaches out a hand tentatively. He shudders, and so do I—the energy beyond this entrance is overwhelming, a million threads to every one in the mortal world, something so intense that I fear it may crush me if I dare to step through. When the priests come searching for this place, is this where they stop? Do they sit under the light of the ice faeries and admire the beads of ice dangling in the cavern? Perhaps mere mortals cannot even tell that this entrance is here. Perhaps the energy here is so strong it is lost on them.

Raffaele stands there for a long moment, hovering between one space and another. Then he looks at us. *He is going to step through.* "We are already ghosts," he whispers. I open my mouth, wanting to stop him, then close it. He is right, as he always is. If this is how we must end, then so be it. Raffaele takes a deep breath, and I study his silhouette in this dim blue light, this magical realm, outlined in a halo as if for the last time. Beside me, Magiano nods and takes my hand. Maeve and Lucent stand together. Teren looks ahead without fear.

There is a space beside me where Violetta would have stood. Without her, I am less afraid of dying. Without her, the world is that much darker.

Raffaele steps through. And we follow.

> It is said that the Dark of Night can be entered solely by those
> who have known and suffered true loss—that only through
> surviving such agony can a mortal understand what it is like
> to set foot inside a realm of the gods.
> —Tales of Travelers to the Dark of Night, *compiled by Ye Tsun Le*

Adelina Amouteru

My boots sink into fresh snow that looks untouched for miles. A forest of frosted trees towers around us, their branches bare and layered with thick blankets of white. What freezes us all in our tracks, though, is the sight of the three moons in the night sky. They are enormous, great and golden and cold, covering half the sky, so large that I feel as if I could reach up and brush my fingers along their marble surfaces. Sheets of stars litter the sky, the constellations impossibly bright. *We are close to the heavens here.* As I stare, a curtain of faint green dances against the stars, undulating, appearing and disappearing in complete silence. I have never seen the night like this. It is as if the realm of the gods were reaching down to greet us here, and our mortal world yearning up in return.

"Gods," Magiano gasps beside me.

We entered, after all.

How is this possible? We shouldn't have. It should have killed us. Beside me, Raffaele stares in astonishment.

When I look over my shoulder, I notice Teren. Like the rest of us, he is frozen in place at the sight. His pale eyes are very wide, and his mouth is open. There are tears in his eyes, and frozen streaks on his face. I can hear him whispering a prayer as he stares, so moved by the beauty of this entrance of the gods.

We make our way through the untouched land. The pulse of the origin is a steady beat now, guiding each of us along. The snow crunches softly under our boots. I tremble in the cold. The whispers in my head burst into chaotic voices with every step I take, growing stronger the closer we get to the origin. I try again to keep them at bay, but gradually, they start to drown out the silence around me, until I can't hear even our footsteps or our breathing anymore. The whispers speak nonsense now, in a language too ancient for me to understand. The trees in this forest seem to blur and shift every time I blink, and I rub my eye, trying to make myself focus.

Now and then, something flashes across my vision. A shape, a figure, I'm not sure. Other times, I see abandoned houses, covered with snow and broken glass. Each time, I shake my head and cast it out of my mind, telling myself to focus. I can control my illusions. This is *my* power, even if we are standing in the realm of the gods.

Another shape darts between the trees and vanishes. I

stop to look for it. No use—it's already gone. I look back at Magiano. "There is something in the forest," I whisper.

He frowns, then glances at the gaps between the trees.

And at that moment, I stop. My stare goes up to the trees. I halt in my tracks. Beside me, Magiano turns and gives me an alarmed look. "What is it?" he asks.

But I can't answer him. All I can do is stare at the dead bodies hanging from the trees.

They hang from the branches all around us, dangling by their necks from ropes. Their bodies look gray, their faces ashen, and as I look on in horror, I start to recognize each one of them. The one closest to me is my father. His chest is skeletal as always, caved in, and drops of blood stain the white snow underneath him. Nearby is Enzo, his hair a deep, black scarlet, his neck broken, the same droplets of blood under his swaying body. Behind him is Gemma, her familiar face still half covered by her purple marking. There is the Night King of Merroutas, whom I'd once run through with a sword. There is Dante, his face contorted in pain. There are Inquisition guards I've killed, soldiers from foreign lands I've conquered, and rebels I've executed for daring to defy my rule. And there is my sister, my latest victim.

They are all here, their eyes open and trained on me, their lips cracked, expressions solemn. The whispers in my head grow to a roar, and I realize that the voices have always been *their* voices, the voices of those I have killed, growing and growing over the years as more have died.

What wolf? You're a little lamb. This whisper was Dante's voice.

Broken so easily. Enzo.

The dead cannot exist in this world on their own. Gemma.

You do not leave until I say so. The Night King of Merroutas.

Go ahead. Finish the job. My father.

All this time, the voices have been the whispers of the dead, growing in number, taunting me, haunting me, driving me to madness for their blood that stains my hands.

I stumble backward with a choked gasp. Magiano rushes to catch me before I fall in the snow. "Adelina!" he exclaims. The others stop to look at me too. "What's happening? What are you seeing?"

"I see everyone," I sob. "Enzo. Gemma. My father. My sister. They're all here, Magiano. Oh gods, I can't do this. I can't go on." My knees give way, and I sink, still unable to tear my gaze from the sight. *This isn't real,* the rational part of me tries to say. *All an illusion. Just an illusion. Just a nightmare. This isn't real.*

Except it *is* real. Except all of these people really *are* dead. And they are dead because of me.

"Don't make me go in there," I whisper, clinging to Magiano's arms as he leans over me.

Raffaele approaches and kneels in the snow beside me, while farther ahead, Maeve, Lucent, and Teren look on. Raffaele takes one of my hands. As I struggle to regain control over my power, he begins to use his. I can feel his threads intertwining with my heart, seeking the panic and fear within

me and pushing it gently down. My desperate stare goes from the hanging bodies to Raffaele's beautiful face, his olive skin, and his black hair framed by snow, the ice lining his long lashes, the green and gold of his eyes.

"Breathe, mi Adelinetta," he whispers. "Breathe."

I try to do as he says. Raffaele is not Violetta—he cannot save me from my power. But slowly, gradually, his soothing begins to smooth over the raging tides of energy in my chest that threaten to drive me mad. I feel the energy settling, and with it, the bodies begin to fade. They look like ghosts, translucent and floating. Then they turn so faint, I can no longer see them. My breath fogs in the air. My limbs feel weak, like I've just been swimming for hours. I lean heavily against Magiano.

Finally, Raffaele stops. He looks exhausted too, as if it were harder to work his magic here against mine. I take a deep breath, then nod and draw away from Magiano. "I'm all right," I say, trying to convince myself of it. "The energy here overwhelms me."

Raffaele nods once. "It pulls at me too," he tells me gently. "In a million different directions. This is not an easy place to be, a realm between us and the gods."

Lucent walks over to me and offers me her hand. I stare in surprise. When I take it, she helps me to my feet. Beside her, Maeve nods at me once. There is something lighting her face, a sudden recognition. "Your sister," she says. "You said you saw her back there, as an illusion. A ghost of the dead."

"Yes," I whisper.

"So that is why," Maeve murmurs. "Of course." She glances at Raffaele. "You said *all* of our alignments to the gods must be in the immortal realm in order for us to be here." Maeve looks back at me. "We were able to enter without Violetta's alignments."

"Because her soul is already *in* the immortal world," Raffaele finishes, understanding. His eyes soften at me. "In the Underworld."

She is already here, I realize. And somehow, this thought sends a wild surge of hope through me. *She is already here. Perhaps I can see her again.*

"We can't be far," Maeve says, turning away from me and continuing again down the snowy path through the forest. "The pulse keeps getting stronger."

The others all feel it too; I am not alone. *We're not far. We're almost there.* I repeat it to myself, letting it comfort me and calm my energy. We are not far from Violetta, where she waits for us in the realm of Moritas.

The others turn away, and I start walking after them. Magiano stays beside me, his hand now intertwined with mine. I try to concentrate on the warmth coming from him. I'm too afraid to look back at the treetops, for fear that I will see the dangling bodies again. I'm afraid that this time I might see bodies of those still alive, those who can still die.

As we go, the moons seem to move in the skies, edging closer together, growing ever larger until they look like they might hurtle right into us. They are going to align, I realize, each overlapping the next, when we reach the entrance to the

origin point. At the edges of my vision, dark shapes still flitter through the forest, vanishing when I try to look at them directly. I grasp for the threads in my chest and then try to hold on as tightly as I can, to stop my unconscious weaving. The figures waver and vanish for a while. But they don't go away altogether.

Finally, ahead of us, Maeve and Teren slow down. Through the forest and the night, a thin shaft of light shines in a clearing. I see it first. It glows against the bark of the trees, and as we round the corner, the glow intensifies, washing the landscape in an ethereal blue-white light. I squint. The trees grow sparse, then stop altogether. We step out into an enormous clearing of pristine snow. From here, we can see a valley nestled deep in the center of sharp, steep mountain ranges, with forests growing wild on either side.

In the middle of this valley is the source of the blue-white light, a narrow beam that seems to be pouring from another realm.

At the same time, the pulse of energy that I have been feeling for the past few days suddenly intensifies a dozenfold, sending a sharp stab of pain through my chest that reminds me of the way Enzo's tether had pulled. I gasp. The others do too—they must have been affected in similar ways. Magiano groans and clutches his head, while Raffaele hunches over and winces. Ahead of us, Maeve falls to a kneel, while Teren stabs his sword into the snow and leans against it. My illusions flare, sending sparks of dark silhouettes dancing through the snow around us.

This is the origin, the point where Laetes had once descended from the heavens to become a mortal, where the energy of the immortal world had originally torn, seeping into our world, where the Dark of Night formed around it, twisted by divine energy. Where the story of the Elites began. Even without Raffaele, I can feel the energy emanating from this place, made of threads from every god—War and Wisdom, Fear and Fury, Ambition and Passion.

I stand closer to Magiano, touch his arm, and move toward Raffaele. As I do, something flickers in the forests of the valley. At first, I think it must be my illusions again. Dark shapes, silhouettes that look like monsters.

Except that Teren also turns to look at them. He raises his sword at the same time Maeve does. "What is that?" he asks.

As the words leave his mouth, one of the shadows wanders out of the forest and into the clearing. It makes a sharp, clicking noise with its teeth. I recoil in horror. The creature has no eyes at all, only two soft, empty sockets where they might once have been, and a wide mouth full of fangs. It skitters forward on four legs, leaving prints in the untouched snow. In its wake hovers a blanket of fury, an energy so dark and vile that it makes me ill. Behind it comes another. Then, a third. They emerge from every corner of the forest, licking their lips.

"They are drawn to our energy," Raffaele whispers, his eyes wide.

Monsters, the whispers of the dead tell me. *Monsters from the Underworld.*

I glance back at the way we came. More shadows stir in

the forests behind us. They are suddenly everywhere, drawn out by our powers. The clicking of their teeth echoes through the trees.

Run.

We all break into a sprint toward the beam of light. Our sudden movement causes several of the creatures to swivel their heads in our direction—they sniff the air, then pull their mouths open to reveal sharp fangs. They bolt.

My breath comes in ragged gasps as the icy air burns my lungs. In front of me, Lucent stumbles in the snow—I reach out and catch her before she goes down. Maeve pulls away from us, leaving some room between herself and Teren, then twirls her blade. Her eyes narrow into slits. She bares her teeth, hefts the weapon as one of the creatures draws near, and swings at it.

The creature snarls and lunges toward her. Maeve's sword slices right across its gaping jaws, slashing deep into each side of its mouth. The creature screams—the sound is deafening. A shudder of fury and fear ripples through me at the attack. It is as if Maeve had cut *me* along with the creature. Maeve herself winces too.

We both align with the Underworld. These creatures *are* monsters from the immortal realm, creatures that are a part of us, connected to us.

Maeve slashes at the creature again. This time, she catches it in its side and sends it tumbling into the snow. There it twitches, while Maeve continues to run. "Hurry!" she shouts. Behind her, the creature starts to rise again.

Teren fans out to our other side. As we hurtle between the trees toward the blue beam, he swings at two creatures that come at us from the right. His swing is so powerful that it slices straight through the first creature's neck, decapitating it, before hacking deep into the second creature's chest. The first falls writhing in the snow, spilling black blood everywhere, while the second screams and thrashes. I gasp at the rush of pain from its death, stumble, and clutch at my neck. Lucent does the same. Maeve staggers to us, hauls us to our feet, and motions for us to keep going. We run faster.

Magiano darts away from my side. He spins around to face a growling creature behind us, draws a pair of daggers, and stabs them deep into the creature's face. Another jolt of pain courses through me. He yanks out the blades. We keep running as the creature collapses, shrieking.

I reach the valley first. Here, the trees are so close together they seem to form a maze leading to the center of the origin point. As we run, I look through the trunks and see my reflection flash by in small pockets of ice amongst the snow, fleeting and distorted. My face is pale, my hair a stream of silver. I look panic-stricken.

"Watch out!" I shout at Raffaele as a creature barrels through the maze of trees toward us. Raffaele jumps back in time for the creature to lodge its face in between a split trunk. It snarls and claws for us through the narrow gap, fangs snapping. Raffaele stumbles backward and falls in the snow. A sword streaks out of nowhere to cut the creature nearly in half. It's Teren, both hands gripping the hilt of his

sword tightly, standing over Raffaele like a strange guardian. More creatures leap for him. He swings at them, forcing them back. Another creature dies by his blade.

"*Move*," Teren snaps over his shoulder at Raffaele. "Don't make me save you again."

Raffaele needs no second warning. He leaps to his feet and continues running for the beam of light. I do the same. Behind us, Teren pulls out a long knife and stabs one more creature.

Then another leaps out in front of us, landing deep in the powder snow. It turns its sightless sockets on us and smiles with its fanged mouth. Beside me, Lucent rises from her painful crouch and grits her teeth, then brandishes her own sword and swings at the creature. The whispers burst to life in my head, and I can almost understand what it wants. It focuses on me.

Kill them, it says.

A shudder ripples through my body. The creature takes a step forward. *No*, I think in return.

You are one of us. You don't need them to visit the Underworld. You belong there yourself. It is your home.

The poison of the whispers seeps deep into my mind. I turn to look at Raffaele, and my thoughts fill with a sudden influx of hatred. Raffaele must see the change in my expression, because he suddenly pulls away from me. Lucent's eyes widen. "No, Adelina!" she shouts. I clench my fists.

No, I think, hanging on to Lucent's cry. *No.*

The creature snarls. It lunges for me—only to skewer

itself on Lucent's blade. She had moved in front of me so quickly that I didn't even see it. The creature screams, even as a spasm of pain shoots through me at its dying throes. Lucent yanks her blade out of its chest with a labored growl, and together with Raffaele, we run around its flailing body.

We are so close to the origin now. But more creatures crowd around from all sides, their hulking shapes gathering near the beam of light and behind us. We continue to run. Ahead of us, a cluster of creatures surrounds the light, and they turn their hideous faces in our direction. Maeve appears, bares her teeth, and flings herself at them—I reach within to weave a cloud of illusions around her and the others, trying to make them as invisible as I can. There are too many of us in motion. I can't hold the illusion, but it is enough to give them some cover.

Then, from somewhere, comes Teren. He is breathing heavily, his eyes wild with fury, his mouth twisted into a wide smile. His blades are covered in black blood, while his own clothes are stained red. He meets my stare, then turns to face the creatures. With a roar, he charges at them.

The creatures swarm him—but even then, they can't seem to take him down. He still fights like a beast while the rest of us gather by the origin. The light is bright enough here that I need to shield my eye from it. I look back at Teren again. One of the creatures sinks its jaws deep into his shoulder—he lets out a roar of agony. In the same moment, he twists around and stabs the creature deep in the neck. I wince. The creature tears its fangs out of his shoulder with a shriek. I throw my

energy out in Teren's direction, trying to prevent him from feeling the pain.

Magiano darts past me, along with Maeve. "Give us some cover!" he shouts back at me. He glances at the others. "Keep going!"

Before I can tell him to stop, he's gone, dashing to where Teren is trying to fend off the monsters. He draws his daggers and flings one at a creature clawing at Teren's back. At the same time, Maeve pulls an arrow from her sheath and aims it at a second creature preparing to lunge at Teren. She fires. Both attacks hit their marks. The creatures scream and fall back—but more continue to come. Through it all, Teren fights like a demon himself. It takes me a moment to realize that he is laughing. He closes his eyes.

"The gods speak!" he shouts as the creatures rip at him. And an instant later, one of the monsters plunges its razor-sharp claws straight through Teren's back, the black nails protruding from his chest.

I shudder, stunned. Maeve lets out a gasp, while Magiano freezes. Then they are on the move again, rushing toward him—but Teren's eyes are wide, his mouth open. Blood trickles from the corners of his lips. His body tries to heal around the creature's claws, but they remain buried in his heart. He trembles. A flash of Enzo's dying moments returns to me, followed by the memory of Giulietta's final breaths.

Magiano flings himself onto the creature still skewering Teren. He's strong enough to knock the creature backward—he is channeling Teren's power. I pull harder, trying

to inflict an illusion of pain on the creatures. They shriek at me, but my illusion cannot bring them down. Maeve swings her sword at the still-advancing creature that Magiano had just attacked—her blade cuts the demon's arm clean off. As the creature writhes, Teren collapses. I know before his body even hits the snow that he will not make it. A ringing blocks out the sound in my ears. I can barely believe it, but Teren is still smiling. His eyes are turned in my direction.

There is a moment of silence. We stand, stunned, at the sight.

Maeve and Magiano carefully roll Teren onto his back, while I hurry forward a few steps to see him. He is limp, his breathing slow and shallow. His eyes are hooded. The wound in his chest is healing, but it is not healing fast enough. "Teren," I say, leaning over him.

His eyes flutter open for a moment. He has trouble focusing on any of us, and instead his gaze ends up resting somewhere on the night sky above. "Now I am forgiven," he murmurs, so quietly that I think I misunderstand him.

I wait for his chest to rise again, but it doesn't.

I find myself looking down at the snow, willing myself to remember my first encounters with him—how he'd tied me to the stake and wished me to burn, how he'd threatened my sister and taken Enzo's life, how even after that, he continued to torment *malfettos* and Elites alike, how I drove him mad enough to take his own lover's life. I know, without a doubt, that he deserved to die.

So why am I sad? I reach up and feel tears on my face.

Why do I care what happens to him? I'd kept him a prisoner of my own, hated him and tortured him. I should be thrilled in this moment to see his blood running through the snow, the vacant, lifeless white of his eyes.

Teren is dead, and I do not know why I cry for him.

I have killed and destroyed too. I have hurt. Perhaps we have always been one and the same, just as he used to tell me. And now that he's gone, I feel a sudden rush of exhaustion, a freeing grief. His death marks the end of a long chapter in my life.

He will be in the Underworld. Waiting for us.

The monsters in the woods are still drawing near. Maeve and Magiano run toward the light. I follow them in a daze, the world still quiet around me, the snow blurring. With the creatures at our backs, gaining on us fast, and the blinding blue-white light before us, I tear my gaze away from him, take a deep breath . . . and step in at the same time as the others.

MEDINA. Have I arrived? Is this, truly, the ocean of the Underworld?

FORMIDITE. Speak, child, for you stand at the gates of death.

MEDINA. O goddess! O angel of Fear! I cannot bear to look upon you.

–Eight Princes, *by Tristan Chirsley*

Adelina Amouteru

Energy floods me. It fills every crevice in my mind and body, threads of power from every god—Fear, Fury, Prosperity and Death, Empathy and Beauty, Love and Wisdom and Time, Joy and War and Greed. I feel everything at once. It burns my insides with its sheer intensity, and for an instant I think I won't be able to stand it. I want to scream. *Where are the others?* I can no longer hear Magiano's voice or Raffaele's shouts. I can no longer sense anything but the light and the energy.

I try to open my eye, and in that instant, I think I see a glimpse of the heavens beyond the sky, and the waters deep below the mortal oceans.

Gradually, the light starts to fade. The air turns cold again, but it is different from the winds in the Dark of Night. It is

a cold that burrows deep into my bones, a numbness that nestles there near my heart and wraps it in a cocoon of ice. Tentatively, I open my eye. The world around me is hazy and gray. I recognize this gray. It is that of the Underworld.

Under my feet is the feeling of cold water. On one side of me is Magiano. On my other is Raffaele, then Maeve and Lucent.

We have crossed into the world of the gods.

Although the Underworld's ocean looms at our feet, we do not sink into the water. Instead, we stand on top of it, as if we were weightless. When I look down at the water, I notice that not a single ripple disturbs its surface. A mirror of the eternal gray sky around it, the realm between the heavens and the earth, the space where you are neither here nor there; the water is dark, almost black, but completely transparent. Far below glide the silhouettes of enormous creatures, the same that I've seen countless times in my nightmares of the Underworld. Except now we are here.

Adelina.

The whisper echoes all around us, reverberating deep in my heart. It is a voice I know well. I look up at the same time everyone else does. There, some distance away, a pale figure with long black hair walks on the surface of the ocean toward us. As she draws near, I am unable to move. The others remain frozen in place. A chill lodges in my chest.

Adelina. Then she whispers the others' names too. *You do not belong here. You are from the world of the living.*

Formidite. The angel of Fear. She has come to claim us.

Her hair trails all across the ocean, stretching on beyond the horizon, so that the sea behind her is nothing but a field of dark strands. She has the body of a child, but skeletal. Her face is featureless, as if skin were stretched tightly across it, and she is whiter than marble. Suddenly I am reminded of the first time I ever saw her in my nightmares, on the evening right after Raffaele had tested me for the Dagger Society.

I bow as she approaches us and the others do the same. Raffaele is the first to address her, his eyes cast down toward the water.

"Holy Formidite," he says. "Gatekeeper to the Underworld." We murmur our own greetings to her.

Beneath her layers of skin, she seems to smile at him. *Return to the mortal world.*

"We are here to save those like ourselves," Raffaele answers. He must be afraid of her, as are we all, but his voice stays steady and gentle, unrelenting. "We are here to *save* the mortal world."

Formidite's smile vanishes. She leans down toward us. The fear building in me grows, and my power grows with it, threatening to undo me. She looks first at Raffaele, and then turns to Maeve. Something about Maeve catches her interest. She steps closer to the Beldish queen, then tilts her head in what can only be described as curiosity. *You have a power, little one. You have pulled souls out of my mother's realm before, and taken them back to the living.*

Maeve bows her head lower. I can see her hand visibly trembling against her sword's hilt. "Forgive me, Holy Formidite," she says. "I was given a power I can only say was from the gods."

I was the one who let you in, Formidite answers. *You have learned since then, I know, that there are consequences for channeling the gods' powers.*

"Please let us enter," Maeve says. "We must fix what we have done."

Still, Formidite waits. She looks at Lucent, then at Raffaele. *Children of the gods,* she says as she goes. And then she looks at me.

The fear in my chest spikes. Formidite takes another step forward, until her figure looms over me and casts a soft shadow across the ocean. She reaches down, one bony hand outstretched, and she touches me gently on my cheek.

I cannot stop my power—an illusion of darkness bursts from all around, silhouettes of ghostly arms and red eyes, visions of rainy nights and a horse's wild eyes, of a burning battleship and long palace corridors. I stumble backward, tearing myself away from her touch.

My child, Formidite says. Her strange, featureless smile returns. *You are my child.*

I am hypnotized by her face. The fear swarming inside me makes me delirious.

Formidite is silent for a moment. The ghostly calls of creatures from the deep echo up to us, as if they had been stirred

to life by our presence. Finally, she nods once at us. When I look down again, the creatures' shapes are closer to the surface, and they crowd one another. My heart pounds faster. I know what this means, and who is waiting for us beneath the surface. Formidite's twin angel.

The water beneath us gives way. I drop into the depths, and my head submerges. The world fills with the sound of being underwater. For an instant, I'm blind in the darkness, and I reach out instinctively for Magiano. For Raffaele. For Maeve and Lucent. I find nothing. The silhouettes of enormous creatures glide around me in a circle. As I continue to sink, I get a glimpse of one of the creatures' faces.

Eyeless, finned, monstrous, fanged. I open my mouth to scream, but only bubbles emerge. *I can't breathe.* The energy of the Underworld pulls me down, tugging hard on my chest, and I have no choice but to follow it.

One of the creatures glides close to my face. It is Caldora herself, the angel of Fury. She opens her jaws at me, and a low, haunting echo reverberates through the water. Even though I can't see the others, I can feel their presence. I am not alone here.

Follow me, Caldora's thoughts say, penetrating my mind. She turns away, and her long, scaly tail makes a loop in the water. I swim deeper and deeper with her.

Follow me, follow me. Caldora's hiss becomes a rhythm in the water. Her voice blends with my own whispers, forming an eerie harmony. The water turns blacker and blacker, until

the pressure builds and I can no longer see anything, not even Caldora swimming ahead of me, not even the silhouettes of other creatures haunting the waters. It is just deep, black, endless space, in all directions, until eternity.

I sink into the realm of Death.

> How noble it must be, the pain of Moritas,
> to stand guardian forever to silent souls,
> to judge a life and choose to take it.
> —Life and Death and Rebirth, *by Scholar Garun*

Adelina Amouteru

I don't remember what happens, or how I arrive. All I know is that I am here, standing on the shore of a flat, gray land, its edges lined by the quiet, unmoving surface of the Underworld's ocean. It is still as a pond.

I look up. Where the sky should be, there is instead the ocean, as if I were standing upside down on the sky and looking down at it.

I turn to face inland. Everything is painted in the same muted tone of gray. The pulse of death beats all around me, the silence ringing rhythmically in my ears. I find myself staring at a flat landscape littered with thousands, millions, *countless* numbers of towering glass pillars. The pillars are iridescent and white.

Each one is in the shape of a quartz and the color of

moonstone, evenly spaced from the next, forming perfect rows that extend outward to the horizon and then tower high up into oblivion. Each pillar seems to shine with a faint silver-white light, a hue that sets it sharply apart from the uniform gray in the rest of this place. As I draw nearer to the first pillar, I see something inside it, suspended in the space of the stone. It is hard to make out the shape, although it seems long and blurred. I step up to the pillar and press one hand against it.

There is a man inside.

My hand jerks away as if the pillar were ice cold—I jump backward. The man's eyes are closed, and his expression is peaceful. Something about his face seems timeless, frozen forever in the prime of his life. I study him a while longer.

This is his soul, I suddenly realize.

I turn away from him and look around at the pillars stretching as far as I can see. Each of these pillars is the final resting place of a soul from the mortal world, the remnants of that person long after flesh and bone have been reclaimed by the land. This is the library of Moritas, all who have ever existed.

My hands start to tremble. If this is where all the souls of the dead reside, then this is also where I will find my sister.

I look around me, searching for the others. It takes me a long moment to notice the beam of light illuminating my body, as if marking me as a moment of life in this world of the deceased. Four other beams are scattered in the midst of this maze of lustrous pillars, their glow distinct against

the backdrop of silver and gray. They seem very far away, each of us separated from the others by what seems like an infinite amount of space.

Everyone enters the realm of Death alone.

Across this eerie landscape comes a whisper. It permeates every empty space around me, echoing up to the ocean in the sky. There is a darkness creeping forward, something greater than anything I have ever seen, a black cloud stretching from the heavens to the sea. It roils onward.

Adelina.

It is Moritas, the goddess of Death. I know, beyond the shadow of a doubt, that this is her voice.

You have come to bargain with me, Adelina.

"Yes," I answer in a whisper. "I've come—we've all come—to heal the tear between your world and ours."

Yes, the others. The cloud towers before me. *Your immortal energy has been missing from our realm for a long time.*

My powers, I start to say, but the words falter on my tongue. Even now—even after coming all this way. The whispers in my head churn, angry that I would consider giving them up.

Step forward, Adelina, Moritas commands.

I hesitate. The cloud before me is a terrifying tangle of black bruises and curves, shapes of monsters all joined together. Terror freezes my body in place. I have walked through forests at midnight. I have traveled through the darkness of caves. But to step into Death herself . . .

Fear is your sword.

My sword, my strength. I take one step after another. The

cloud looms closer, closer still. I take another step, and then I am inside it, consumed whole.

I walk in a land of black mist and silver-white pillars. Within each pearly structure, a person hovers in eternal sleep, and over them I can see a faint reflection of myself peering in, wondering how their mortal life used to be. My heart pounds rhythmically in my chest. I'm grateful to feel it, to know that I am not dead here. A whisper floats through the mist now and then, the voice of Moritas, calling out for me. I follow it, even though I don't know where she is leading me. I pass one row of pillars after another. Their luminous glow reflects against my skin. I walk until I lose count of how many rows I've passed, and when I look over my shoulder in the direction I first came, I can see nothing but rows of these pillars all around.

Are the others wandering through their own nightmare of pillars, searching for me? Now and then, I see ghostly figures walking the paths amongst the moonstone too, figures that I can never look at directly. Perhaps those are lost souls, ghosts. Perhaps Moritas is speaking to the others, each in turn.

Adelina.

Moritas sounds closer now. I turn back to the path before me—and then I stop short. The face inside the pillar closest to me, her eyes closed and her expression peaceful, belongs to the former queen of Kenettra. Giulietta. Her dark hair seems to float inside the column of moonstone, and her bare arms are crossed over her chest. I take a hesitant step toward her.

There are no signs of any wounds on her body, no evidence of Teren's sword cutting through her chest. She is pristine, forever preserved in the Underworld. I study her face in a way I never did when she was alive. She was beautiful. *Enzo looked so much like her.*

I continue walking. Then I realize that the pillars now nearest to me are all people I once knew.

There are Inquisition soldiers. The Night King of Merroutas is here as well, his brows no longer furrowed in anger. Dante hovers nearby too. There is Gemma, her purple marking stretching across her peaceful face. I utter a whisper of a prayer as I pass her, asking for her forgiveness, and then force myself onward, recognizing one face after another. I pause for a moment on Teren, who now stays encased in his own pillar, arms crossed over his chest, lost to eternal night. It is the most serene I have ever seen him, and I find myself hoping that he has at last found some semblance of peace.

And there is Enzo. I stop before his pillar. He looks like he is merely asleep, his face calm and flawless. His arms still bear the burns he has always had, his skin there ruined and scarred. I stand there for a long moment, as if perhaps he would wake up if I stare long enough. But he doesn't.

Finally, I continue on. The faces seem to blur together around me.

I stop again when I reach my mother, who is entombed beside my father. It has been so long since I've seen her that I might not even have recognized her—except that Violetta looked exactly like her younger self. My lips part slightly,

and my chest tightens in grief. I lay a hand against the cold surface of the pillar. If I concentrate hard enough, I feel as if I could hear her voice, her soft, sweet singing, a tune I remember from when I was very small. I can remember her hands on the swell of her belly, can recall wondering who would emerge from it. I stare at her for a long time, perhaps an eternity, before I am finally able to move on.

I do not bother looking at my father. I'm searching for someone much more important.

Then, I find *her*. Violetta.

She is lovely. Stunning. Her eyes are closed, but if they could open, I know I would be staring into familiar brown eyes, not the lifeless gray ones she'd had toward the end of her life. I reach out for her, but the moonstone blocks my way—and I have to settle for pressing my hand against the surface, staring within at my sister's face. My face is wet with tears. She is here, in the Underworld. I can see her again.

Adelina.

I tear my gaze away. And there, I see it. I know instantly that this is what we came for.

In the center of this landscape of iridescent pillars is a dark slab, a black column in the midst of the moonstone. It cuts through the air and into the sky, as high as I can see, and around it is a swirl of dark mist, a wound stretching from the Underworld, up to the mortal world, and higher into the heavens. Raffaele's words return to me in a flash. This is the cut—the ancient tear—that opened the immortal world into the mortal, when Joy descended to the earth as a human and

then passed through the Underworld again. This black pillar is where Joy himself had been encased after his mortal death, before returning to the heavens. Where the blood fever first originated. Even here, I can feel the dark power, the wrongness of it. I can remember the feel of a wooden table beneath my body, the taste of brandy on my lips that the doctor prescribed for my illness, the sound of him coming into my chambers when I was only four years of age, holding a red-hot knife over my infected eye even as I screamed and cried and pleaded with him not to do it.

This is the origin of the fever that has touched each of our lives. The closer I step, the darker the space behind the pillar turns, until it seems like I am walking directly into a world of night, being swallowed by this fog.

I reach the pillar. As I do, the swirling darkness changes, morphing into the shape of a towering figure, dark and elegant, her body shrouded in robes of fog and mist, a pair of horns twisting high over her head. She stares at me with eyes of black. I open my mouth to say something, but nothing comes out.

Moritas, the goddess of Death.

My child, she says. Her black-eyed stare focuses on me. Her voice is deep and powerful, a sound that echoes across the landscape and inside my chest, a vibration so ancient that it aches in my bones. *The children of the gods.* To either side of her, other figures now appear, tall and silent. I recognize Formidite, with her long black hair and featureless face. Caldora, her fins huge and monstrous.

Then, a man clad in a cloak of gold and jewels. Denarius, the angel of Greed. Fortuna, goddess of Prosperity, in a sheet of glitter and diamond. Amare, god of Love, impossibly breathtaking. Tristius, angel of War, with his sword and shield. Sapientus, god of Wisdom. There is Aevietes, god of Time, and Pulchritas, angel of Beauty. Compasia, angel of Empathy.

Laetes, angel of Joy.

The gods and goddesses are all here, come to claim their children.

"Moritas," I whisper, the word barely a sound from my lips. My power seethes in her presence, threatening to destroy my dying, mortal body.

You were never meant to wield our powers, she says. *We have watched from the immortal realm as your presence changed the mortal world.*

Moritas lowers her head and closes her eyes. To my side, the others now materialize out of the black mist. Raffaele, Lucent, Maeve. Magiano. I want to step forward, aching to go to them, to *him* . . . but all I can do is look on. They, too, seem to be in a trance.

"What do you want, in order to fix this?" I whisper. I know the answer, but somehow, I cannot bring myself to say it.

Moritas opens her eyes again. Her voice echoes in unison with her siblings. *Your powers. Relinquish them, and you shall all be returned to the living realm. Give them to us, and the world will be healed.*

In order to repair the world, we must hand back our powers. We will be the last of the Young Elites.

The whispers rear in my head, clawing, hooking deep into my flesh. *No.* I cry out from the pain. *How dare you,* they roar. *After all we've done for you. How* dare *you think of life without us. You cannot survive without our help. Have you forgotten what it feels like to have us taken from you? Don't you remember?*

I do. The memory of Violetta wrenching away my power now hits me so hard that I take an unsteady step back. It feels a hundred times worse than I'd remembered, even—as if someone had ripped into the hollow of my chest, closed a fist around my beating heart, and tried to pull it out. I tremble at the pain. It is unbearable.

And for what? To protect the rest of the world? You owe them nothing; you rule *them. Return to your palace and continue your reign.*

It is such a tempting offer.

"I cannot do this," I say to Moritas as my voice falters. "I cannot give you my power."

Then you will die here. Moritas raises her arms. *If you offer your power, willingly, you may step out of our realm and back into your mortal world, alive. Your powers cannot return with you. Each of you must do this.*

Each of us. If we all give up our powers, we will be allowed to return to the living world.

The landscape around us is engulfed in darkness. I take a deep breath, filling myself with it, and shake at the feeling. The power within me, all the darkness I have ever felt, and all the darkness that I have ever been able to call upon, pale in comparison to the power of the darkness from the goddess

of Death. Moritas wields a million, billion infinite threads all at once, and under the terrible influence of her power, I can see in one glance all of the suffering that has occurred since the beginning of time. The visions swallow me whole.

I see the fires that created the world, the great ocean that existed before the gods created land. There is the descent of Joy to the mortal world, and the first spread of the blood fever. It sweeps through the villages and towns and kingdoms, infecting the living with its touches of immortality, killing many, scarring a cursed few . . . gifting immortal powers to even fewer. I see the screams and the moans of terror from Kenettra. I see the *malfettos* who burn at the stake, and then the Elites, who fight back. I see *me*.

I see the darkness that the world inflicted upon us, and we onto them.

Poor child, Moritas says. Beside her, the forms of Caldora and Formidite watch me silently. *You would die with darkness clutched in your hands?*

No. I wrap my arms around myself and look behind me desperately, as if someone might come to save me. *Violetta.* She had been there for me, once. We had loved each other, once.

Moritas tilts her head in my direction curiously. *You are bound to your sister.*

And then, something occurs to me. We had to enter the realm of the dead with *all* of our alignments, together, even those who had perished on the way. Teren. Violetta. If we return our powers to the gods, then we are given our lives in

exchange, can walk out of this immortal realm and return to the living. Does that mean . . . if we do give up our powers, if *I* give up mine, that *all* of us who had come to offer up our powers can return to the mortal world? That even Teren would live again?

That *Violetta* could return? *Would this bring my sister back?*

The scene changes again. I am a child, walking hand in hand with Violetta. I am lying in bed, losing my fight with the blood fever. I watch my hair color shift from dark to light, settling into silver. I see my scarred face, watch myself shatter my mirror into a million pieces. Then I see my future. I am Queen of Kenettra, ruler of sea, sun, and sky. I sit alone on my throne, looking out over my empire. The sight stirs my ambition, and the whispers in my head coo. *Yes, this is what you want. This is all you have ever wanted.*

But then I see myself curled on the marble floor of the throne room, sobbing, surrounded by illusions that I cannot erase. I look on in horror as I chase my own sister out of the room, as I hold a knife to her throat and threaten her life. I see myself lashing out at Magiano, ordering his execution after he tries to stop me from hurting myself. I see myself sobbing, wishing I could take back what I've done. I look on as I lock myself in my own chambers, screaming for the illusions that claw with their long black talons to leave me alone. I stay locked away forever, mad and terrified, until, finally one night, I have my nightmare once more.

I wake to the horror of it, over and over again, only to be lost in another layer of the dream. I run to the door, trying in

vain to keep the darkness outside. I wake, and do the same thing again. I cry out for help. I wake. I push uselessly against the yawning door. I wake. I cycle again and again—except, this time, I cannot pull myself out of it. I cannot wake up in reality. Instead, I cycle until I finally can no longer keep the door closed and it swings open. On the other side of it is a never-ending darkness, the gaping mouth of the Underworld, Death come to claim me. I try once again to shut the door, but the darkness pushes in. It bares its teeth at me. Then it lunges, and even as I try to shield myself, it tears me to pieces and devours my soul.

This would be my life.

I think of the pile of stones we had to leave behind in the mountains. I remember the feeling of my sister's body cradled in my arms, of myself sobbing into her frozen hair, telling her over and over again that I am sorry, begging her not to leave me.

If I give my powers to the goddess of Death, if we all do, then perhaps, just perhaps, she will return my sister to me. Violetta might live again; perhaps we will all walk out of here. The possibility is fleeting, but it is there and it sends a shudder of wild hope through me. *She might live. I can, at least, undo this one wrong. I can fix what I have broken between us.*

And I can save myself.

Slowly, I rise to my feet. I am still afraid, but I lift my head high. The whispers in my head suddenly start to howl. They call to me, begging me not to leave them, hissing at me for my betrayal. *What are you doing!* they scream. *Have you forgotten?*

Your father's hands, beating at you—your enemies, laughing at you? The burning stake? This is life without power.

I stand firm against their onslaught. No, that is not my life without power. My life without power will be one of walking through a crowd without darkness tugging at my heart. It will be seeing Violetta in the living world, smiling again. It will be riding on the back of a horse with Magiano as we crest another mountain, searching for adventure. It will be a life without these whispers in my head. It will be a life without my father's ghost.

It will be a *life*.

I look at Moritas. Then I reach deep within myself, grasp the threads that have entwined themselves around my heart since I was a child. I pull them away. And I relinquish them.

The whispers shriek.

At the same time, I see—somehow, I *see*—the others do the same. I see Magiano offering his power of mimicry to the immortal world; I see Raffaele sacrificing his connection; I see Lucent returning her mastery of wind; I see Maeve give up her right to the Underworld.

The world around me erupts. The power of it throws me to the ground. I suck in my breath and scream at the pain of my power being wrenched away from me. Darkness swirls— and the whispers are suddenly deafening. They scream in my ears, their pain my own. I curl in on myself in defense.

Then—all of a sudden—they are gone. The whispers that have haunted me for so long. Every word, every hiss, every

claw. Every tendril of darkness that wrapped itself in the corners of my chest.

Gone.

A piercing sensation, one of fury and grief and joy, fills my heart, replacing the hollow. I reach, but there is nothing on the other end. No threads to grasp. I am no longer an Elite.

Go, Moritas says, the other gods' voices echoing hers. *Return to the mortal world with the others. You do not yet belong here.*

I clutch my chest, overwhelmed at the emptiness in my heart. We are going home.

Then I see, across the shattered remains of the darkened pillar, the figure of my sister. Violetta. She is still encased in her opalescent tomb, her face peaceful in death, her arms folded across her chest. She hovers there before me. I reach out for her. I look for her to stir back to life.

But Violetta does not wake. My eagerness wavers. In this overwhelming silence, I wait desperately for her to open her eyes.

Moritas looks at me again. I can barely see her through the black, churning mist.

Your time in the Underworld has not come, Adelina, she says. *In giving up your power, I offer you your life back.* She turns to Violetta. *But her time in the mortal world is past.*

My elation fades. Violetta has already died. Moritas will not give up her soul. She will not return to the surface with us.

"Please," I whisper, turning back to the goddess. "There must be something I can do."

Moritas stares down at me with her silent black eyes. *A soul must be replaced with a soul.*

In order for Violetta to live, I must sacrifice something that does not give myself gain.

In order for Violetta to live, I must give Moritas my life.

No. I pull away, stumbling backward. All these things I have seen for my future, all that I can have. I think of Magiano, of laughing with him, of him smiling at me and pulling me close. Never will I do that again, if I give up my soul. Never will I walk the streets with my hand looped through his arm or hear the music of his lute. My heart twists in agony. I will not see another sunrise, or another sunset. I will not see the stars again, or feel the wind against my face.

I shake my head. I cannot take my sister's place.

And yet.

I find myself staring at Violetta's lifeless figure, forever sealed away. I know, with searing conviction, that the Violetta who had come with us on this journey would never hesitate to offer her life for mine.

I have killed and hurt. I have conquered and pillaged. I have done all of this in the name of my own desires, have done everything in life because of my own selfishness. I have always taken what I wanted, and it has never given me happiness. If I return to the surface, alone, I will forever remember this moment, the moment I decided to choose my own life over my sister's. It will haunt me, even with Magiano at my side, until my death. What I saw for myself

in my future is a future I cannot have, not with the past that I have already created. It is an illusion. Nothing more.

Perhaps, after all the lives I have taken, my atonement is to restore life to one.

I reach out instinctively for my sister. I stand up, walk toward her through the mist, and place my hand against the silver-white pillar.

She opens her eyes.

"Adelina?" she whispers, blinking. And all I can see before me is the little sister who used to braid my hair, who sang to me and whimpered under the stairs, who bandaged my broken finger and came to me when the thunder rolled outside. She is my sister, always, even in death, even beyond.

My heart twists again as I think of what I am doing, and I choke back a sob. *Oh, Magiano. I will miss all the days we will never have, all the moments we will never share. Forgive me, forgive me, forgive me.*

I open my mouth. I mean to tell my sister I'm sorry, sorry I couldn't save her in the mountains, sorry I didn't listen to her, I didn't tell her more often that I loved her. I am ready to say a thousand words.

But I say none of them. Instead, I say, "The deal is done."

A faint glow encircles Violetta. The pillar vanishes. She sucks in a deep gasp of air, then falls to her knees. She is *alive*. I can even sense the beating of her heart, the life that it gives her, that permeates through her like a wave, adding color to her skin and light to her eyes. She shakes her head, then reaches out to grasp my hand as I kneel beside her. "What

happened?" she murmurs. She looks around. Behind her hovers the shape of Moritas, waiting patiently for me.

The deal is done.

Violetta tugs on my hand. "Let's go," she says, her fingers wrapped tightly around mine.

But I can already feel the weakness invading my body. My shoulders hunch. I struggle to draw in my next breath. All around me, the threads of darkness once tied to my body now anchor deep into the gray ground, and when I try to push against them, it feels as if each had pierced my flesh, a million hooks in a million places. Death has already come for me.

"I can't," I whisper to her.

"What do you mean?" Violetta frowns at me, not understanding. "Here, let me help you," she replies, bending down to me, looping one of her arms around my shoulders and trying to lift me up. Her pull only strengthens the tug of the threads, and I cry out as pain lances through me.

"I am tied here, Violetta," I murmur. "It is my bargain with Moritas."

Violetta's eyes widen. She looks at the looming darkness all around, the towering, faded image of Moritas silently watching us. Then Violetta turns back to me. *Now* she understands. "You traded your life for mine," she says. "You came here for *me*."

I shake my head. No, I'd come here for myself. That was my goal from the beginning, to save myself under the guise of saving the world. I spent my entire life fighting for my

welfare and power, destroying in order to make it happen. I wanted to live. I *still* want to live.

But I don't want to live as I had.

Violetta grabs my shoulders. She shakes me once, hard. "I was meant to go!" she cries. "I was weak, dying. You are the Queen of the Sealands, you had everything ahead of you. Why did you do it?" Tears swell in her eyes. They are the same as our mother's, sad and kind.

I smile at her weakly. The darkness pulses, waiting for me, and the strings tying me down continue to pull. "It's all right," I whisper, taking Violetta's hand off my shoulder and squeezing it in my own. "It's all right, little sister, it's all right."

Violetta turns her face up to Moritas in desperation. "Give her back," she says. A sob distorts her words. "Please. This is not the way—I am not supposed to live. Let her. I don't want to return to the mortal world without her."

But Moritas just stays silent, watching. The bargain is done.

Violetta cries. She looks back down at me, then curls her body around mine, pulling me to her. I reach out and wrap my arms around her, and, here in the mist, we cling together. My strength wanes; even the act of hanging on to Violetta seems to take all my effort, but I refuse to let go. Tears roll down my face. The realization sinks in that I am dying, and I hold on to Violetta tighter. *I will never see the surface again. Will never see Magiano again.* I can feel my heart breaking, and I am suddenly afraid.

Fear is your sword.

"Stay with me," I murmur. "Just for a little while."

Violetta nods against my shoulder. She starts to hum an old song, a familiar song, one I haven't heard in a long time. It is the same lullaby I used to sing to her when we were small, the one Raffaele had once sung for me along the banks of an Estenzian canal, a story about a river maiden. "The first Spring Moons," she whispers. "Do you remember?"

And I do. It was a sun-drenched evening, and I pulled Violetta through the fields of great golden grass that spanned the land behind our home. She laughed, asking me repeatedly where I was taking her, but I just giggled and pressed a finger to my lips. We made our way across the expanse until we reached a sharp outcropping of rock that overlooked the center of our city. As the sun threw purple, pink, and orange across the sky, we crawled on our bellies to the very edge of the rock. Sparks of color and light danced on the city streets below. It was the first night of the Spring Moons, and the revelers had started to appear. We looked on with delight as early fireworks lit up the sky, bursting in great explosions of every color in the world, the sound deafening us with its joy.

I remember our laughter, the way we casually held hands, the unspoken feeling between us that we were, for a moment in time, free from our father's grasp.

"Sisters forever," Violetta declared, in her tiny, young voice.

Until death, even in death, even beyond.

"I love you," Violetta says, hanging fiercely on to me even as my strength dies.

I love you too. I lean against her, exhausted. "Violetta," I murmur. I feel strange, delirious, as if a fever had wrapped me in a dream. Words emerge, faint and ethereal, from someone who reminds me of myself, but I can no longer be sure I am still here.

Am I good? I am trying to ask her.

Tears fall from Violetta's eyes. She says nothing. Perhaps she can no longer hear me. I am small in this moment, turning smaller. My lips can barely move.

After a lifetime of darkness, I want to leave something behind that is made of light.

Both of her hands cup my face. Violetta stares at me with a look of determination, and then she brings me to her and hugs me close. "You are a light," she replies gently. "And when you shine, you shine bright."

Her words are starting to turn soft, and she is beginning to fade. Or perhaps I am the one fading. The whispers in my mind are gone now, leaving the inside of me quiet, but I don't miss them. In their place, there is the warmth of Violetta's arms, the beating of her heart that I can hear against her chest, the knowledge that she will leave this place and return to the living.

Please, I whisper, and my voice comes out as quiet as a ghost's. *Tell Magiano I love him. Tell him I'm sorry. That I'm grateful.*

"Adelina," Violetta says, alarmed as she continues to fade away. The feel of her is growing faint. "Wait. I can't—"

Go, I say gently, giving her a sad smile. Violetta and I stare at each other until I can hardly see her. Then she disappears into the darkness, and the world around me blurs.

I feel the cold ground beneath my cheek. I feel the pulse of my heart die down. Over me, the looming figure of Moritas bends to enfold me in her embrace, covering me in a merciful blanket of night. I take a slow breath.

Someday, when I am nothing but dust and wind, what tale will they tell about me?

Another slow breath.

Another.

A final exhale.

Violetta Amouteru

There is an old legend about Compasia and Eratosthenes. As Violetta crouches, crying, over her sister's dying soul, she thinks of it.

Adelina had first told this story when they were very small, on a bright afternoon in the gardens of their old home. Violetta remembers listening contentedly while she braided her sister's silver hair, wishing her own hair could look so beautiful, grateful and guilty that she did not have to bear the consequences of it. Long ago, Adelina had said, when the world was young, the god Amare created a kingdom of people, who ungratefully turned their backs on him. Hurt and furious, Amare called on the lightning and thunder, and pushed up the seas to drown the kingdom beneath the waves.

But he did not know that his daughter, Compasia, the angel of Empathy, had fallen in love with Eratosthenes, a boy in the kingdom. Only Compasia dared to defy Holy Amare. Even as her father drowned mankind in his floods, Compasia reached down to her mortal lover and transformed him into a swan. He flew high above the floodwaters, above the moons, and then higher still, until his feathers turned to stardust.

Every night, when the world was quiet and only the stars were awake, Compasia would descend from the heavens to the earth, and the constellation of Compasia's Swan would transform back into Eratosthenes; and together, the two would walk the world until the dawn separated them again.

Violetta does not know why she thinks of this story now. But as Adelina made a bargain with Moritas for her life, so does Violetta find herself kneeling at the feet of Compasia, her own goddess, begging for the sister who had once cast her out, who had struck at her, who had nevertheless fought and hurt for her. She finds herself dreaming of the night they stood together, sailing through a sea and sky of stars.

Violetta aligns with Compasia, the angel of Empathy. And she makes a bargain of her own.

I am death. And through death, I understand life.

— Letter from General Eliseo Barsanti to his wife

Adelina Amouteru

There is a small, singular light somewhere in the distance. It is brilliant and blue-white, something reminiscent of the color I'd seen when we entered the immortal realm through the origin. It is a light of immortality, a light of the gods, a star in the sky among billions. I find myself yearning toward it, struggling through the night in order to grasp that spark of warmth. I can see, for a moment, the world beyond ours, the heavens, the stars that burn alongside me.

Somewhere in the darkness, I hear voices. They are unlike any voices I've ever heard—clear as glass, mighty and deep, so unbearable in their beauty that I am afraid it might drive me mad. I think they speak my name.

As I draw closer to the beam, it splits into various colors. Red and gold, amber and black, deep blue and pale summer

green. They gather around me in shafts of color, until it seems as if I were on the ground and the colors surround me in a circle.

The gods.

Adelina, one of them says. I know it is Compasia, the angel of Empathy. *There has been another bargain.*

I don't understand, I reply. They are so tall, and I am so small.

There is a feeling of light under my body, of wind and stars. There is the disintegration of my form. Then, there is sky.

You will.

Raffaele Laurent Bessette

There is a brilliant flash of light, and a ringing that reverberates outward from the origin. Raffaele falls to his knees. The world spins around him — the snow and monsters and forest all blending into one — and for a moment, he cannot move. Tears run down his face.

Through his blurred gaze, he sees the monsters slow in their attacks, their bodies hunched, their gaping jaws closed, and their eyeless sockets turned away. They seem confused, as if something had taken their energy and left them as hollow shells. One of them stumbles forward, letting out a low moan. Then it falls. As it does, its body disintegrates into tiny shards of black, scattering across the snow like broken glass.

The same happens to another creature, and another. All around them, the monsters that had seemed unstoppable

now crumble into pieces. Raffaele looks down toward the origin. The beam of light—the merging of the mortal and immortal worlds—has disappeared.

Raffaele takes a deep breath of cold air and tries to clear his head. Everything had seemed like a dream, a streak of events painted on canvas. What had happened? He remembers falling through the depths of a dead ocean into the Underworld, arriving on the still shores of another world. There were an infinite number of silver-white pillars reaching up forever into gray sky, and a black mist that shrouded everything around him, the tendrils of fog curling near his feet in anticipation of his death.

He remembers seeing his mother and father asleep, encased in moonstone. He saw old companions and friends from the Fortunata Court. He saw Enzo. He knelt at each of their feet, weeping. There was the sight of distant lights, his other companions that he could not reach. The gods and goddesses gathered before him, with their bright light and overwhelming voices.

Most of all, he remembers reaching into his heart and severing his connection to the immortal world, returning his power to the gods.

Had it *really* happened? Raffaele pushes himself into a sitting position in the snow. He holds out one hand. His grasp captures only the cold air, and his fingers touch nothing. There is an emptiness in his chest now, a lightness, and when he reaches out for his threads of energy, he finds that they are

gone. It is as if a part of him had died, allowing the rest of him to live on.

The Dark of Night is eerily silent. All that remains are the snow and the forest, the remnants of creatures slowly fading away, sinking into white. Time floats past. His vision sharpens. Finally, Raffaele finds the strength to stand. Around him are the others. He sees Lucent first, shaking snow from her curls, and beside her, Maeve, pushing herself up with her sword planted deep in the snow. Magiano crouches nearby, clutching his head. They must be feeling the same emptiness that Raffaele now feels, all trying in vain to reach for the powers that had once always simmered right at their fingertips. On instinct, Raffaele reaches out to sense their emotions . . . but all he feels is the bite of the cold.

It is strange, this new reality.

"It's gone," Maeve whispers first. She closes her eyes, takes a deep breath, and lifts her head to the heavens. A strange expression is on her face, one that Raffaele instantly understands. It is a look of grief. Of peace.

"Where is Adelina?" It is Magiano's voice now. He looks around frantically, trying to find her. Raffaele frowns. He had seen Adelina—he was sure of it. Her silver hair, glinting in the black mist; her white lashes, scarred face; her chin, always up. She had been in the Underworld with them. Raffaele scans the landscape, a knot tightening in his stomach, as Magiano calls for her again.

There she is.

There is a girl stirring nearby, her hair is dusted silver and white with snow, and it falls across her face. Raffaele feels immediate relief at the sight of her — until she lifts her head.

No, it is not Adelina. It is *Violetta*, with the snow hiding the color of her dark hair. The markings that had blemished her skin are now gone, and the color has returned to her cheeks. She shakes her head, blinking, and looks around. Her eyes are red from crying, but she is here and whole, *alive*.

Raffaele can only stare in silence. *Impossible.* How did she come here?

Where is Adelina?

Magiano has already struggled to his feet and is making his way through the snow toward her. "Violetta," he calls. His eyes are wide, pupils dilated. He looks as if he can't believe what he is seeing. Then he embraces her, lifting her clear off the snow. Violetta makes a surprised sound. "What happened? How are you . . . ?"

Impossible, Raffaele repeats to himself. How did Violetta return from the Underworld? She does not look like Enzo did when Maeve pulled him out, with pools of black in his eyes and an energy about him that felt like death. No, Violetta looks healthy and alive, even radiant, the way she had once looked when Raffaele first met her. He wants to cheer, to be joyous for her return —

— but her expression tells him otherwise.

Magiano puts her down and holds her at arm's length. He furrows his brow at her. "How are you here?" he exclaims. "Where's Adelina?"

Violetta returns his stare with an unbearable look in her eyes. At that, Magiano's smile wavers. He shakes her once. "Where's Adelina?" he asks again.

"She made a deal with Moritas," Violetta finally says, her voice cracking.

Magiano frowns, still not understanding. "We all made a deal with Moritas," he replies. "I was there in the Under-world—*we* were there, with the gods and goddesses." He looks to where Maeve and Lucent stand, still dazed, and pauses to hold up one palm. He turns his hand over. "Like stripping a layer of my heart."

Violetta looks toward the sky. She can't seem to bear meeting Magiano's eyes. "No," she says. "Adelina traded her *life*."

Even when the realization hits Magiano, he doesn't dare acknowledge it aloud. Instead, they all stand frozen in the snow, trying to grasp the weight of Violetta's words, hoping that Violetta is wrong and that Adelina will somehow emerge from the forest and rejoin them. But she doesn't.

Magiano gives an imperceptible nod, then releases Violetta. He slowly slides down to sit in the snow.

The first time Raffaele ever saw Adelina, it was a storm-wracked night that changed her life and, indeed, the world. He recalls looking down from a window in his Dalia lodging to see a girl with silver-bright hair, conjuring an illusion of darkness such that he had never seen. He remembers the day she first came to his chambers in Estenzia, when Enzo was still alive and she was still innocent, and the way she looked up at him with her uncertain, damaged gaze. He remembers

her test, and what he said to Enzo that night. How long ago that had been. How he had judged her wrongly.

Raffaele looks around the clearing, searching for one last figure. He looks high and low, hoping for footprints in the snow or shadows in the forest line. He wishes he could still sense the energy of the living, could pinpoint where she is. But even then, he knows that he would arrive at the same answer as the others.

Adelina is gone.

After she was gone, I sheathed her sword at my belt,
draped her cloak over my shoulders, carried her heart
in my arms, and, somehow, went on.
  —The Journey of a Thousand Days, *by Lia Navarra*

Violetta Amouteru

My name is Violetta. I am the sister to the White Wolf, and I am the one who returned.

It is a quiet journey back through the Karra passages. Raffaele had said that time in the immortal realms passes differently from time in our own world. What felt like a flash of lightning to us had been months for Maeve's soldiers—but even so, they stayed, faithfully waiting for her all this time. I look on as she smiles and greets her troops, as they cheer her in turn. Raffaele stands with the rest of us, his expression solemn and sober. Our return did not come easily.

There is an empty space between Magiano and me that pains both of us, a lingering silence that neither of us can break. We walk without talking. We look without seeing. We eat without tasting. I want to say something to him, to

reach out to him during evenings around our fire, but I don't know what. What difference would it make? She is gone. All I can do is turn my eyes skyward, starward, searching for my sister. Time may be different here, but my goddess made me a promise. A bargain of our own. I search and search the skies until sleep claims me, until I can search again the next night, and the night after that. Magiano watches me quietly when I do. He does not ask what I am searching for, though, and I cannot bear to tell him. I am too afraid to raise his hopes.

One starlit midnight, as we at last begin our voyage back to Kenettra, I find Magiano standing alone on deck, his head bowed. He stirs, then looks away as I join his side. "The ship is too still," he mutters, as if I had asked him why he is awake. "I need some waves to sleep properly."

I shake my head. "I know," I reply. "You are searching for her too."

We stand for a moment, staring out at the stars mirrored in the calm seas. I know why Magiano doesn't look at me. I remind him too much of her.

"I'm sorry," I whisper, after a long pause.

"Don't be." A small, sad smile touches his lips. "She chose it."

I turn away from him to study the constellations again. They are particularly bright this evening, visible even as the three moons hang in a great and golden triangle. I find Compasia's Swan, the delicate curve of stars standing out in the blackness like torchlight. I had knelt at the feet of my

goddess, begging with a voice choked by tears, and she had made me a promise. Had she not? *What if none of it were real? What if I dreamed it?*

Then, Magiano straightens beside me. His eyes focus on something far away.

I look too. And I finally see what I have been waiting for.

There, prominently in the sky . . . is a new constellation. It is made of seven bright stars, alternately blue and orange-red, forming a slender pair of loops that aligns with Compasia's Swan.

My hands cover my mouth. Tears well in my eyes.

When Compasia took pity on her human lover, she saved him from the drowning world and placed him in the sky, where he turned to stardust.

When Compasia took pity on *me*, she reached down into the Underworld, touched the shoulder of Moritas, and asked her forgiveness. Then Compasia took my sister in her arms and placed her in the sky, where she, too, turned to stardust.

Magiano looks at me, his eyes wide. It seems as if he already, somehow, understands.

"My goddess made me a promise," I whisper.

Only now do I realize that I have never seen him cry before.

In the stories, Compasia and her human lover would descend each night from the stars to walk the mortal world, before vanishing with the dawn. So, together, we stare at the sky, waiting.

Over the span of a few months, the color of Magiano's remarkable golden eyes fade into hazel. His pupils stay round, unchanging. Raffaele's sapphire strands grow out raven black, blending in with the rest of his hair. His jewel-toned eyes, one the color of honey under sunlight, settle into an identical pair of emerald green. Maeve's hair, half black and half gold, gradually becomes pale blond. Michel's nails, once striped deep black and blue, have changed into the color of flesh. Sergio's eyes transition from gray to a forest brown. And the dark, swirling lines on Lucent's arm fade, lighter and lighter, until one day they are gone altogether.

The Young Elites were the flash of light in a stormy sky, the fleeting darkness before dawn. Never have they existed before, nor shall they ever exist again.

Across Estenzia, Kenettra, and the rest of the world, the last touches of the blood fever and the immortal world fade, leaving little difference between the marked and the unmarked. But you can never truly forget. I can hear it in our voices, the sound of another age, the memories of darker times, when immortal power walked the world.

Six months after we return to Kenettra, when twilight is descending on the day, I stop in the palace gardens to see Magiano swinging two canvas packs over the back of a horse. He pauses when he notices me. After a brief hesitation, he bows his head.

"Your Majesty," he says.

I fold my hands in front of me and approach him. I knew this day would come, although I did not think he would leave so soon. "You can stay, you know—" I start to say, knowing my words will be in vain. "There is always a place for you in the palace, and the people love you. If there is something you want, tell me, and it will be yours."

Magiano laughs a little and shakes his head. The gold bands in his braids clink musically. "Lucent has already returned to Beldain with her queen. Perhaps it is my turn now."

Lucent. Across the oceans, Queen Maeve had decreed her eventual successor to be her niece, the newborn daughter of her brother Augustine. Thus, finally, she was free to wed Lucent, returning the Windwalker to the birth nation that had exiled her for so long.

"I've always been a wanderer," Magiano adds in the silence. "I grow restless here in the palace, even among such fine company." He pauses, and his smile softens. "It is time for me to go. There are adventures waiting for me."

I will miss the sound of his lute, the ease of his laughter. But I don't try to persuade him to stay. I know whom he misses, whom we *both* miss; I've seen him walking alone in the gardens at sunset, perched on the roofs at midnight, standing at the piers at dawn. "The others—Raffaele, Sergio—they will want to see you before you leave," I say instead.

Magiano nods. "Don't worry. I'll say my proper farewells." He reaches out and lays his hand on my shoulder. "You are

kind, Your Majesty. I imagine Adelina could have ruled like you, in a different life." He studies my face, as he often does now, searching for a glimpse of my sister. "Adelina would want to see you carry this torch. You will be a good queen."

I lower my head. "I'm afraid," I admit. "There is still so much broken, and so much to fix. I don't know if I can do this."

"You have Sergio at your side. You have Raffaele as your adviser. That's quite a formidable team."

"Where will you go?" I ask.

At that, Magiano puts his hand down and turns his eyes up to the sky. It is a habit now that my eyes instinctively turn skyward, too, to where the first stars have begun to appear. "I'm going to follow her, of course," Magiano says. "As the night sky turns. When she appears on the other side of the world, I will be there, and when she returns here, so will I." Magiano smiles at me. "This farewell is not forever. I will see you again, Violetta."

I smile back at him, then step forward and wrap my arms around his neck. We embrace each other tightly. "Until you return, then," I whisper.

"Until I return."

Then we move apart. I leave Magiano alone to prepare for his journey, his boots already turned in the direction where Adelina's constellation will appear in the sky. I hope, when he comes back, she will return with him, and we might see each other once again.

The tale is told by royalty and vagabonds alike, nobles and peasants, hunters and farmers, the old and the young. The tale comes from every corner of the world, but no matter where it is told, it is always the same story.

A boy on horseback, wandering at night, in the woods or on the plains or along the shores. The sound of a lute drifts in the evening air. Overhead are the stars of a clear sky, a sheet of light so bright that he reaches up, trying to touch them. He stops and descends from his horse. Then he waits. He waits until exactly midnight, when the newest constellation in the sky blinks into existence.

If you are very quiet and do not look away, you may see the brightest star in the constellation glow steadily brighter. It brightens until it overwhelms every other star in the sky, brightens until it seems to touch the ground, and then the glow is gone, and in its place is a girl.

Her hair and lashes are painted a shifting silver, and a scar crosses one side of her face. She is dressed in Sealand silks and a necklace of sapphire. Some say that, once upon a time, she had a prince, a father, a society of friends. Others say that she was once a wicked queen, a worker of illusions, a girl who brought darkness across the lands. Still others say that she once had a sister, and that she loved her dearly. Perhaps all of these are true.

She walks to the boy, tilts her head up at him, and smiles. He bends down to kiss her. Then he helps her onto the horse, and she rides away with him to a faraway place, until they can no longer be seen.

These are only rumors, of course, and make little more than a story to tell around the fire. But it is *told.* And thus they live on.

—*"The Midnight Star,"* a folktale

Acknowledgments

I'm frequently asked if Adelina was inspired by anyone, and I'm always a bit embarrassed to admit that—while Adelina and I share very different life circumstances—she is absolutely molded from myself. My stories are all a piece of who I was and who I am. They are what I regret being, what I'm proud to be, and what I want to be more like. So, Adelina *is* me. She is a memory of all the times I've been angry or sad, bitter or disillusioned, and all the times the best people in my life have pulled me out of it with patience and kindness.

I won't lie—this series was by far the hardest thing I've ever written. I want to thank the many people in my life who helped me along this path, professionally and personally:

To my agent and champion, Kristin Nelson—thank you for always traveling alongside me, ever since that first

writer's conference so many years ago! Adelina would not exist in her final form without your early input; I'm forever grateful to know you. To my incredible editor and friend Jen Besser, thank you for always guiding my girl Adelina even through her darkest moments. You're an inspiration in a million ways. To Kate, editor extraordinaire—I can't exaggerate how grateful I am for all of your attention and insight! To my genius copyeditor Anne, you are the opposite of Jon Snow— you know everything, especially how to put a smile on my face. To Marisa, I don't know how you always manage to accomplish so much, but you do, and I can't thank you enough for it. To the inimitable and tireless and badass Team Putnam, Team Penguin, Team Speak, my international publishers, my wonderful, *wonderful* film agent Kassie Evashevski, my incredible producer Isaac Klausner and Team Temple Hill, the bookstore community and librarians and teachers, and everyone who puts stories into as many hands as possible, who fight every day to break down barriers: thank you. I owe you all more than I can say.

Thank you, darling Amie, for reading the early drafts of this final book and for being an incredible friend, always, without question. Onsenmosis!! To JJ, my very first writing friend, I'm forever grateful for your encouragement and intelligence and awesomeness. To Tahereh and Ransom, thank you for your laughter and warmth and themed dates and endless kindness. To Leigh—some people just light up a room, and that's you; thank you for always knowing exactly how to cheer me up and make me laugh. To Cassie, Holly, Sarah,

and Ally: I remember struggling through the muddy waters of this draft on retreat with you all, and am forever grateful for your help, wisdom, insight, and hilarious wit (and K-dramas). To Sandy—I think you might have seen the *earliest* draft ever of *The Young Elites;* thank you for all of those early words (and for being awesome). To Kami, Margie, and Mel—you set the bar for goodness in this world. I'm so honored to know all of you, and I'm inspired by you every day.

To my husband, Primo—I love you for every wonderful moment. To my mom, Andre, and my fam bam, for your unwavering support and love. To my friends, without whom I don't know what I would do. I'm reminded every moment how lucky I am.

Finally, to my readers: thank you so, so, so much for following me on this journey, and for the gift of telling you stories.

For loads more about the things you love, make sure you follow Penguin Platform.

🐦 @penguinplatform

▶ youtube.com/penguinplatform
YouTube

📷 @penguinplatform

tumblr. penguin-platform.tumblr.com

SHARE, CREATE, DISCOVER AND DEBATE.

HE IS A
LEGEND
SHE IS A
PRODIGY
WHO WILL BE
CHAMPION
?

WWW.LEGENDTHESERIES.COM

PENGUIN BOOKS

THE
MIDNIGHT
STAR